THE MONDAY THEORY

DOUGLAS CLARK

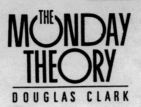

THE MONDAY THEORY

DOUGLAS CLARK

PERENNIAL LIBRARY
Harper & Row, Publishers
New York, Cambridge, Philadelphia, San Francisco
London, Mexico City, São Paulo, Singapore, Sydney

THE MONDAY THEORY. Copyright © 1983 by Douglas Clark. All rights reserved. Printed in the United States of America. No part of this book may be used or reproduced in any manner whatsoever without written permission except in the case of brief quotations embodied in critical articles and reviews. For information address John Farquharson Ltd., 250 West 57th Street, Room 410, New York, N.Y. 10107.

First PERENNIAL LIBRARY edition published 1985.

Library of Congress Cataloging in Publication Data

Clark, Douglas.
    The Monday theory.

    Reprint. Originally published: London : Gollancz, 1983.
    I. Title.
PR6053.L294M6   1985   823′.914   84-48146
ISBN 0-06-080737-7 (pbk.)

85 86 87 88 89 10 9 8 7 6 5 4 3 2 1

FOR
KATHARINE EMMA

THE MONDAY THEORY

— 1 —

Rhoda Carvell was wearing a rust-coloured, fine worsted suit, severely cut to fit her slim figure and heavily saddle-stitched, in fawn, a quarter of an inch in from every edge and turning. Her chestnut-coloured hair, worn long, with only its natural waves to break its symmetry, was topped with a little cap cut on Juliet lines, carried out by some skilled milliner in a fawn material to match the stitching on the suit. The decoration—classical little pearl shapes —had been built up from the thread of the same rust red as the suit. As she entered the main, open-plan editorial office of the *Daily View* she caused a couple of subs to give her exactly similar wolf whistles, which she ignored. She spoke to no one as she made her way in the long swinging stride of an athlete past tight-packed desks, to the Women's Page corner of the office. There, she placed the envelope she was carrying on the desk of the Women's Page editor, Golly Lugano.

"You're a day early," said Golly. "Today's Monday."

Golly Lugano was a middle-aged butch who dyed her hair ginger and used black eye shadow inside her nostrils. Nobody knew quite why, though it was generally be-lieved that Golly had at one time appeared on the music-halls in some minor act as a male impersonator and the black nostrils were the last vestiges of the stage make-up she favoured at that time.

"The divorce comes up tomorrow, so I won't be coming in."

"There's no need for you to go to the court, is there?"

The voice crackled as Golly spoke. The audible result of years of chain-smoking.

"I've said I'll be there. There could be some good background copy in it. You never know, I might even get a piece from it."

"All's grist," agreed Golly, stubbing out a cigarette with her left hand and withdrawing another from the open packet on her desk with the right. "And if you appear in court in that rig-out, you'll wow the judge."

Rhoda made no reply. Instead she turned to a young man sitting at a desk scarcely four feet away from Golly's. "And how's Nettle today, my little Stinging Nettle?"

"I'm fine, Mrs Carvell. You look great, too."

"I feel well, Nettle. I'm about to get my freedom."

"You're divorcing the professor because you don't get enough freedom, Mrs Carvell? He seemed a pretty easy-going chap to me. I know I only met him once…"

"He's divorcing me, Nettle. You wouldn't understand, but an easy-going man can curb a woman's freedom just as much as an old stickler. Not that the dear professor is easy-going. Just preoccupied most of the time."

"He may be a professor, but I reckon he's a fool if he's divorcing you, Mrs Carvell."

"Why, thank you, Nettle. That's a pretty compliment."

Golly Lugano pushed aside the article she had been reading and drew Rhoda's attention back to the business in hand. "What's the ploy this week, dearie?"

"The Conservative Woman. They've just had their conference."

"Dreary, dearie. All wearing those abortions of hats they seem to affect on these occasions."

"Oh, I agree, Golly. But I think it is time I took the directoire knickers off them over their views on capital punishment and birching."

"Mmm…It sounds promising, but it's been done before. What exactly had you in mind?"

Rhoda perched on the corner of Golly's desk, so that she was only half facing the editor. But she turned her

2

head towards her and used her elegant hands to gesture as she spoke.

"I've thought up this idea of what I've called The Restoration Garden Party—to be held in the afternoon of the day of the first execution. Side shows—guess the length of the rope; play the new game, Backhangman, etcetera. Tea menu, drop scones..."

"Long-drop scones."

"If you like. And gallows gâteau. That sort of thing."

"I like it. There's more, I hope?"

"The second half is The Birching Coffee Morning—to be attended by all the Cats. Strike a blow for law and order! Lashings of coffee. Stroke by stroke account of the great occasion. It's the Weal Thing!"

"Lovely," gabbled Golly, and then grinned, a movement which tipped upwards the end of her current cigarette to such a degree that the smoke went straight into her eyes. "Damn!" she said and then, when she had recovered from the smart, "I can hardly wait to get going on it, dearie. I'll lay on cartoon illustrations. One typical specimen called the Black Widow and another the Trap-Door Spider."

"Play it any way you like, Golly, but don't go over the score with the cartoons."

"A typeface with a nice, twisty, rope effect for the headline and crossheads?"

"I'll leave it to you. I've got quite a lot to do before tomorrow, so I must rush."

As Rhoda prepared to go, Golly put out her hand for the envelope. "It's all in here, is it?"

"Yes." Rhoda started to pull on one glove. "And I've got an idea for next week. I shall probably post it in."

Golly looked up from the script she was by now reading. "Why's that, dearie?"

"I'm going down to the cottage to stay for a few days."

"Understandable. You'll want to rejoice a bit, I expect. You'll be taking Woodruff with you?"

"Ralph will be with me," admitted Rhoda. "I should be

3

able to catch the Saturday collection with my piece. Anyway, I'll see you get it in good time."

"Ta. And if it's as good as this ..."

"You like it?"

"Just what I wanted."

"In that case ... 'bye, Golly. Don't smoke yourself to death."

Rhoda Carvell turned and threaded her way back, through the desks, to the door.

Detective Superintendent George Masters lay in bed for a minute or two after his wife, Wanda, had got up to attend to their young son, Michael, who was causing some disturbance in his own small room next door. Masters guessed at some sort of stick or toy being dragged across the spells of the cot interspersed with occasional drum beats with the same instrument on the more solid head or foot boards of the cot.

Masters, unusually for him, felt grumpy. It was not the noise that caused the feeling. He was used to that by now. Michael played happily every morning—had done ever since he was able to pull himself up and prance about in his cot—but he timed his playing very nicely to coincide with the time when his parents should be thinking of getting up. So his exploits caused no ill feeling. But Masters definitely felt slightly less than cheerful as he padded to the window to look out at the day.

It was a beautiful October morning. The sun was already up, and as he stripped off his pyjama jacket, ran his fingers through his hair and stifled a yawn, he could sense that it was going to be a bright, crisp day. Just the sort of day he should have revelled in, because he liked autumn best of all the seasons. The autumn reds and yellows and dry rustly leaves, not the wet, misty days with leaves slippery underfoot and trees dripping as one passed under them.

But despite the day, Masters still felt grumpy, though he had the sense to realise why. Last night he had been obliged to suffer the Cartwrights. He mentally used the word suffer with conscious exactitude. Cartwright was the headmaster of a nearby comprehensive school. Somehow, Mrs Cartwright had cottoned on to Wanda over some business to do with an adoption society in which Wanda was interested. Short of downright rudeness, Wanda had been unable to shake off the older woman who had shown herself determined to become a friend of the Masters' family. Mrs Cartwright had succeeded so well, that from time to time she and her husband had perforce to be invited for supper. Much to Masters' annoyance the compliment was returned with unfailing regularity.

And last night Masters had come off second best in a conversation with Cartwright simply because he, as host, had felt obliged to tone down his argument out of courtesy to guests who, in return, had presumed upon such leniency by stepping-up the power of their verbal attack.

Masters went across to the bathroom. As he cleaned his teeth, he recalled some of the exchanges of the previous evening. Several times Cartwright had started sentences with: 'In your profession...'. It had irritated Masters who always insisted that though he was a professional policeman, police work was not, of itself, a profession. Cartwright had told him he was old hat if he still believed the Church, Medicine, Law and Education were the only professions and had called on Mrs Cartwright to support him. Mrs Cartwright, who was also a schoolteacher, had been examining a Vogue pattern book with Wanda on the other side of the small room. They had been choosing a style for Mrs Cartwright's new winter coat, which she was to make herself, so she knew nothing of the subject under discussion, but she was the know-all type and had jumped in feet first to support her husband.

By now Masters was lathering his face. The memory of the conversation caused him to wield the brush so angrily that a large dollop of foaming soap shot across and hit the mirror. He wiped it away irritably. The only point he had been trying to make was that, in his experience, the older

5

professions were often jealous of their image to the point of obstructiveness whereas other members of the community—again in his experience—were, by and large, more helpful. He had wanted to explain that he had on occasions found the youngest of lawyers treating him as a nit-wit when a point of law arose; young medics had read him lectures when it came to injuries; and some pedagogues always assumed nobody but themselves had ever entered a seat of learning and knew anything of education.

That's what life had taught Masters. His remarks were to have been merely an observation based on his own wide experience, but he had been shouted down before he could produce it. The truth was—as he well knew—that he didn't like the Cartwrights whom he suspected of adopting an entirely spurious air of erudition. But it seemed they had managed to get their hooks into Wanda so, to avoid unpleasantness, he tried to tolerate them. He nevertheless found it a very, very difficult role to play.

He was towelling off when Wanda brought him a cup of black coffee upstairs. As she kissed him and murmured a compliment about nice smooth cheeks and nice smells of shaving soap, he asked: "What's all this? Are we late?"

"No."

"What then?"

"It's to say sorry for subjecting you to the Cartwrights last night. They get up your nose, don't they?"

"That's a ladylike way of putting it."

She grimaced. "What can I do about them?"

He put his arm round her waist. "Nothing, my sweet. I'm away from home so often that to choke off people who drop in and keep you company from time to time would be silly. Really I should be as grateful to them as I am to Doris Green for their kindness while you are house-tied by young Michael, but they do rub me up the wrong way."

"That's because they are basically anti-police and..."

"Anti-everything else? I know."

6

He kissed her again and let her go. She left him, humming to herself as she went. He mentally berated himself for feeling grumpy. He reckoned he had no right to indulge in such feelings when he was blessed with a wife like Wanda. He returned to the bedroom to dress.

Wanda saw him off half an hour later as he prepared to walk the short distance to the Yard. It was a lovely morning with just a nip in the air. Wanda had insisted that he should wear his light coat—a fawn houndstooth raglan that had cost the earth from Aquascutum.

Green met him in the corridor outside his office. Formerly a DCI, Green was now a Senior Scene of Crime Officer, a title bestowed on him so that the Yard could retain his services beyond police retirement age.

"Anderson wants to see you, George."

"He's in? So early?" It was barely ten to nine, and the Assistant Commissioner (Crime) was not noted for arriving before the streets were aired.

"He sounded a bit mardy."

"Did he now?" Masters entered his office to take off his coat. "Did you get the impression that I have done something to upset him? Or is there some other minor cause that got him out of bed on the wrong side this morning?"

"Some young cub reporter rang him up before seven."

"Good Lord! Whatever for?" Masters was by now beginning to feel more cheerful. He took out his pipe and started to charge it with newly-rubbed Warlock Flake. Green carefully selected one from among a number of crumpled cigarettes in a crushed carton before replying.

"He only said he wanted to ask the AC's opinion on the deaths of two people."

"What two people?"

"A woman called Rhoda Carvell and a chap called Woodruff."

"Rhoda Carvell? Isn't she some sort of journalist?"

"That's the girl," said Green. "Writes a so-called dy-

7

namic weekly column for women in the *Daily View*. Actually it's not half as dynamic as most of the over-the-garden-wall variety of conversations normal women get into. But they haven't the gall to put it into writing. The average washerwoman is slightly more sensitive than Rhoda Carvell."

"I know. Fishwife. Female bummaree."

"You know her stuff do you?" asked Green. "That surprises me. I wouldn't have thought her rubbish would have been up your street."

"It isn't. But that woman Cartwright who visits Wanda is an avid reader of the Rhoda Carvell column."

"That figures."

"Whenever she comes to the house she quotes bits at me. Always the bits that seem to march with some particular opinion of her own."

"She would." Green looked across at Masters. "George," he said hesitantly, "I know it's no business of mine and you also know I'd be the last person on earth to criticize anything Wanda did..."

"But?"

"Can't you get her to drop that Cartwright woman? She's not a fit companion for Wanda or young Michael."

"Or me," grinned Masters. "Don't worry, Bill. I've decided to work on it. But what is it that makes you think La Cartwright—apart from being an unlikeable woman—is likely to be a bad acquaintance for Wanda? Assuming you meant she would be bad?"

"I've overheard her talking to Wanda," said Green cryptically.

"What about?"

"She's a clever propagandist."

"Is she now?"

"She's always getting at Wanda about how repressive the police are."

"Wanda wouldn't swallow that, Bill."

"Maybe not. But Cartwright butters her up about you."

"How on earth..."

8

"She's always telling Wanda that you, of course, are wonderful, but you're not typical. Tells the lass that living with you blinds her to the faults of the force at large. Says because her husband is a reasonable man she is not in a position to judge critically the corruption that is rife in the police. And so on. I tell you, it's clever, George, because naturally Wanda thinks you're the cat's whiskers and it makes pleasant hearing to have this other woman say so."

"Meaning that if Wanda knows—or believes—half of what she's told to be true, she'll swallow the other half?"

"Not right off. She's too smart for that. But anything said often enough..."

"Begins to assume the trappings of truth?"

"Something like that."

Masters tapped his pipe out and laid it in the big ashtray on his desk. He looked across at Green. "Thanks for telling me, Bill. I know what you think of Wanda so I'd never think of questioning your motive or your judgement. But why haven't you mentioned this before?"

"Because you've never blasted off about the Cartwrights before. For all I knew you could have approved of them, so it wasn't for me to criticize your family friends."

Masters nodded. "Understood, chum. Now, I suppose I'd better report to Anderson or he'll be getting even more disgruntled than he was when he arrived. While I'm away, Bill, would you see what you can dredge up about this Carvell woman—just in case we need it?"

As Green had said, Anderson was testy. "Nothing to do with us," he growled. "The pair were found dead in a deserted cottage in West Sussex. The young fool who rang me didn't mention that. He simply said they'd been found dead last night, and before I knew where I was, I was in a discussion with the dam' fellow. And me only half awake."

"Why did he ring you, sir, and not the Yard direct?"

"Because the woman was one of the regular contributors to their paper. Writes a weekly article blasting everybody

9

and everything in sight. Does it indiscriminately so that she's bound to please somebody every issue. Got a reputation for plain speaking based upon nothing more than filling a page with vitriolic rubbish. And there was this chap wanting to know what I was going to do about it and hinting I should have been up all night investigating."

Masters heard him out and then asked: "He thought you should become involved because she's a journalist, sir?"

"Something of the sort."

"You said 'found dead'. Two of them."

"In bed."

"Accident? Suicide pact? Murder? Did your young informant suggest which, sir?"

"Lord knows. It wouldn't surprise me if somebody she'd written about had murdered her. But as there were two of them, I'd say it was an accident. Rhoda Carvell wouldn't commit suicide. Too sure of herself, if you take my meaning, George. Capable of beating hell out of life and everybody in it. No need to yield to weakness. That sort of thing."

Masters allowed a moment or two of silence before asking: "So you favour accident, sir. Gas leak, perhaps?"

"No gas in the damned cottage according to the local police."

"Not even butane or something like it? These out-of-the-way houses often use bottle gas."

The AC shook his head. "Nothing like that. There is a generator and batteries for light and cooking and open fires for warmth."

Masters grimaced. "Presumably the West Sussex people are dealing with it, sir. So what do you want me to do? Speak to the *Daily View* and explain things?"

"Quite frankly, I don't know, George. The journalist who rang me up didn't say so, but I got the impression he could have been hinting at—or hoping for—murder. I want you to find out how and why he knew about the deaths and, in general, sort him out. And while you're at it, tell him and his colleagues not to ring me at seven o'clock in the morning. I don't want that sort of thing to become a habit."

"Do the West Sussex people assume it was murder, sir?"

"Too early for them to say, George. I rang them immediately I'd got rid of that reporter. They promised to ring back as soon as they had anything to go on."

"I'd prefer to know the score before I go to see this journalist. You haven't given me his name, by the way, sir."

"Sorry. Heddle."

"Is that his christian name or surname?"

"Surname. Why do you ask?"

"There was a famous singer..."

"Ah, yes! Forgotten him for the moment. Got an old record of him somewhere singing *The Fair Maid of Perth.* My missus likes it. So do I, come to that."

Masters let the AC talk on without interruption. A few years earlier, when on holiday in Scotland, the Andersons had visited the Fair Maid's cottage. The AC rambled on, talking about the North Inch and the South Inch in Perth, explaining as he went that these were really tracts of riverside meadowland and ideal for picnics if the weather was clement. Masters listened gravely, though itching to be away. He was extremely grateful when the clamour of the external phone cut Anderson short.

The AC took the call and listened for a few moments before asking: "Arsine? That's a gas isn't it? Arsenical gas?"

It seemed he got a yes in answer to this query and he listened a little longer, making a scribbled note on his pad as he did so. Then he, in turn, gave a yes or two and Masters guessed that his senior officer was agreeing either to help or take over the case completely. The conversation was too broken for Masters to be sure which, but he realised that he and his team were to be implicated in the investigation in some way.

Anderson put the phone down.

11

"You heard, George? It was a gas, after all. Or so they think. Arsine."

"They're not sure, sir?"

"Educated guess on the part of the medics apparently. In advance of the full laboratory tests."

"Did they say why they suspect arsine?"

Anderson consulted his pad. "The bodies smelt of garlic, apparently, and...hang on a moment while I interpret this...ah, yes...and the eyelids of both were noticeably oedematous." He looked up. "That means swollen, doesn't it? Full of watery fluid?"

Masters nodded. "I thought we'd finished with arsenic for murder years ago, sir. I hope it's not going to start cropping up again."

"These things can go in cycles, George. Somebody will always be there to copy what others have done before them."

"So, West Sussex are definitely treating it as murder, sir, and you think it will help them if we can find out how one of Rhoda Carvell's colleagues knew it was murder, or hinted that it was, before ever the local police knew what to think?"

"It can't do any harm, George."

"Do they know you're proposing to help them, sir?"

"Not me. You. They asked me if we would take it."

"The entire investigation, sir? Do they think we're touting for business? The crime was committed in West Sussex."

"They reckon on it being largely connected with London. The cottage was only the Carvells' second home."

"The Carvells? Plural? She was married?"

"And found dead in bed with a man other than her husband! Actually it isn't as bad as it sounds, George. Carvell divorced her a week or so ago and this Woodruff character was the man in the case. Or so I'm told."

"I see." Masters realised he still felt as he had done earlier in the day—rather glum. The case seemed likely to turn out to be one of those he was still old-fashioned

12

enough to regard as unsavoury. It bade fair to be even worse when the AC asked: "You know who Carvell is, of course?"

"No, sir." Somebody important, otherwise the AC wouldn't have mentioned him in quite that way.

"Professor Ernest Carvell. Big-wig at the university. Gaine Professor of something or other at Disraeli College."

Masters' spirits sank even further. The conversation with Cartwright last night! Cartwright didactically laying down the law! His wife acting the part of the pedagogue's mate! 'My goodness, Chief Superintendent, how very out of date you are.' Insinuating that they should know better than he did because they were school teachers. He groaned inwardly. A professor in the case! And though the overall responsibility belonged to the West Sussex County force, it appeared he had been offered the tarry end of the stick not only here in London, but on their patch as well.

"Not that Carvell is likely to come into it very much, George, but when you see him, walk on eggs, because he's a haughty bastard."

"You know him, sir?"

"Met him. The Great-I-Am. Lectures at the Royal Society and that sort of thing. Writes learned papers. And talking of papers, watch it with those dam' journalists, too, or anything you say will be taken down and twisted into a rod for our own backs." The AC sniffed as though he had the beginnings of a cold, but Masters recognized it as the usual sign of the hidden anger that seized him whenever it seemed likely that an investigation might be hampered by considerations other than those of strict police work.

"I'll have to start with this young man, Heddle, sir."

"He's probably some youngster horning in on what he probably thinks will be a scandal."

"Very likely, sir." Masters got to his feet. "I'd say he made the call off his own bat before the day staff got in. Now, if you could tell me who is dealing with the case for the West Sussex people, I'll be on my way, sir."

"A DCI at Chichester called Robson."

"Thank you, sir. I'll call him for a few more details and arrange to meet."

Masters, Green, and Detective Sergeants Reed and Berger used the police Rover to get to Fleet Street. Reed drove. Masters was in no mood to appreciate the glorious day. Instead of thinking about the case, he was wondering how Mrs Cartwright was faring in Oxford Street. She had announced that she proposed to get up early this morning to go to the stores to buy the material for the new coat she and Wanda had been discussing last night. Masters had asked if the school was closed for a holiday thus allowing her the time to go shopping on a Wednesday morning. The answer had done little to endear her to him. 'How little you know of what goes on today, Chief Superintendent. School teachers are not confined to the school premises as if in a prison, as they were in your time. We go and come as and when we have work to do. I have no classes tomorrow morning until after play-time. Have no fear, I shall be in my place by a quarter to eleven to give my lesson in Civics.' Masters doubted the assurance she had seen fit to give him. If he read Mrs Cartwright correctly, choosing coat material to suit her head as well as her body and pocket would be a long-drawn-out penance for the shop assistants.

"A penny for them," said Green. "Or aren't you proposing to talk to us in case it cuts your handicap down?"

"Sorry. I wasn't thinking about it. My mind was on that damned Cartwright woman."

"No wonder you look fit to kick somebody. Forget her, George. Forget what I said about her."

"I'll go down the side alley, Chief," said Reed. "Better than leaving it at the kerb."

Masters grunted. It could have meant acquiescence or that he couldn't care less about what the sergeant did with the car. Reed made his choice and manoeuvred into the *Daily View*'s loading bay.

"You can't leave it here, mate."

"Police. We're going inside."

"I don't give a toss where you're going. We have paper coming in here, mate. Big rolls of it. Somebody might just fancy rolling one on a fuzz car."

Green got out and glared balefully at the man in the apron. "I don't like you, and I don't like your tone."

"Only trying to be helpful. Take it or leave it."

"We'll leave it. Here. And if there's a scratch on it when we come out, or anything in the way to hold us up, I'll blame you, Dixon. And when I blame people, I make them pay."

"Here, how d'you know..." Dixon grinned, showing an incomplete set of very stained teeth. "I'm slipping, and no error. It's Green. I didn't recognize you with grey hair. It's been a few years since you were plodding round here."

"You'll likely remember, too, that I didn't stand for any nonsense. I still don't, grey hair or no grey hair." Green turned to join Masters who had started to stroll towards the street, hands in coat pockets, head down and still grumpy. Reed, still in the car, started up and manoeuvred it into a corner of the bay. When he and Berger caught up with the other two, they were waiting in the foyer by the enquiry desk.

"Thanks for waiting," said Berger to Green.

"Don't kid yourself, lad. We're only here because that cub reporter hasn't got down here to fetch us yet." He turned to Reed. "Did as the man asked, did you?"

"The Chief says to co-operate whenever possible."

"You'll learn. Co-operation means doing what you want to do and letting others conform to you."

Reed didn't reply. There was no need. They were joined by a young man.

"Chief Superintendent Masters?"

"Are you Mr Heddle?"

"Derek Heddle to my friends."

"Don't count your chickens, lad," said Green. "We're not universal aunties."

15

Heddle was in a chocolate-brown suit with a heavy, wide-spaced chalk stripe and flare-bottomed trousers. His hair was pale yellow and thin, in shoulder-length straggles. The white, tired face looked as if a spot of open-air and exercise would do it no harm.

"Do you rate a private office in this beehive?" asked Masters.

"No. But there's an interview room we can use on the first floor."

They followed him up the stairs.

"Are you the cub reporter?"

"Crime junior, actually." Heddle offered chairs and French cigarettes. Masters refused both and walked over to the window of the little room. Green accepted the Gitane and straddled the chair. The sergeants followed suit and waited for Masters who was looking out of the window. At last he turned to face Heddle who was sitting behind the desk, apparently not the least put out by the presence of the four Yard men.

"Did you know Rhoda Carvell?" asked Masters.

"Of course. Well, not socially, exactly, but I often saw her here. She came in about once a week."

"Was she a good looking woman?"

"Very good looking with a smashing figure and nice legs. She was your real open-air type."

"Did you ever try to get to know her better?"

"How do you mean?"

"Did you ever ask her out for a drink or a meal?"

"What are you getting at?"

"It's a simple question, lad," growled Green.

"But not relevant," announced Heddle.

"Not relevant to what?" demanded Green.

Heddle was at a loss, but he tried. "Not relevant to telling me what the police are doing about her death."

"We're doing better than that, son. We're showing you the police in action investigating her death."

"How do you mean? Asking me if I'd tried to get next to her? That's investigating?"

"Did you?" said Masters.

"Did I what?"

"Fancy her, or whatever the current term is? And knowing she wasn't too strict in her behaviour, hope you might succeed?"

Heddle looked round the others in disbelief. All three stared back, poker faced. "This," he asked incredulously, "is a murder investigation?" He gave a nervous laugh. "Now I know why the undetected crime figures are rising."

"Oh? Why? Please tell me, Mr Heddle. It's a problem that has been exercising my mind for years. But if you have the answer, why not let me know what it is?"

"You! Spending your time asking me personal questions instead of being out chasing a murderer."

"I suspect I may be questioning one now."

Heddle was astounded.

"Me? You suspect me?"

"Why not, Mr Heddle? You knew Mrs Carvell had been murdered before ever the police did. Such knowledge is a factor common to all murderers. I can think of no other material link so absolute as that. So how did you know she had been murdered?"

"I didn't know she'd been murdered. Not for sure. Not like that."

"I find that hard to believe, Mr Heddle."

"Why?"

"You rang up the AC (Crime) at his home while he was still in bed and gabbled about murder..."

"I never mentioned murder."

"You'll have to do slightly better than that. You accused the AC of lying down on the job..."

"Well..."

"Well what? He could hardly be said to be lying down on the job if the deaths were due to natural causes or accident, could he? So you must have been sure it was murder."

"I didn't know for sure."

17

"Then we'd better take you in for being a public nuisance, lad," said Green. "Making alarming and unfounded phone calls is an offence."

"I'm the press," screamed Heddle, his voice cracking on the top note. "I'm a crime reporter. I was calling in the line of business."

"If that is so," said Masters, "tell me why you, a crime reporter, don't know the police system in this country?"

"I do."

"Obviously you don't, or you'd have known that unexplained deaths in West Sussex are the responsibility of the West Sussex force, not the Metropolitan Police. And another thing, I have never heard of a crime reporter, however senior, ringing up the Assistant Commissioner when he's at home, in bed. There's a press bureau at the Yard, though you apparently have never heard of it."

"Yes, well…"

"So what little game did you think you were playing, Mr Heddle?"

Heddle answered disconsolately: "I wanted a story. A big one."

"And that's your only excuse for, or explanation of, such odd behaviour? You killed Mrs Rhoda Carvell because she wouldn't have you? And then, like a lot of killers, you couldn't resist letting people know you knew she had been murdered? It often happens with psychopaths, Mr Heddle, and they often select some big bug to show off to, like you chose the Assistant Commissioner."

Heddle didn't reply because he was incapable of speech. He sat, mouth hanging open, staring at Masters like a frightened youth awaiting the hiding of his life.

"Nothing to say, lad?" asked Green, selecting a crumpled Kensitas. "Cat got your tongue? Oh, and I'd close my mouth if I were you. If the wind changes it could stick like that."

"Eh? No. I mean, this is all wrong."

"Is it? Well now, suppose you tell Mr Masters and the rest of us all about it. Right from the very beginning,

18

leaving nothing to the imagination, or we might start imagining some weird and wonderful things. Show us where we've gone wrong, because the Chief Superintendent seemed to me to have a lot going for him. It sounded very feasible, his theory."

"Where? I mean when shall I start?"

"Suppose we say the last time you saw her alive."

"Well...she came up to the desk of the editor of the Women's Page and..."

"Everything, laddie," said Green wearily. "The day, the time of day, what she was wearing, who she spoke to on the way in, what she said. The lot. Start again."

"You can't possibly want to know..."

"Everything," asserted Green. "You're in a hole, lad. You'll have to work hard to climb out of it."

"It was a week last Monday," said Heddle at last. "In the morning."

"What time in the morning?"

"About eleven o'clock, I think, because the coffee trolley was on its second round, and I remember she was offered some by Kath—that's the woman who takes it round—and she said she couldn't drink the institutional plastic variety out of greasy cardboard. I'd been wanting to say that myself for a long time, but it carried more weight coming from her."

"Go on," said Masters, coming into the circle to take the chair that had been left for him. "How do you remember it was a week last Monday?"

"Because she always comes in to file her copy on Tuesdays. Or she did, I should say."

"Are you saying that last week she broke the habit and came in a day early?"

"Yes. Her column appears on Wednesdays, you see, so Golly Lugano—that's her editor—has to have it on Tuesday. But I heard Mrs Carvell tell Golly last week that her divorce from the Professor was coming up on the Tuesday and she wanted to be in court, though she hadn't got to be, in case she could get some material for a future article. So she delivered her piece on Monday."

"I think I've understood that," said Masters. "What I'd like to know is how you were near enough to hear this conversation between Mrs Carvell and the Lugano woman."

"My desk is only about four feet away from Golly's. We're packed in there like...well, we're short on space but our editor says with the price one has to pay for every square foot of room in London offices he's going to install double-decker desks and make us..."

"So you are seated near enough to...what is she? Miss or Mrs? Lugano's desk to overhear all that goes on?"

"She calls herself Mizz actually—you know, emm ess. I can hear every word she says to anybody. And she smokes like a chimney."

"I see. Mrs Carvell came in a week last Monday morning at eleven o'clock. What did you overhear on that occasion?"

Heddle gave a fairly accurate account of the meeting between Golly Lugano and Rhoda Carvell. He mentioned the proposed article on the restoration of capital punishment and the fact that Rhoda intended to spend some time at the cottage celebrating with Woodruff her freedom from the Professor.

"Then what?" demanded Masters.

Heddle looked slightly uncomfortable. "She turned to me and asked me how I was."

"Mrs Carvell did?"

"Yes."

"What did she say, lad?" asked Green. "Good morning Mr Heddle. How are you?"

"What she said exactly was..."

"I'm listening, lad."

"And how's Nettle today, my little Stinging Nettle?"

"She said what?" demanded Green. "Nettle? Was that you?"

"Yes."

"So this smart, well-dressed woman, who ignored all

20

the other men on the floor, spoke to you, did she? My little Stinging Nettle!"

"She'd called me that for about four months."

"Why?"

"It was just her way."

"She'd got some reason, son. Why you and nobody else?"

There was a moment or two of silence.

"Answer please," said Masters. "Otherwise I shall assume there was something going between the two of you. Four months ago, you said. That would make it June. What happened in June?"

"It was nothing," said Heddle truculently. "I'd gone down to her cottage on the Sunday."

"Why?" demanded Green. "I thought you said you'd never got next to her?"

"I went to pick up her copy. She was going on holiday on the Monday and asked Golly if she could send somebody down to collect it because she didn't want the fag of coming back to town."

"She could have posted it," accused Green. "So why did you go? You're not a messenger."

"I was there when she came in and spoke to Golly about it," expostulated Heddle. "Golly said she couldn't send anybody. Not on Sunday. Mrs Carvell would have to post it. Mrs Carvell said the last post out was midday on Saturday and the copy wouldn't be ready then because there was some event on the Saturday afternoon which would be featured—something to do with tennis or Ascot or something."

"And?"

"She said God knew when the next post went out from that area and there'd be some artwork she didn't want bending in the post."

"So?"

"So I said I was doing nothing on the Sunday and I'd fetch the material if she'd tell me where the cottage was."

"You went out there, spent the day with her and came back? Did you go to bed with her?"

"There was nothing like that."

"No?" demanded Green. "What was there something like?"

"We sunbathed."

"Ah! She got into a bikini, I suppose? One of those that showed the top half of her bottom at the back and the top half of her top at the front?"

"Something like that."

"And the two of you sunbathed all day, with you lying next door to a tasty bit of capurtle that you've admitted to admiring and you want us to believe that nothing else happened? Not even a cuddle? Not even a bit of smoochy talk? Come on lad! Why should she keep you there all day when all you'd gone for was to collect a parcel? Come to think of it, why did you go prepared to sunbathe if you hadn't thought there was something in it for you?"

"Her husband was there."

"Sunbathing?"

"No."

"He was in the house?"

"No."

"So where was he exactly?"

"About."

"Please be a little more forthcoming, Mr Heddle," said Masters. "If you persist in being evasive, your attitude will only reinforce our belief that you have something to hide. Where was Professor Carvell that day?"

"He'd gone down there, along the beach, looking for fossils or rocks or something. I don't know what he was after exactly, but he didn't show up till late in the afternoon. Rhoda said she didn't even know he was there."

"Thank you. I take it the cottage is near the sea?"

"About two hundred yards inland."

"Right," said Green. "So where does this stinging nettle come in?"

"Perhaps," said Reed, "you did try it on, but the only bed you managed to get her into was a bed of nettles."

Heddle looked round wildly. "Why won't you believe

22

me? I tell you I didn't do anything like that."

"There must have been some reason for her to give you a nickname like that."

"I'd bought a pound of strawberries on the way down there. From one of those stalls they set up on the roadside outside country cottages. She ate a lot of them, straight out of the bag, while we were lying out in the garden. About an hour later she'd developed a rash across her stomach. It looked like nettle rash. She said she'd had it once before with strawberries and she thought it could be because she hadn't washed them before she ate them."

"I've heard of that in other people," growled Green. "So Mrs Carvell fooled about saying you'd caused it? Did you?"

"Did I what?"

"Doctor those strawberries? Put something on them?"

"Of course not."

"Then why did she blame you for causing the rash on her belly?"

"I told you it looked like nettle rash, and as she'd already started to call me Nettle, for some reason..."

"I think I understand," said Masters. "Did Mrs Carvell ever invite you to her cottage again?"

"No."

"But you did see Professor Carvell there that day?"

"He came back just before tea. We talked a bit."

"Did he dislike the idea of his wife spending the day sunbathing with another man?"

"Not that I could tell. He was a nice enough chap, I seem to remember. There was no aggro about me being there."

"Doddering old professor, is he, looking for fossils?" asked Green.

"He's a strong-looking, well set-up chap of not much more than forty. A bit thick set and wearing nothing but a pair of navy-blue shorts, white tennis shoes and a terry towelling sun hat. He was as brown as a berry, with muscles like a weight-lifter and his hair was just going grey

23

at the temples. If that sounds to you like a doddering old professor, you wait till you see him."

"Had he found any fossils?"

"Yes. He had a cloth bag with him. One of those with a draw-string top, and I could see he'd got bits of something in it. He told me they were bits of rock. Oh, and he had a hammer, too. One of those with a flat end and a pick end. It looked a dangerous weapon to me."

"Why?"

"I'd never seen a geologist's hammer before. I thought they were little things like those they used to use in shops for breaking up slabs of toffee. But this was much bigger and heavier than that, with a shortish, stubby handle. The way he held it I reckon he could have felled an ox with it."

"So he did threaten you, if not directly, then perhaps by implication?" said Masters.

"No. No, he didn't."

"You felt quite safe even though the hammer he held looked dangerous—to use your own words? Mr Heddle, a geologist's hammer cannot be considered dangerous unless it is held or wielded in a dangerous or potentially dangerous manner."

"Well, he didn't threaten me. It was just that I sensed that were he ever to use it..."

"What you are trying to say, Mr Heddle, is that the professor was himself a bit of an intimidating figure. Isn't that it? He looked a bit of a pirate, dressed as you've described him, and pirates are, by tradition, bloodthirsty fellows?"

"That's exactly right," gabbled Heddle, pleased that at least somebody seemed to be understanding and believing what he was saying. "I wouldn't have liked to have crossed swords with him."

"Cutlasses," grunted Green. "Pirates used cutlasses."

"Oh, yes. Of course."

"Right, lad. Let's get back to the last time you saw her.

24

She'd asked you how you were—her little Stinging Nettle."

"I said I was fine and that she looked well dressed in that suit, and she said she felt well and was looking forward to getting her freedom. I was a bit shocked because I hadn't heard about the divorce, so I said she couldn't be divorcing the professor just to get her freedom, because he'd seemed pretty easy-going to me. What I mean was he'd not worried about me being there all that Sunday, where some chaps might have.

"And then she told me he was divorcing her. She said I wouldn't understand, but easy-going men can curb a woman's freedom just as much as an old stickler. Then she added that the dear professor wasn't easy-going, just preoccupied with other things rather than her."

"Hold it there please," said Masters. "What did you understand from that conversation? Was Mrs Carvell the sort of woman who pretended she liked her own way, but in reality would have been happier if her husband had been stricter or far more attentive?"

Heddle thought for a moment or two before replying. "I'd never thought of it that way, Mr Masters, but I think you're right."

"On what do you base your conclusion?"

"I'd never been able to guess what it was about her that made her sort of unsettled, but now you come to mention it..."

"Please say whatever it was you were about to tell me."

"One day I heard Mrs Carvell say to Golly, who was making some derogatory remark about one of our girls who was going to get married to Purby, who's a real no-nonsense character we have round here, I heard her say that this girl would likely be very happy with a man who took the trouble to be jealous about her. Just as if she, Rhoda, wouldn't have minded somebody laying down the law to her once in a while. I must say it surprised me a bit at the time."

25

"You're a very observant young man, Mr Heddle."

"I'm a reporter. I have to be, don't I?"

"It doesn't necessarily follow. But please go on. Mrs Carvell had told you the professor was divorcing her and not *vice versa*. What then?"

"I said I thought he was a fool if he was divorcing her, and she said that I'd paid her a pretty compliment. And that was about it. She had a few more words with Golly about her article, and then said she had to rush away because she'd got quite a lot to do before the divorce next day after which she was going off to her cottage for a few days to celebrate with Ralph Woodruff, her boyfriend."

"Did she leave the office then?"

"She went straight out."

"And that was the last time you saw her?"

"Well—not quite."

"Make up your mind, son," growled Green. "You told us her visit to the office was the last time you'd seen her."

"It was—alive."

"You mean you've seen her body?"

Heddle grimaced. "I discovered it."

There was a long moment of silence.

At last, Masters spoke. "The West Sussex police have already interviewed you, Mr Heddle?"

Heddle shuffled in his seat and a faint tinge of colour rose in his pale cheeks. "Well...no, they haven't," he confessed.

"No? Are you saying they don't know you've seen the two bodies?"

Heddle didn't reply.

"You're not very forthcoming, are you lad?" said Green. "I wonder what else you're keeping hidden under that straggly thatch of yours?"

"I haven't hidden anything." He looked from one to the other of the detectives in turn as if seeking some sympathetic glance. "Honest."

"We've been talking to you for thirty-five minutes,"

growled Green, "and we've only just got to know that you discovered the bodies." He put a pudgy clenched fist on the table. "In my book, boy, the discoverer of dead bodies shouts it from the housetops—if he's innocent. And I'll add something every budding crime reporter should know before he's been in the job a week. And that is that people who discover murdered bodies are very often the people who have done the murdering."

"No."

"Yes. They can't wait to show off their handiwork, so if nobody else will oblige with a rapid discovery, they come across their victims themselves—accidentally on purpose."

Heddle swallowed. "It wasn't like that at all."

"Wasn't it?" asked Masters. "Then suppose you tell us what it was like. We'll be grateful to hear your version. To see how it stands up."

"How do you mean, stands up?"

"Hasn't it occurred to you, Mr Heddle, that people who discover bodies are usually invited along to the nearest police station and questioned rather closely by the local CID? Yet you don't appear to have been to any police station or even to have been interviewed by so much as a constable. In fact, you were free to ring the Assistant Commissioner before he was out of bed this morning. I find that slightly...shall we say, unusual?"

"I told the local police."

"Did you now? When?"

"Late last night—about eleven o'clock, I think."

"And after helping the local police you were back here in London before seven o'clock, making a nuisance of yourself?"

"Yes."

"When the West Sussex police spoke to me they didn't mention your name, and I must say they let you go surprisingly quickly."

"I never saw them."

27

"How about stopping the story of what you didn't do," said Green wearily, "and starting to tell us what you did do?"

"I did my duty as a citizen. I rang the police at Chichester and told them there were two dead bodies in the cottage."

"And they didn't ask you to wait at the scene or call at the police station?"

"No."

Green sighed heavily. "So what did they do, lad? Tell you to forget it and go home?"

"They asked me my name."

"And they haven't been in touch with you yet?" asked Masters. "That does surprise me."

"They couldn't get in touch. I didn't give them my name."

Masters shook his head. "You're a very foolish fellow, Mr Heddle. Foolish and irresponsible. How long do you suppose it would be before the West Sussex police tracked you down?"

"I . . . I didn't . . ."

"You didn't think they would find you?"

"Oh, I knew they would, but . . ."

"You wanted to hold them off for a bit. I wonder why?"

"Because I was scared," flared Heddle. "And after meeting you lot, I was right to be."

"You can hardly say we've beaten you up, can you?" asked Reed.

"Let's get back to business," said Masters. "You say you made an anonymous phone call, Mr Heddle?"

"Yes."

"You seem to like the telephone. I hope the *Daily View* can afford to pay the bill even if it can't afford to rent more office space. I take it you did phone from here, and not at your own expense?"

"Well . . ."

"At about eleven o'clock last night, you said?"

"Roughly."

"Presumably after returning from a visit to Mrs Carvell's cottage?"

"Yes."

"Let's have it, son," urged Green. "What were you doing down there last night in the dark. What were you hoping to find or get?"

"Copy."

Green groaned again. "Oh, no! Not playing the volunteer messenger boy again for this Lugano dame?"

"I didn't volunteer. Rhoda's copy should have been in yesterday morning for today's issue. It didn't come. By the time the last delivery of mail had been, Golly was tearing her hair and cursing the Post Office for having lost it or held it up because Rhoda would never let her down."

"Didn't she try to get in touch with Mrs Carvell?" asked Masters. "You people seem to like using the phone, so why not ring her?"

"Golly tried. She knew Rhoda was down at the cottage and she rang umpteen times. There was no reply. And Golly got more and more angry. You don't know her, but she's a...well, she lives with another woman and she's always sounding off against men and marriage, and she was saying some pretty basic things about Rhoda and her Ralph Woodruff being more interested in you-know-what than they were in business. It was a pretty acid display, I can tell you. I was quite pleased when I had to go out on a job in the afternoon, believe me."

Masters suddenly felt a surge of sympathy with young Heddle. He had not met Golly Lugano, but the memory of Mrs Cartwright still lingered with him, and he imagined that each, in her own way, could have the same effect upon men. So it was in a gentler, more conversational way that he urged the young reporter to continue with his account.

"I got back to my desk about half-past five. I'd just got a few bits and pieces to file and after that I hoped to get away, but Golly grabbed me as soon as I got in. She'd been to see the editor about Rhoda's piece not having turned up..Her column was popular, you know, and it was a bit of a disaster not having it for its regular Wednesday spot. The editor had said they could hold the space until everything else was ready to be put to bed. I suppose that meant until half-past ten or eleven. So he and Golly between them had decided that I should go down to the cottage as I knew where it was. I was to pick up Rhoda's copy, bring it back, and everything would be fine."

"Seems like a good idea to me," said Green. "But there were obvious snags."

"You're telling me. I told Golly to phone Rhoda and get it dictated. Golly said how the hell could she do that if Rhoda wasn't there, so I asked how the hell I was to get the carbons in that case. She told me I'd got to get into the cottage and find them. She said they were sure to be on her desk or filed on top of everything else as they would be the latest thing she'd done."

"Are you saying, lad, that you were told to break into that cottage?"

"Golly said the door would likely be on the latch because they always are in the country. I said not these days they aren't, but she insisted that Rhoda's always was. When I said that I doubted that, she said if I had to I'd got to break a window to get in. I didn't like the idea at all. I know enough about crime to know it's an offence even if I had been told to do it."

"How did you get in?" asked Masters.

"The door wasn't locked—just like Golly said. But the house was all in darkness and the lights wouldn't work. Thank heaven I'd had enough common sense to take a torch with me. We keep a few here, you know, for people who have to go out on assignments at night. To write by if you're in the open away from lights."

"You pressed a switch and got nothing?"

"That's right. But I could use the torch to see my way around and I knew something of the lay-out, which was

30

a help. When I went from room to room I tried all the switches. There was no power."

"Did that surprise you?"

"Yes, it did, because I got the impression the place hadn't been occupied for a bit. And that was strange because Golly—all of us, in fact—thought Rhoda had installed herself down there with her boyfriend."

"Apart from the fact that the batteries were flat—I take it there were batteries . . . ?"

"Yes. Big storage dags which were charged by the engine. A bit old-fashioned, of course. Not like your modern generators."

"Dags?" queried Masters.

"Heavy wet batteries," grunted Green.

"Apart from the fact that the storage batteries were flat, which would seem to indicate that the generator had not been run for some time, and which accordingly supports the impression you had that nobody had been in residence for some time, what else added to that belief?"

"It could have been my imagination, but the place felt cold —dampish, in fact."

Green intervened. "You've said that this Lugano bird expected the door to be on the latch. But only when Mrs Carvell was staying down there, surely? Nobody would leave a cottage unlocked if they were leaving it for any length of time."

"That's what I thought—exactly," gabbled Heddle. "That's why I couldn't understand the air of desolation. If I'd had to break in, I'd have understood it better."

"Desolation?" asked Masters. "Is that an exact description or journalistic hyperbole?"

"If you mean am I exaggerating, I'm not. The place was as dusty as makes no matter and there was a rotten, fusty smell as though the windows hadn't been opened for ages. And that wasn't like Rhoda. She was a fresh-air fiend. She was always writing about people who frowst away, sleeping in rooms with doors and windows shut. One of the

31

characters she invented and used to refer to a lot was Stale Air Stella, the high smelling housewife of the high rise block. You must have seen her articles."

"Not him," grunted Green. "He reads proper newspapers, not adult comics."

"Here, I say..." began Heddle.

"What about the carbons you went for?" asked Masters. "Did you find them?"

"No, I didn't. There was nothing in the typewriter on her desk and the top thing in the tray was last week's article."

"So you assumed she hadn't written her column?"

"Not right away. I know it looked as if she'd not done it, but Golly was right. Rhoda wouldn't just barge off on some spree and neglect her spot. I knew that, too. She was a professional and bloody proud of what she did. So I thought maybe the carbons would be upstairs."

"For any particular reason?"

"Not really. I suppose I thought she might have taken the article itself upstairs to correct in bed, in which case she might have left the carbons lying about because she was too busy with Ralph Woodruff to do her filing. You see, I still thought she must have posted the top copy but probably just hadn't got round to putting the carbons in the tray."

"If she had posted the top copies, surely Ms Lugano would have received them?"

"Things have been known to go astray in the post."

Masters inclined his head to acknowledge the truth of this assertion and, to Heddle's great relief, it seemed to indicate that the DCS thought his entire explanation reasonable.

"You went upstairs to look around. What did you find?"

"I'd been up to use the bathroom and loo that Sunday in June, so I knew where to go. But it was bloody eerie, creeping..."

"Quite. We can imagine your feelings. Please go on."

"There were three bedrooms. Two of the doors were ajar, so I decided to try those to begin with. The first room I went into was not very big, and though it had a bed and the usual things in it, it looked as though it had been used as a junk room. Cases and boxes and heaps of books on the floor...

"The second open room was the guest bedroom, I suppose. It was quite big and furnished with a double bed, wardrobe, dressing table and so on. But the bed wasn't made up and I got the impression it hadn't been used for a bit. It looked sort of unlived-in, if you know what I mean. Of course, I only had a torch..."

"And then you tackled the room with the closed door?"

Heddle grimaced in distaste. "When I opened that door I didn't have to wonder any longer where the smell came from. God, it was awful. I held my nose and held the torch in at arm's length. I saw two bodies in the bed and I knew they must be dead. That stink! I've heard about it. The stench of death! But I'd never come across it before. I have now, though, and I never want to again." He looked directly at Masters. "I knew they were dead. They just had to be."

Masters said kindly: "Such experiences are not pleasant, Mr Heddle. But try to forget your repugnance and tell me what you did."

"I held my handkerchief over my nose and mouth and went in for a closer look."

"That was very brave of you."

"Brave? Bloody stupid more likely. I didn't touch anything and I didn't touch them. I just had a closer look and then..."

"And then" said Green, "you got a bit scared and scooted from the room, down the stairs and out to your car as if all the fiends in hell were after you, and you didn't stop to phone the police."

"I never thought about it. Honest!" said Heddle, wildly. "All I wanted to do was get away. To get out of the house and away from that ghastly smell. I just got into the car and drove away." Although basically more composed than earlier, the reporter was showing some signs of panic at the memory of the events of the previous evening. He was breathing gaspily.

"Take it easy, son," said Green. "Forget what you saw, if you can. You'll find you'll feel a lot better about it now you've told us. Getting it off your chest's as good a remedy as any. And have one of my fags. If you smoke your own you'll choke." Green got up to give him the cigarette and the light. "Look on it as good experience, son," went on Green, continuing to humour the younger man. "In your line of business, what happened to you should help a lot. It'll add a bit of colour to your reporting. Give it an air of authenticity."

"I suppose it will."

"If you're ready, Mr Heddle, I should like to get on," said Masters.

"Yes, of course. Sorry."

"You said you got back here to the office at about half-past five yesterday afternoon. When did you set out for the cottage?"

"Sixish, I think. I only had a few little things to do and Golly was trying to rush me."

"How long would it have taken you to drive to the cottage?"

"No more than an hour and three quarters or two hours, normally, but it was rush hour when I set off from here. I lost a bit of time at this end of the journey. I'd say two and a quarter hours at least."

"That would mean that you arrived at the cottage at a quarter or half past eight."

"Yes. I remember looking at my watch a mile or two before I got there and wondering if I'd be too late."

"Too late for what?"

"Supper with Rhoda, of course. I'd eaten nothing since lunchtime and I thought that the least she could do would be to give me a meal for running her errands for her."

"Which you would then claim for on expenses?" asked Green with a grin.

"Perhaps I would. But I'd rather have had supper with her."

"What time was it when you looked at your watch?" asked Masters.

"Ten past eight."

"You are very precise, Mr Heddle. Most people when questioned are a little hazy about times."

"It was only last night," complained Heddle. "And I can tell you I'm not going to forget the salient facts of what happened last night. Minor things may go, perhaps, but the others..." He shuddered at the memory.

"I'll accept that for the moment. How long were you at the cottage?"

"Too long."

"Please don't be flippant, Mr Heddle. Half an hour?"

"It seemed like it, but I don't think in reality it could have been more than six or seven minutes."

"So you were away from there soon after half-past eight and, from the way you described it earlier, driving like the clappers. The rush hour would be over by then so you would have arrived here by ten or soon after. You rang the Chichester police at something after eleven. What happened to that hour between ten and eleven?"

"I didn't come straight back here."

"Ah!"

"I didn't do anything," protested Heddle.

"Anything?"

"Look, when I got away from the cottage and I began to feel a bit less scared, I began to feel hungry, so I stopped at one of those Inns. You know, where you can get a set meal and a drink..."

"I know the sort of place. Berni, Schooner and various others. Please give me the name so that we can check your story and timings."

Heddle gave the required information.

"I had a steak and half a bottle of red wine."

35

"And was it while you were eating your meal that you cooked up the idea of ringing the police at Chichester anonymously?"

Heddle nodded. "I realized that perhaps I'd been a bit of a fool not to do anything about the two bodies immediately. And because of that I thought that if I went back then I might be in trouble it would take some time to get out of."

"Meaning what, lad?" asked Green.

"I suppose I felt I would be safer doing something about it from here with the *View* behind me and the editor and so on. If I'd turned round and gone back to Chichester I'd have been alone with nobody knowing where I was."

"And frightened of the police, lad?"

"I'd rather have somebody powerful watching my interests if I was in their hands. Besides I had to get back here to see Golly."

"You'd a lot on your mind," said Masters drily. "But please go on, Mr Heddle."

"While I was having supper I decided that the best thing was to come back here and phone the Chichester police without giving my name. That way, they'd get to know of the deaths, and as I'd had nothing to do with them they'd be no worse off not knowing who their informant was."

Masters shook his head sadly. "You didn't think very far ahead, Mr Heddle, did you? You forgot to consider that as soon as the news of Mrs Carvell's death broke, your colleagues here would remember you'd been to the cottage last night and they would tell the police of your journey. And that, I'm afraid, would make your situation much worse than it would have been if you'd gone to Chichester after you'd finished supper."

"Yes," whispered Heddle. "When I got back here soon after eleven, I was told Golly had got fed up of waiting for me and had gone out to eat, leaving a message to say she'd be back later. I was really thankful, I can tell you, not to have to face her with the story. Her absence gave

36

me the chance to ring the Chichester police and then to scribble her a note. I just said: 'No luck at the cottage. Nothing in the typewriter or Rhoda's tray'. I left it for her to make of it what she liked. Then I hid. One of my colleagues told me she came steaming back, read the note, crumpled it up and just rang down to the presses. She'd had a stand-by page made up in case I didn't get the copy, so there was no delay. They ran it and Golly went off home."

"Was it then that you realised you hadn't thought far enough ahead?"

Heddle nodded miserably.

"So what did you think up next?"

"I thought—all of a sudden—that this might become a bit of a scoop for us and I could say I'd acted properly by letting the police know about the deaths and at the same time I'd done the right thing in withholding my name until the crime editor could be told and decide what was best to do in the interests of the paper."

"Clutching at straws, lad," said Green.

"Specious, Mr Heddle," added Masters.

"A bit specious, I know. But I am supposed to refer to him before I do anything big or important."

"Then please tell me why you rang the Assistant Commissioner."

"I stayed here all night, thinking. Honestly, I did come to the decision that I ought to let somebody in the police know about me. I reckoned it was no good giving information to the press office at the Yard. They're there to dish it out. So I looked up our phone list and found the Assistant Commissioner Crime. He seemed to be the one who ought to be told, so I waited until I thought he might be up and then I rang. Then if questions were asked about my journey to the cottage..."

"But you didn't tell the AC you were the one who had found the bodies, did you?"

"No, I didn't. I'd meant to, but honestly I didn't know whether I was coming or going. I said who I was and that

I was from the *View* and mentioned the two bodies and where they were, and then I funked telling him I'd found them. I didn't know what to do, so I pretended I'd rung to ask questions for a report. Honestly, Mr Masters, that's how it happened."

"If you say so. But I shall have your story tested at every possible point, and if I find you've told me the merest hint of an untruth I shall take you up either as an accessory or for impeding the police. Is that clear, Mr Heddle?"

"Yes. Yes, thank you."

"And one more thing. No writing this up for your rag until I give the word. If you do, I'll take you in, even if it's only for breaking faith."

"I'll have to tell my bosses. They know I went there."

"Mr Green will see them and he will tell your editor he is at liberty to put in a piece about you finding the bodies. But there will be no details because you are a witness and, despite the chance of a scoop, you are not permitted to talk. If they'll let you, you can write them an account later. Meantime, as I said, you are to regard yourself as a witness and to keep absolutely quiet, on that account. Mr Green will tell your bosses that, too, so they will not press you to act unlawfully."

"I understand."

"And now, Mr Heddle, we are taking you to the Yard."

Heddle looked thoroughly frightened. "What for? I've told you the truth. I thought you'd believed me."

"Your finger prints will be all over the cottage," said Reed. "On every door handle and light switch. I want to take your prints for elimination purposes, and I can't take them here."

"We shall also need a written statement from you," added Masters.

Heddle got to his feet looking slightly happier.

Green slapped him down again immediately. "Before we go, lad, just tell us why you were so sure it was murder, right from the word go."

Heddle blinked.

"Because I knew it couldn't be suicide. At least I decided it wasn't after I'd thought about it. Rhoda told me she was looking forward to her freedom, so I reckoned she wouldn't have killed herself as soon as she'd got it. And I couldn't see her joining in a suicide pact with a man. I mean, they were in bed. Suicides don't go to bed, do they, unless they're taking an overdose of sleeping pills? And knowing Rhoda, I'll bet she didn't take pills—not sleeping ones. But even if she had done, would that Woodruff chap have let her die and then taken an overdose himself?"

"All right, so it wasn't suicide in your book. What about accident?"

"I don't really know, but it didn't look like an accident if you know what I mean. They were lying there peacefully in bed. I knew there was no gas in the house and that home-made current of theirs wouldn't have electrocuted a mouse I'd have thought—well, not two grown people lying in bed it wouldn't. They were just there, with no disturbance or anything. I know it sounds as if I'm describing people who'd just laid down and died, but people don't, do they? Not people like Rhoda Carvell, anyway."

"So you decided on murder."

"I didn't see what else it could be."

"Right, lad, we'll be on our way."

"You believe him, George?" asked the AC.

"I'm inclined to do so, sir. He was in a blue funk, he was tired from being up all night and he'd had a hell of a shock, so when he rang you he really didn't know what he was doing. At that time he wasn't thinking straight, sir, and I don't think he was in any condition to dissemble when we tackled him."

"Long-haired character, you say?"

"A straggly youth, certainly, but all things considered, he didn't put up a bad show when the four of us confronted him."

39

"Pleased to hear it. There's a lot of good in most of these lads if only they weren't too ashamed to show it. Now what?"

"Heddle's given us a start and some background detail, sir. I'm thankful for that. It'll give me a basis for working on."

"You'll be visiting the cottage?"

"Probably this afternoon."

"I'd make it definitely this afternoon. Not only to see the place for yourself, but to make your number with the West Sussex people. I'll get in touch to tell them to expect you."

"Right, sir." Masters got to his feet. "We'll go now, before lunch. It will give us a bit more daylight to play around in."

When he got back to his office, he rang his home. He told Wanda he might be late for supper.

"Will you get lunch, darling?"

"Perhaps."

"Only perhaps?"

"I've got to scoot off to West Sussex."

"When do you expect to get back?"

"I really can't say. Seven maybe, or eight."

"That's a pity."

"Why?"

"Because I thought we'd have that beef pie you've been asking for for so long and I haven't given you because of your no-fat diet..."

"That's over, now."

"Only just. I stewed the beef all yesterday afternoon ready for supper tonight. But I can't keep a pie hot. The crust would burn. So if you don't know when you'll be back..."

"I'll ring you. It will take an hour and a half to get home after that. Does that give you time?"

"Plenty."

"White sauce on the cauliflower?"

"Men and their stomachs! You're getting to be as bad as William."

"I hope not."

"Is it that murder you're investigating?"

"Which murder?"

"I've been shopping. The early edition placards say 'Double tragedy in seaside cottage. Murder feared'."

"That's it."

"I heard somebody say it's Rhoda Carvell, the one who writes for the *View*. Mrs Cartwright will be upset. You know how she adored that column."

"I know. She'll be cut up, but she'll have her new coat to console her."

"She won't, you know. She rang me to say she couldn't find any material she liked anywhere."

"Not in the whole of Oxford Street and its environs?"

"Well, she only had two hours..."

Masters felt a lightening of his spirits as he put the phone down. Even Mrs Cartwright could be worsted—even if it took half a dozen of the biggest stores in the world to do it.

— 2 —

Reed was driving and driving fast. For once Green did not complain.

"Did anybody get lunch?" asked Masters.

"In the time it took you to make a phone call to your missus?" demanded Green. "Come off it."

"There wasn't time and it wasn't time, Chief," said Berger. "Ten-to-twelve is a bit early and we had to put the bags in the car."

"Good."

"Good?" demanded Green, "What's good about it?"

"I was thinking I could do with a drink. That's a good idea, isn't it?"

"Chief," said Reed, "we've all been too long with you to be fooled."

"Meaning?"

"Why tell us now that you would like a drink? Don't bother to answer that. I'll answer it myself. We're about three miles from the Inn where young Heddle claims he ate last night. It'll be open for lunches till two or half past and it will have a bar. As it is now coming up for one o'clock we find ourselves, seemingly by chance, just where you want to be when you want to be—at drinkies time."

"Clever lad," said Green. "If you thought his nibs was trying to be smart, that's your pigeon. But if he's anything like me, he simply wants a drink. He talked too long to young Heddle. Of course, after the first drink on you, I shall want a sandwich."

"With your second drink?"

"That's right."

"These Inn places don't serve sandwiches. They have set meals."

"No matter," said Masters. "We'll manage."

"You're sounding a bit more chirpy, George."

"I feel it. That call to Wanda..."

"Caused you to perk up a bit, did it? I'm not surprised."

"She gave me a bit of good news."

"Oh, yes? What?"

"Mrs Cartwright can't find any material for her new winter coat in the whole of Oxford Street and Regent Street. I have visions of her chilling her beef this winter at all sorts of outdoor rallies in aid of..."

"Of what?"

"All those protest groups she supports."

"And that cheers you up?"

"Yes. I think do-gooders should suffer for their causes. A bit of cold might stiffen up their soft centres. The idea pleases me."

"Like deep-frozen ice cream. I know. Or rather I don't know."

"Don't know what?" asked Berger.

"Why they're all as soft as Joe Soap."

"What do you want them to be? Hard hearted?"

"Like Icicle Joe, lad."

"Should I know him?"

"No," replied Green. "He's staunchly teetotal. Not your type at all."

"I see."

"Heddle's Inn coming up, Chief. I take it you want me to pull in."

"Yes, please."

"This Icicle Joe..." began Berger. "Do you know him, Chief?"

"He's not one of my acquaintances nor, I suspect, is he very friendly with the SSCO if he's a total abstainer."

"You mean to say you don't know him, George?"

"No. Who or what is he?"

"An Eskimo."

Reed pulled on the parking brake. "I know scads of Eskimos. The road where I live's full of them. The trouble is they're forever taking their blasted polar bears for walks. I have to be very careful where I plant my snow shoes or..."

"Cut it out," growled Green. "And let's get on with mixing business with pleasure."

The manager of the Inn was a man of indeterminate age. He looked youngish. Thirty-five or so? But Masters had the impression that the positively young styles he affected should by now have been left behind. Too much heavy black hair—albeit carefully trimmed and lacquered into place with, one supposed, one of the stronger strength hair sprays produced for women. And a pale blue denim, two-piece suit cut on battle-dress lines. In the evening he would, no doubt, be in a dinner jacket with a cascade shirt front, but he obviously thought this less formal attire more suitable for lunchtime. Probably because he felt that it lopped five years off his age at a casual glance. But Masters read faces rather more than clothes. This one had been browned under a sun lamp and looked superficially healthy enough, but it was beginning to show the ravages wrought by too much rich food and strong drink—presumably on the house.

"My name is Masters. I am a detective chief superintendent from Scotland Yard."

"Glad to meet you, Mr Masters. And your colleagues. My name is Brice. You're not here on business, I hope?"

As he spoke, he looked about him to see if there was anybody to overhear. But the bar was almost empty. The man behind the counter was polishing glasses and the only other two occupants were seated at a small table in the window. The dining room, of which the bar was merely an extension, showed more signs of activity. The tables were in chest-high alcoves, the partitions just low enough

44

to show at a glance that a number of places were still occupied.

"I wouldn't bother to tell you who I am if I weren't here on duty, Mr Brice," replied Masters.

"I see. Or at least I think I do."

"Meaning what exactly, chum?" asked Green.

"Well, I mean...Scotland Yard! That sounds to me as if whatever you're doing here isn't just concerned with local village crime."

"It isn't. We've come to see you."

"Can we have a drink?" interrupted Masters. "Best bitter for all of us?"

"Certainly. On the house."

"No, thank you. But I'll be glad to take one off you some time when we're not making enquiries."

"You think I'm trying to...to influence you?" He'd nearly said bribe, but had thought better of it. Influence was more delicate. "I honestly haven't a clue what you're here for, so I don't see how buying you a drink could affect anything any way."

"Let's have the drinks, chum," grated Green. "Then we'll enlighten you."

Brice himself rounded the bar to serve. His hand was noticeably unsteady as he held the tankards. Reed said quietly to Berger: "I wouldn't back him in an egg-and-spoon race. I wonder what he's been up to that's giving him nerves?"

"Probably nothing except a bit of VAT dodging. It's the Chief's presence."

"You reckon he intimidates them? Even the innocents?"

"Everybody's bound to wonder what they've done when he arrives and announces he's on an official visit."

Masters paid for the round and lifted the last of the tankards. After a sipped tester, he put it down again. "I'm sure you don't know why I'm here, Mr Brice. Nor am I suggesting, either by my presence here or by my refusal

45

to accept a free drink, that I think you are in any way implicated in crime."

"I'm glad to hear it. If you don't mind, I think I'll join you gentlemen." He busied himself pouring a lager and lime. "But you did introduce yourselves as police officers and you did say you were here on business, so what can I do for you?"

"Help me, I hope. I want a few words with you and a plate of sandwiches for four."

"Sandwiches? We don't...oh, wait just a minute. If a couple of dinner rolls with a steak in each would do you, you can have those immediately."

"Capital," said Masters.

"Just the jobbo," added Green. "And don't forget the mustard."

Brice nodded and went to the end of the bar to call into the dining room. "Helga! Helga!" When the waitress arrived he gave her his instructions and then returned to Masters to await the food.

Helga was a pretty blonde. Brice explained she was a Norwegian who had come over as an au pair, but had found working as a waitress more to her liking and more lucrative. When she arrived, carrying two oval platters with the unusual looking fare, she glanced curiously at Masters with large, blue, bold eyes.

"The mustard pot, love," reminded Green.

"French?"

"Proper mustard, love. English."

She jiggled away. Masters turned to Brice. "A young man we're interested in claims he called here last night for a meal. He says he had a steak and a half bottle of red wine."

"Then he'd have eaten in this dining room. We've got just the three restaurants—Steak, Duck and Fish. What time did he say he came?"

"He reckons about nine, and that he stayed until ten or thereabouts."

46

"Alone?"

"So he says."

"Excuse me." Brice picked up an internal phone below the bar counter. "Jessie? A tab last night for one steak, one half bottle of red of some sort. Somewhere about the middle of the invoice numbers. Let me know right away, love, please." He put the phone down and turned to Masters. "He'd get his bill as soon as he was served. That would be about a quarter past nine if he arrived when you said. All the bills are numbered and that time is about half-way through the dining period—half-past six to eleven, but the rush is from eight to ten."

"That's all very clear, Mr Brice, thank you. I take it that if you find the invoice we shall know who served him?"

Brice nodded. "If he came we will," he said confidently. "We don't get all that many eating alone. No more than two or three a night, so it will be a case of..."

The internal phone interrupted him.

"Yes? Only one for a steak and half a bottle. Two singles for scampi...no, just the steak. Who served him? Helga? Thanks, Jessie."

"Did I hear you say Helga served him? The girl who brought our sandwiches?"

"Yes. Perhaps a relief if Helga was away having a whizz at the time, but reliefs don't usually do bills. Tips, you know. But the regular girls do have to sneak a couple of minutes to powder their noses now and then. I tell them to do it while the chefs are cooking the orders."

"Thank you. I'd like to speak to Helga, please."

"And she to him, I'll bet," said Berger in a whisper to Reed. "Those eyes—she gave the Chief the old green light with them."

"Give me a couple of minutes to arrange a relief."

"You're not expecting to get anything here, are you, Chief?" asked Reed. "It's ten to one Heddle was telling us the truth about this place."

Masters merely shrugged. Green said to Reed. "It's always a mystery to me why young jacks, like yourself and Berger here, most of you good at your jobs as far as it goes..."

"Thanks."

"...can never be content unless they're scrabbling around trying to unearth material clues. You never take time to immerse yourself in a case like me and his nibs here, to soak up atmosphere until there's a feel—almost a texture—to the job."

"Hark who's talking! Rabbiting on about Icicle Joe! What had that got to do with the case?"

"With the case, nothing. With the business in hand, everything."

"I'm listening."

"We wanted a drink didn't we?"

"You said this Joe was a teetotaller."

"That's right. But he was always in the right place at the right time."

"So?"

"As I said, you lads aren't happy unless you're finding material clues or collating circumstantial evidence. But take this case for instance. Have you two appreciated the fear young Heddle must have felt? His experience probably didn't panic him, exactly, but it drove him to this place to recover."

"So?"

"For his nibs this place still reeks of the nervousness young Heddle shed here. He can feel it, or the results of it. For me, its stealthy. Yes, stealthy is the word. His nibs is beginning to feel a creepiness about the crime. But do you lads feel that? Or is murder just murder to you, whether it is open assault or murder by craft and stealth?"

"You're making all this up."

"I'm not. To feel the difference is everything to his nibs. It changes his viewpoint, if not his approach."

Masters had not been privy to this conversation. He had been down the other end of the bar examining the prints on the walls. He turned to join them as Brice returned.

"Here's Helga," the manager announced, "and she'll be cross if she sees you haven't eaten the sandwiches she prepared for you."

Green picked up one of the doorstep sandwiches. "You talk to her, George. I've got a sore hand."

"So it would seem." Masters turned to Helga who had donned a clean white overall for the interview. It was held in so tightly at the waist that the size of her large bust was even more accentuated. Berger whistled almost silently through his front teeth at the sight and Reed whispered: "She'd make Marilyn Monroe look undernourished."

"Do you speak English, Helga?" asked Masters.

A smiled affirmative.

"Last evening, about nine o'clock, a young man came into your dining room alone. He ordered a half bottle of red wine with his steak."

"He sat there." She pointed to a cubicle that held a table for two.

"You remember him?"

"A little bit. He was upset. I think he was angry because his girl had not come with him."

"Did he tell you that?"

"No, but what else could there be to upset him?"

"You said he was angry."

"Maybe angry. Maybe something else. Not happy."

"Could he have been afraid—frightened?"

"He had a white face. Very white. That is frightened?"

"What else did you notice about him?"

"He had hair like this—nearly." She flicked the cascade of fair hair at the side of her neck. "But not so pretty," she added hastily.

"Can you remember what he was wearing?"

"It is not easy. We have not big lights. Only little lights on the tables to see faces."

"Sweater and jeans, perhaps?"

"Oh, no, a suit and a tie."

"What colour?"

"I don't know. It had white lines in it I think."

Green, who had been munching away quietly in the background, but never taking his eyes off the girl's face, emptied his mouth and asked. "After he gave his order, how long did he have to wait?"

Helga pouted. "Ten minutes for his steak. But I took his wine to him before it."

"And you passed him several times?"

"Oh, yes. When I was serving other diners."

"What was he doing?"

"He was thinking. He was not here, you know. When I showed him the wine he was...he jumped a bit."

"Startled, was he?"

"Yes. And again when I brought his steak."

"Thank you." Green picked up the remains of his sandwich. Masters looked round to make sure Green had finished his interruption and then turned again to Helga.

"He came in about nine o'clock, you think?"

She shrugged, as if to convey that she would be too busy at that time of night to notice the comings and goings of customers.

Brice said: "Judging by the number on the bill you can reckon that's not far out—give or take a quarter of an hour."

"Thank you, Mr Brice. How long did the customer stay, Helga?"

"A long time. When people come in pairs they sit and talk or smoke together or hold hands. But when a man comes without his girl he gobbles up fast and goes quick. This one did not. He was thinking, like a man with a big problem. I thought he had had a quarrel perhaps with his girl and he was thinking about that."

"Thank you, Helga. That's all. While I have my sandwich, would you fetch my bill, please?"

As Helga went off to sort out this unaccustomed transaction, Brice asked: "What's this chap done? Or oughtn't I to ask?"

"Nothing," replied Masters and bit into his bun.

"Nothing?" Brice looked at Reed in amazement. "Nothing?"

"He's a witness," said Reed. "To a very serious crime. We had to check his evidence."

"That's all right then. I'm glad the Inn doesn't figure in it, whatever it is."

Following the instructions given earlier by the Chichester police, Berger drove straight to Climping and then westwards along a stony track for almost a mile. There was no chance of missing the cottage. It was the only building in sight.

"Lonely," grunted Green. "Away from the crowds of visitors and day trippers. What's it been?"

"Farmhouse, perhaps," suggested Masters. "It doesn't look like a labourer's cottage. They may call it a cottage, but it looks like a very substantial dwelling to me."

The fields round about were plough. A whitish-greyish soil that had been turned over for winter sowing or weathering according to what the crop was to be. But the earth didn't seem to have the strength of wholesome soil that holds the pattern of the plough for weeks, much as good thick cream will hold the pattern of a whisk. Too friable or sandy or chalky, Masters supposed. He couldn't decide which. He was no farmer and an unskilled gardener. Wanda kept the plants in their little home garden, and most of her soil came in bags—peat and potting compost. Masters, still somewhat depressed, realized he suddenly felt sad he had never really learned much about nature, despite his academic knowledge of the biological sciences. Out here, in the autumn afternoon, he sensed the yawning gap between his knowledge and practical experience. The loneliness around the building seemed to be drawing him nearer to Mother Earth. He wondered about it with a kind of silent, melancholy philosophy. How near to Mother Earth was truth? How near to truth would he get at this isolated house?

A black Rover saloon was drawn up at the front gate of

the house, which was neighboured by a pair of tarred, weather-beaten sheds which stood like gatehouses to the property. Behind them was a still pleasant garden with passable lawn about fifty feet square—presumably the one on which Rhoda and Heddle had sunbathed. There was a border of shrubs to the east, four or five gnarled apple trees still bearing some fruit, while windfalls dotted both the grass and the garden path. The deadening stalks of perennials stood up among chrysanthemums bearing small, old blossoms.

"Robson," said the Chichester DI, introducing himself. "And DS Middleton. I was glad when you said you'd come today, sir."

"Why?"

"Why, sir?"

Masters grinned. "Yes, why today particularly?"

He was aware that Robson and Middleton were staring at him in amazement. They obviously thought his question bizarre, if not stupid. The first question from a senior detective investigating a serious crime. "Why are you glad I've come this afternoon?" Bathos! He stood waiting for a reply looking quizzically at Robson with such an intensity of expectation that the DI, suspecting there must be more reason for the question than first appeared, stopped to think before answering.

"I don't like the feel of this place," he managed at length.

"Ah! Not just pleasure at handing over the case?"

"I'm not really handing it over. I'm to work with you."

Masters nodded. "I'm pleased to hear your answer. I felt spooky myself. If you feel it, too, I know it's not just me being fanciful. Can we go in?"

Robson led the way through the open front door and into the large room on the left of the hall. Masters looked about him, hands in the pockets of his overcoat.

"What's it called?"

"Abbot's Hall."

"Hall? Not cottage?"

"Abbot's Hall, sir."

"It's got a history, I suppose?"

The Chichester man nodded. "Look at the windows, sir. Four-inch oak. Look at this floor."

It was of red brick, and though evenly laid, the whole area of it dipped, saucer-like, from the walls to the middle. The Carvells had covered it with a number of rush mats, with a conventional hearthrug in front of the wide fireplace. A half-burnt log, over a yard long, sat across the top of the wrought iron fire-basket from which the ash had fallen as the fire died.

"Abbot's?" asked Green. "Sounds religious."

"Some old boy from the Abbey which used to be round here is said to have built it as a love-nest about four hundred years ago. The story had it he installed women here—fallen women—under the pretence he was trying to make them see the error of their ways and to restore them as good citizens."

Green grunted. "Whereas, in reality, what he was doing was giving them food and lodging in return for the favours he wasn't allowed to enjoy in the Abbey?"

"That's why it's so isolated," admitted Robson. "It became a farm later on, and remained so until about six or seven years ago when the Carvells bought it. The house and land were sold separately."

"You've been doing your homework," said Masters approvingly.

"We thought you'd like to know the score, sir."

"You never spoke a truer word, son," said Green. "I was only telling these two lads of ours an hour ago that his nibs likes to get the feeling of a case. The texture if you like. All the background detail. It affects the way he thinks."

"That's what my boss said."

"Then your boss is a wise bloke. Have a fag." Green drew out his usual battered packet of Kensitas and offered it to the DI.

Masters was wandering round the room. It was a large apartment, with windows piercing the stone walls at both ends. The frames Robson had mentioned may have been original, but the windows themselves were modern. He tried one. It opened outwards very easily on its stretcher bar. He remembered that Rhoda Carvell had enjoyed the reputation of being a fresh-air fiend. He supposed he should have expected her windows to open easily.

"Nice furniture," said Reed who had recently become interested in antiques.

"It all looks like old second-hand stuff to me," said Sergeant Middleton who hitherto had found little to say. "Junk picked up for a seaside cottage."

"Pay no attention to him," said Robson. "He wouldn't know the difference between Hepplewhite and kitchen units you buy in packs to put together yourself."

Masters turned and said to Middleton: "You're not interested in material things, like good bits of furniture?"

"They don't help with a case like this, sir, do they? I mean whether that glass-fronted cupboard was made two hundred years ago or last month is neither here nor there when you're looking for a murderer."

"You've said the wrong thing, chum," said Reed.

"Have I? How? Why? New or old, we can still dust it for prints if that's what we have to do."

"You're interested in people rather than things, Sergeant? Is that it?" asked Masters mildly.

"Yes, sir."

"I have no quarrel with that except..."

"Except what, sir?" asked Middleton.

"You can't separate the two. You heard Sergeant Reed say that this furniture is nice, meaning that it is all probably quite old and valuable."

"I'll take his word for it, sir, not knowing anything about it myself."

"But surely the fact that the Carvells had good taste, and indulged it here, tells you something about them as people. Doesn't it?"

Middleton scratched his head. "I don't know what you're getting at, sir." He looked around at the faces of the other four detectives as if seeking help. He got none, but Green said: "Just keep on listening, son."

"Reed's observation about the furniture and my own nosing about the room have cleared up a very important point for me, Sergeant. I'll explain, so as not to leave you too mystified. People who like good furniture usually look after it and the comfort of the house in which they install it. Agreed?"

"It sounds logical, sir."

"The Carvells have put new windows into the old original frames either because the former ones were rotten or because they were ill-fitting. I favour the latter reason. Why will become obvious in a moment.

"Ill-fitting windows would definitely detract from the comfort of a lonely house only two or three hundred yards from the sea. On-shore gales would make a place such as this almost uninhabitable if the windows let in draughts. And the same goes for doors. But doors don't rot, so if they have been replaced, it must have been because they were ill-fitting.

"In a fireplace like this one, you could build a fire big enough to roast an ox, but if the room door wasn't snug in its frame, you'd get scorched in front and frozen at the back. Now come and look at the door."

"It's new, sir," admitted Middleton.

"Quite so. Not only is the door new, but so is the frame. See how the edge of the door itself is chamfered to fit snug. The frame is of modern design." Masters indicated the strips of sponge-loaded green felt, an inch and a half wide, let in all round, and drew their attention to the new threshold of four-inch, chamfered oak. "When this door is closed and the catch is in position, the room would be almost hermetically sealed if it weren't for the chimney." Masters turned to Robson. "Have they put doors like this in all the rooms?"

"Everywhere. It must have cost a bomb."

"Upstairs? In the bedrooms?"

"Everywhere, sir." Robson sounded slightly irritated that he had to repeat himself.

"As I thought." Masters turned again to Middleton. "Now to get to the point or moral of my lecture. This morning when I interviewed the young man who discovered these bodies, a chap called Heddle, I was inclined to believe his story except for the fact that there was one point in it that didn't ring true. So I decided that if one bit sounded distinctly off, all the rest could be a tissue of lies."

"Understandable, sir."

"So I set out to test Heddle's story. On the way down here we stopped to check events at the restaurant where he said he had supper last evening. That part of his account was true—vouched for by the manager and a waitress. But there remained the doubtful point I mentioned a moment ago."

"Sir?"

"Now I've cleared it up. Would you like to know what it was?"

"Yes, I would sir. You've been nowhere except this room. Spoken to nobody except us about pieces of furniture..."

"And consequently doors and windows.

"Yes, sir."

"Young Mr Heddle told me that when he came into the house last night all he got was what he called a rotten, fusty smell down here. Now that seemed wrong to me, because the stink of death after corpses have lain unattended for some time would pervade an ordinary house. There would be no mistaking it. But Heddle said he suspected nothing wrong until he opened the bedroom door and got the full blast of it. But it appears that he didn't dream up that account. It was true, because the doors are so well fitting. Now, Sergeant, if a witness told you something that sounds patently wrong but which subsequently turned out to be true, what would be your reaction?"

"I reckon I could risk believing everything he had told me, sir."

"Fine. I don't think I need waste any more time on checking Mr Heddle's statement. At least for the time being. So we are free to push ahead with other things."

"Yes sir."

"So don't despise Hepplewhite, lad," said Green.

"The stench is hanging about down here now," said Berger. "It shows that once the bedroom door was opened..."

"We've had enough lectures for today, son," said Green. "Hand over one of your fags. Oh, and have one yourself. The more of us who smoke, the less of that pong there will be."

Masters led the way upstairs. He went slowly, as if so deep in thought that his brain had no spare capacity for directing his feet. The three sergeants followed. Robson, hanging back to talk to Green, whispered: "Your guv'nor sounds a bit of a charlatan to me."

"Oh, yes?"

"Anybody could have guessed that if the doors fit well the stench wouldn't percolate out of the room. All that rubbish about old furniture leading him to conclusions was so much eyewash."

"Was it?" asked Green blandly.

"You don't think so?"

"Well, I didn't pick the hole in Heddle's story, and I didn't inspect the doors to check it, so what his nibs sussed out of it all seems fair enough to me. But perhaps I'm old-fashioned."

"Look at him now. He looks to me as if he couldn't move fast enough to catch cold—either mentally or physically—let alone solve a baffling case of double murder."

"Have you decided who did it, chum?"

"Of course I bloody-well haven't."

"Then why criticize him?"

"He's supposed to be the greatest. I'm not."

"I get you. You're not the most expert of jacks, but you can see enough of what's going on to know he's not going to succeed?"

"I can see enough of what's not going on."

"We'll have to wait and see then, won't we?"

They followed up the stairs.

"This the room?" asked Masters.

"That's it."

Masters opened the door and entered.

"Have you touched the windows, Mr Robson?"

"No. They were closed when we came."

"Mrs Carvell was a fresh-air fiend."

"So she may have been, but there was no fresh air in here."

Masters turned to Middleton. "What was the weather like a week ago?"

"Round here, sir?"

"We're not talking about Ashby-de-la-Zouch, lad," said Green.

"A week ago!" The sergeant looked at his DI. "There was a southerly gale, wasn't there?"

"High winds, at any rate. They lasted for several days. But why a week ago, sir?"

Masters mused for a moment and then turned to Middleton. "Go to the phone and get to know exactly. From the Coast Guard people. From five to seven days ago, please."

Middleton went. Robson stood quiet until Masters addressed him. "Putrefaction," he said laconically.

"What?"

"The decomposition of organic matter under the influence of micro-organisms, accompanied by the development of disagreeable odours." He still looked at Robson. "That's a quotation from the Police Pathology Manual— if you hadn't already guessed."

"I still don't see..."

"Have you had the medical report yet?"

"Only the verbal while they were here."

"They? Police Surgeon and pathologist?"

Robson nodded. "They told us that they suspected arsine straight away and that's really all we've had."

58

"Did they say why they suspected arsine?"

"The pathologist said that apart from all the other stinks in the room there was a strong smell of garlic."

"What else did they say?"

"The pathologist said that most arsenical vapours smell like a Spaniard's breath after Sunday dinner. That's exactly how he put it, and said that's why he suspected arsine."

"Then what?"

"He said he'd had some experience of non-fatal bouts of arsine poisoning. He gave our police surgeon a lecture on how the use of arsenical agricultural preparations constitutes a constant hazard, not only to the farmer, but to the consumer. Evidently agricultural workers can get arsine poisoning from dust or sprays or whatever they use to keep down weeds and pests."

"Did they examine the eyes closely?"

"Yes, they did now you come to mention it. The path bloke said one of the things he looks for in these cases is...er..."

"Oedema?"

"That's it. I'd forgotten the word for a moment. Oedema in the eyelids, particularly the bottom ones."

"He suggested that oedema round the eyes was one of the obvious signs of arsine poisoning?"

"So he said. They both looked at the eyes on both the bodies and nodded to each other. Definite signs of fluid swelling one of them called it. So the pathologist turned to me and said, 'Off the top, DI, we suspect arsine. But don't take it for granted, because neither of them appears to have vomited, which seems a bit strange when there's any form of arsenic involved.'"

"Anything else?"

"He said the post-mortem would take a long time because with arsine it can be quite difficult to make a diagnosis without their histories and with apparently so few symptoms."

"No hint as to how long they'd been dead?"

"I asked, naturally. But they merely said more than forty-eight hours. Too diffcult to say with any accuracy beyond that until after the p.m."

"So," said Masters, "putrefaction."

"You're back on that again, sir. Why?"

"Don't buy it, lad," said Green.

Robson replied: "I want to know what's going on. And that includes what people are thinking about."

"Very well," said Masters, his hands still in the pockets of his overcoat. "It's autumn. It's not hot weather. Yet the bodies were stinking. In your experience, how long does it take for corpses to smell?"

"Several days, I suppose. Funerals aren't held for three or four days usually."

"They would be if there was any chance of decomposition being so far advanced in that time as to be unpleasant. Ignoring any form of embalming or cold storage, that is. So though the pathologist won't be more precise, I'm guessing they've been here a week, or the best part of a week. If Middleton tells me there were gales a week ago, that will tie in, because otherwise Mrs Carvell would have had her windows open when she went to bed."

"Logical," agreed Green. "Closed windows, airtight door, no fireplace and death by gassing. Just what the old suicides tried to achieve when they gassed themselves."

"But where does it get us?" demanded Middleton.

"First off," said Green, "his nibs has probably determined the time of death—to the night, if not the minute. Second he has raised the question of whether the death was accidental..."

"A combination of circumstances, you mean?"

"Right, lad. The first time ever this Carvell bird goes to bed in an airtight room, she's gassed. Would it have happened a year ago if she'd done the same? Are we in danger at this moment—the door being shut?"

"Meaning there could be some source of arsine under the floorboards?"

"Or in the paint or the plaster. We don't know, son, but

the questions have to be considered. That's always the result of the thought processes you are so keen on following."

Middleton nodded. "Okay. So what can we do about it? Tear the place to bits?"

"Not yet," said Masters. "But your people could make some enquiries as to if and when either of them was seen alive or anybody noticed activity about the house—lights on or cars coming and going."

"Talking about cars," said Robson, "there's one in one of the outbuildings. We've checked it. It belonged to Ralph Woodruff."

Masters nodded his thanks for this piece of information and turned to leave the bedroom. The others followed him downstairs. He passed across the square, brick-floored hall to the front door which had been left open to help clear the house of its unpleasant odours. He paused to examine it. It was not new. Not the original door either, Masters guessed, but still a door of some antiquity. Probably dating from 1880 or thereabouts, he supposed. Then he found himself wondering why that particular date should have come into his mind. He was not knowledgeable about such things, but the date persisted, and he was too curious a man to accept the fact without searching for a reason. The door was of oak, planked and untreated. Grey with age and from its proximity to the salt sea air. Each join in the planks had been covered by a baton little more than an inch wide. It was a common enough sort of door, he supposed, and had it been his he would have applied linseed oil for the wood to soak up and thus regain some of the vitality which the Carvells had apparently been content to allow to ebb away. He stood staring at it moodily, the others standing by watching him quietly. Then he got it. The latch on the door. A wrought iron ring on the outside, with a biggish drop-bar inside. But it was the pivot below this bar that he must have noticed subliminally and which must have brought the date to mind. A little curved length of iron with wrought finials. It pivoted as the catch bar lifted and fell which would, he knew, give a very individual sound to the movement every time the handle was turned. He tried it for himself and listened. How many times had he heard it in his youth? The latch was the twin of the one on the little, narrow, outer vestry door of the church in which he had been a choirboy for several years long ago. How many times had he gone through that door to and from choir practices and services? The church had been an architectural horror. Its arches faced with alternate black and red bricks, and elsewhere there had been similar Victorian mistakes. Victorian— built in 1880, as he knew. He'd learned that as a small boy of seven years old, at Sunday School. He knew he had subconsciously stopped to examine not the door itself, but the latch which young Heddle claimed he had found ready for lifting. He had wanted to check whether this was true or false. He reckoned it was true. People with door latches like that don't bother to lock up overnight. The strength of the thing gave an entirely spurious air of safety which a flimsy but more secure spring lock could never have imparted.

Without a word to his companions, hands still in his coat pockets, he left the house and headed along the garden path. They followed him through the gate between the old sheds across the track and on to the scrubland where a well-beaten path, not much more than a foot wide, led towards the sea.

"What now, George?" Green was stumbling over the low scrub, trying to keep abreast.

"I thought it would be as well to see if anybody could approach from this way, Bill."

"Without being seen, you mean?"

"If they were to leave a car, come along the beach and then strike inland."

"At night they could, I reckon. There's nobody anywhere in sight now, so it would be easy to get here unnoticed at night."

The miniature cliffs were scarcely four feet high, standing above a stretch of pebbles and then a sandstrip. The wind, not strong, but blowing just enough to make its presence felt, moved the skirts of Masters' coat. The westering sun was red-gold. Despite the brightness there was an air of desolation about the area.

"I suppose it's crowded in the summer," said Green, "but it's bloody lonely now."

"Never crowded just here." Robson had come up behind. "At Littlehampton, to the east, the trippers crowd in. And, of course, we get scads of people at Hayling Island and boating people in the Chichester Harbour area, also, to the west. But not here. They're frightened to move out of the herd, most of them."

"That's probably why the Carvells bought the place," mused Masters. "The tide is going out, isn't it?"

"Ebbing fast."

In the few moments they had been standing there, a curious development had been taking place below high water mark. As the water shallowed over the clay-sand, greyish-white lumps started to show. Upturned bowls of lumpy grey rock, looking like giant turtles stranded, half buried in mud. First one and then another broke the surface, showing knobbly protuberances like the ball and socket joints of the thigh bones of long dead animals. The water fretted between them and gradually subsided. Masters stood and watched as more and more of the mounds were exposed.

"What are they made of?" he asked Robson. "Chalk or limestone?"

"Chalk," replied Robson. "They're the outcrop of the hills." He turned and pointed inland at the distant, rounded shapes, low down on the skyline and nearly lost in the pre-twilight haze. "The strata dip under the soil and come up again here. Not that I know a lot about it, mind, but I suppose they were a lot higher at one time. The sea will have worn them away almost down to the level of its bed. Those things sticking up are flints. They used to be used for building years ago."

Masters nodded his thanks for the information and remained silent for some minutes as if fascinated by the receding water. Though he had four colleagues with him, he was conscious of the autumn solitude. But, liking this time of the year as he did, he was cheered rather than saddened by the grey water dropping back, leaving only shallow pools between the chalk formations. His companions remained silent, waiting on him as if unwilling to interrupt his thoughts lest he should be considering some point in the case as yet not recognized by them.

Masters turned as he heard Middleton coming along the little path. The sergeant's footfalls, though light enough, still made a sound audible above the noise of wind, sea and mewing gulls.

"Sou'sou'west gale, sir," reported Middleton, consulting his notebook. "A week last Sunday and Monday. Straight in to this part of the coast. By Tuesday midday it had lessened considerably and veered to the west. It blew itself out over Tuesday night. That's the coastguard's log report, sir."

Masters thanked Middleton and led the way back to Abbot's Hall, now standing silhouetted against the last of the light in the sky. He stopped suddenly and said to Middleton: "You're sure the coastguard said Sunday and Monday?"

"That's right, sir. Lessening and veering by Tuesday noon."

Masters continued his way towards the house. As they reached the car, Robson asked: "Shall you call in for the pathologist's report, sir?"

"No. Leave it for the moment—until they've had time to write it up fully. They'll want to examine all the organs of both bodies. It'll take time to do and write up."

"You'll be coming down again?"

"Maybe tomorrow. We shall let you know. Don't forget to ask round about when they were last seen."

"Tomorrow morning? Then I'll be on hand if you come down."

"Tonight, chum," said Green. "You'll get everybody at home in the evening. Half the men, at least, will be away by day."

Robson looked as if he could have kicked himself for not seeing so obvious a reason for choosing evening for his house-to-house enquiries. If either Rhoda Carvell or Ralph Woodruff had been noticed in person, it would more than likely be at night time as they went to or returned from some social occasion, or at the weekend when they might be expected to journey about. In any case it could well be men, going to or from one of the local pubs, who might have seen them in the car, or might have noticed a distant light in an uncurtained window of Abbot's Hall.

Masters pretended not to notice the local man's discomfiture. He opened the door of the Rover and settled himself into the rear offside seat. As he was about to shut the door he said to Middleton: "Would you do me a favour, please, Sergeant? Ring my home and let my wife know we are setting out for London now. She wanted to know because of preparing supper."

"Number, sir, please?"

Masters gave it to him, drew his coat close around him and closed the door. He lifted one hand in a gesture of farewell to Robson and Middleton as Reed started up and drew away.

"Funny one, that, sir," said Middleton to Robson. "His wife sounded okay. A bit la-di-dah, perhaps, but nice with it."

"How d'you mean, funny? I didn't get many laughs."

"What I mean is I wouldn't put any money on him successfully investigating a theft of toffee apples from a street barrow."

"You wouldn't, wouldn't you? Then you'd be a bit of a fool. He's a highly successful jack."

"Got a reputation up in the smoke has he?"

"He's the whizz kid. Once he's set on, he never lets go.

65

He's reckoned to be spectacular with it and none of his files get put away marked unsolved."

Middleton slowed the car to enter the road from the track. "I wouldn't have believed all that, sir, if you hadn't told me. I thought he just mooned about."

"That's what it seemed like to me, too, but I got the impression that every word he said and every question he asked was pertinent. The trouble was I couldn't always see why. Even when he asked me if those ridges on the shore were chalk or limestone."

"Are you sure you weren't reading more into what he asked because of his reputation?"

"Maybe."

"All that rubbish about furniture! And why send me off to find out what the weather was like a week ago?"

"That's easy. It's obvious he doesn't expect the pathologist to come up with a precise time of death."

Middleton swung the car left on to the main road. "They never do. So what's clever in knowing that? We always get a time bracket for unnatural deaths. Between ten and twelve or not earlier than six and not later than nine."

"You're talking about hours, Bert. This time the bracket will be days—not less than five, not more than eight. Masters knows that's what he's going to hear. That's why he isn't visiting the pathologist tonight."

"Seems keener on his supper being ready for him when he gets home than bothering with the pathologist."

"Don't you believe it. He intends to cut that bracket down a bit himself, and finding out about the weather was one way of doing it."

"How come?"

"If a woman is a fresh-air fiend and sleeps with her window open whenever possible, the night she shuts it is the night when there's a gale blowing straight in."

"Two nights. Sunday and Monday."

"Right. Two nights. So he says to himself, she was killed either last Sunday or Monday, seeing the medics can't be sure."

"Oh, come on, sir. Whoever killed those two could have closed the windows if they'd been open."

"True. But what if he didn't? It's worth thinking about."

"Maybe."

"Not maybe, Bert. Think of the mechanics of the job. To steal into a room where two people are in bed to close the windows is pretty risky. It's a damn-sight easier not to have to."

"I agree with that, sir, but it still isn't fact."

"Nobody pretends it is. Least of all Masters, I'd say. But he's bearing it in mind, I'll bet. And if anything crops up to support his theory, he's in clover, isn't he?"

Robson lit two cigarettes and gave one to Middleton as the car approached Chichester.

"Yes," continued the DI musingly. "I'll bet he's discussing those closed windows with his pals all the way to London."

"Not Sunday night," said Masters, swaying with the swinging of the car as Reed made what speed he could along the track from Abbot's Hall. "We know Mrs Carvell was in the *View* office on Monday morning handing in all that gup about Conservative women."

Green grunted agreement, and said: "Heddle told us she was going to attend the divorce court on Tuesday morning, so she couldn't have died before Tuesday night at the earliest, and by that time the gale had blown itself out."

"So we're on the wrong track?"

"Looks like it."

Masters didn't reply. He took out his pipe and started to fill it with Warlock Flake. By now it was dark and he performed the operation more by touch than sight. The flame of his match as he struck it gave him a sense of cosiness in this great, warm car, protected from the night outside. He settled more comfortably in his seat. There didn't seem to be much more to say about the case at this point, and his thoughts travelled ahead of him to Wanda and home. The others seemed to recognise his mood and they travelled in silence for some time. Then Berger asked: "Are we going to Chichester early tomorrow, Chief. If we are, I'll see the car's filled up tonight."

"We'll be out soon after nine. But not to Chichester straight away. We'll try to see Professor Carvell first."

"Why him?" demanded Green. "He got rid of her through the divorce court. He's not likely to have been sniffing around her since. Not if she was camping out with the boy friend."

"Right enough, Bill, but the professor might have known something of her plans."

"Like what?"

"Had she laid on some sort of celebration party last Tuesday night? Could there have been other people at Abbot's Hall then? Did she speak to him after the divorce hearing? If so, what did she say?"

Green grunted his acceptance of the point. "Will you contact Carvell to set up a meeting or do we just blow in on him?"

"Descend on him, I think. He must be expecting us to call, but we might as well surprise him."

They continued on their way, stopping to drop Green at his home.

"The Yard, Chief?"

"No, drop me, please. Then take the car on."

They stopped at the end of the narrow way that led down to Master's tiny house. "'Night, Chief."

"Goodnight."

When Masters was out of earshot, Reed said, "I wish to hell I knew what's been biting him all day. He's been grumpy ever since he heard of Rhoda Carvell's death."

"Before that," replied Berger. "He was a bit off when he arrived, according to Bill Green. He's probably had a row with his missus."

"Unlikely," said Reed. "Not with her. They just don't have rows."

Masters, hunched up in his overcoat, walked along the dark, narrow street to his front door. With night had come a hint of frost. With no blanket of cloud to mar the day, there was nothing to keep the earth warm once the sun had gone. The nip in the air made the prospect of home seem all the cosier.

— 3 —

Wanda appeared in the tiny hall as he opened the door. She had heard his key in the lock and had come to greet him.

"Is Michael in bed?" he asked as he kissed her.

"By now, darling? He has been for nearly two hours. Your face feels cold."

"I was glad you persuaded me to take a coat."

"Come into the dining room and have your drink. I can talk to you there from the kitchen."

He knew she wouldn't have put the cauliflower on the stove until he arrived, but everything else would be ready and waiting. "Give me a couple of minutes. I'll change and sluice."

As he sat down at the end of the beautifully laid table, she asked—through the archway leading to the kitchen: "Have you had a good trip, darling?"

"Not bad." Even as he said it, he felt it was a somewhat churlish reply. All about him was comfort and warmth. The highly polished table with spotless white napkins, gleaming silver and glass...Wanda cared for him, their son, and this little house in a way that, had he wanted to, he could never have faulted. "How have you been?"

She came through to join him and accepted her glass of sherry to sip while standing up.

"Michael and I had a good day. We went out for a walk in the park. It was a sort of walky day if you know what I mean. A day for coats and hats but not all shivery and cold. And such lovely colours and the setting sun was glorious. Michael called it a ball. I think he wanted me to get it down for him to play with."

"I saw it, too. From the cliffs at Climping."

"Rhoda Carvell?"

He nodded. "You've seen some reports?"

"The evening paper had it. You said you would be taking the case, remember? Is it nasty?"

"I don't know yet."

"Why not?"

He grinned. "Because I've been grumpy all day."

"I guessed you might be." She kissed his forehead. "I don't know why I thought so, because I've never known you like that before."

"No."

"The Cartwrights?"

"Yes. I'm sorry, poppet, but I just don't care for them."

"It goes beyond that, doesn't it, George? You actively dislike them. See them as some sort of threat to us?"

He looked up at her. "I won't admit that anything or anybody could be a threat to us, but I'm a believer in influences. Influences for good, influences for bad and so on. Not all black and white, of course. Some grey."

"The power of evil?"

"I don't put the Cartwrights in that category, but yes, in my job one comes to sense the power of evil. One would have to be very insensitive not to. Small pockets of it. Not the big overwhelming clouds of evil that emanated from Hitler and his gang for so long."

"I think I understand."

"I'm sure you understand fully, because you're a very clever, not to say wise, girl."

She smiled down at him. "They are inimical to all you stand for, aren't they? The rotten apples. Not actively harmful in themselves but liable to taint their neighbours and eventually the whole barrel."

He nodded. "They provide succour for all sorts of nasties, too, allowing them to multiply..."

"Oh!" Wanda put down her glass and dashed into the

kitchen to turn off a gas tap. "Just in time," she said, relieved. "I thought I smelt it. Your precious cauliflower has nearly boiled dry."

A few minutes later they sat down to their meal. The pie was glorious. Deep, with no bottom crust. Golden pastry with added, decorative leaves made from the overs; well-stewed beef cooked in nothing more than its own tea; stalkless florets of cauliflower in white sauce and boiled potatoes. He had come to regard this as his favourite meal, and his anticipation of pleasure was so great that his knife and fork, as he lifted them, almost groaned with desire. But as he was lifting the first mouthful, the front doorbell rang.

Masters himself answered it as he always did after darkness had fallen, preferring Wanda not to open up to unknown or unexpected callers at night.

He found Mr and Mrs Cartwright on the doorstep.

Edna Cartwright gatecrashed. She usurped the role of the invited guest, assuming that the opened door was an implicit invitation to enter. She brushed past Masters in the tiny hall, exclaiming at how cold it was outside and saying she had come for a few words with Wanda.

Wanda, hearing the voices, appeared at the door of the dining room. Mrs Cartwright made straight for her as Masters closed the door behind Cyril Cartwright. Then they were all four grouped near the dining table.

"Still at supper?" shrilled Mrs Cartwright. "You've usually finished by now."

"We've hardly begun," said Masters coldly.

"Don't let us interrupt you." She turned to Wanda. "We just had to come, my dear. It was too much! On top of this morning's disappointment over the coat material, this dreadful business about Rhoda Carvell. One of the outstanding journalistic figures of our time! She will be missed." She turned to her husband. "She will be missed, won't she, Cyril?"

"Undoubtedly," replied Cartwright. "Her last piece on The Conservative Woman. Masterly!"

Masters couldn't help the jibe. "Aren't you contravening the equal opportunity laws by calling it masterly?"

"Am I? Oh, I see. But I can hardly say mistressly, can I?" Cartwright gave a little grin at his own quip.

"In Mrs Carvell's case it would be quite appropriate," said Masters coldly.

"You could use faultless, Cyril," said his wife, rising to the bait. "Or impeccable."

"Or pitch of perfection," said Masters facetiously.

"Now, now," said Cartwright waggishly. "We all know you wouldn't like her article, George, you being in sympathy with the restoration of hanging and flogging."

"Oh, I don't know. Not all the time at any rate. But I can envisage occasions..."

"So you are not entirely beyond redemption," shrilled Mrs Cartwright. "Whom would you not hang among murderers?"

Masters looked straight at her and said slowly: "Whoever killed Rhoda Carvell, to begin with."

"Why! You..." For once Mrs Cartwright was lost for a reply. Her husband said placatingly: "Pay no attention to George, Edna, can't you see he's pulling your leg? You left yourself wide open there, my dear. The Chief Superintendent got home a shrewd blow."

Mrs Cartwright had gone sulky. Wanda was trying to usher her out of the dining room and into the sitting room so that George could eat in private.

"You have your supper, darling."

"I think I'll give it a miss."

She looked unhappily at him. He shrugged to reassure her and to show that he appreciated her situation. Wanda turned to Cartwright. "George is investigating Rhoda Carvell's death, you know. He's been down to the house where she died. That's why we're late with supper."

Cartwright looked sheepish. "Oh, I say, we are sorry. Most...most inconsiderate of us to bring the matter up."

"Not at all," said Masters. "It's all in the day's work to me. The stink of corruption is almost routine. So you don't

73

upset me. But I am interested in the fact that neither you nor Mrs Cartwright appears to appreciate the macabre significance of Rhoda Carvell's last published article. In it she poked fun at and poured scorn on those who would hang murderers, little dreaming that by the time the piece appeared she would herself be the victim of a murderer whom—one must assume—she would not have wished to be hanged for his crime. Tell me, Mrs Cartwright, if that same man murders you and your husband in bed tonight..."

"Don't, don't!"

"Don't what? Don't go on or don't hang your murderer?"

Masters got no reply. After a long moment of silence, he kissed Wanda lightly on the forehead. "I'll see you later, poppet," he said, and left the dining room, closing the door behind him.

Cartwright said: "I'm afraid the Chief Superintendent is a little overwrought as a result of his experiences today. It's a thought that had never occurred to me before that our police officers could be so affected by what they encounter in the course of their duties. One must not forget to appreciate that, Edna, and one must make allowances. Their lives are so very different from our own daily round among merry, if sometimes boisterous, children."

"Yes, indeed," murmured Mrs Cartwright who had obviously not yet forgotten the possibility of herself being murdered in her bed, as mentioned by Masters.

They heard the front door slam.

Masters had decided to get out of the house because he felt that his presence in his unwonted irritable mood would put an unnecessary strain on Wanda. Without him there to worry her she would cope admirably with the Cartwrights. And he had a sneaking sense of shame that he should be trying to dictate to her in any way concerning her personal relationships with friends and acquaintances. It had never happened before. He prayed it never would again.

74

His feet started to take him to the Yard. Not that he was conscious of the direction. He mentally blasted the Cartwrights. They had annoyed him last night, the memory had ruined his day and now they had spoiled his supper. It was Edna Cartwright who riled him most: her obsession with the desire to be considered one of the intelligentsia. At least he supposed it was that. She was as bad in every way as the women with right-wing views whom she scoffed at. And Cartwright himself was little better to allow a woman like that to rule his life.

Masters entered the Yard and went up in a deserted lift to a deserted corridor. Some of the offices would be occupied, he knew, while various parts of the building would be as busy as Piccadilly underground station in the rush hour, with messages coming in and going out every minute. But once in his own office, he felt cut off from the world. On his desk was a new file cover. A typed stick-on label on the top right hand corner stated simply: Carvell/Woodruff. He sat down and opened it. A typed report from the AC Crime was listed as insert one. His own notes on the interview with Heddle were two. An information memo from somebody gave a breakdown on Rhoda Carvell, Ralph Woodruff, and lastly Professor Carvell. It gave little more than a list of his degrees and appointments as noted in *Who's Who* and his address. This last surprised him. Gladstone Hall of Residence, Tutors' Set I, 3rd Floor. It struck him as odd. Gladstone Hall was for students and, as he well knew, the Tutors' Sets were there to house young, unmarried lecturers who acted in the capacity of wardens, simply because it was thought wise to have a few mature, more responsible people among the many undergraduates who lived there.

He looked at his watch. He was a little surprised to find it not yet nine o'clock. It seemed later, but when he remembered that he hadn't spent time eating supper and that the Cartwrights' intrusion had only lasted a few minutes, the surprise lessened. He lifted the phone, asked for a line, and dialled his home number.

"Have they gone yet?"

"I'm afraid my husband isn't at home at the moment."

"So they're still there? Have they got their sitting britches on?"

"Yes, I think George would say that was right."

"I'm in my office. I'll ring off."

"How long did you say?"

"An hour? Will they be gone by then?"

"Right. I'll tell him. Thank you for ringing."

It was not a code, just an instant understanding. It comforted Masters to know that he and Wanda were still so much in accord, despite the slight disharmony caused by the Cartwrights. He sat for a moment or two thinking about this after he had put the phone down. Was he right to have shown his dislike of the Cartwrights? What should be a husband's attitude towards acquaintances of his wife whom he finds not merely uncongenial but positively inimical? He knew the answers. He should not interfere. He should leave well alone. And yet... after all, Bill Green, too, had thought that something should be done.

Whilst this problem was still worrying him, another thought sprang to mind. It occurred to him that if he were to take a tube to Euston, he might be lucky enough to find Professor Carvell in his set at Gladstone Hall. The visit would use up the hour he had told Wanda he would wait before returning home.

"I can't say if the professor is in."

The porter was in a glass box situated in the foyer between the two main entrance doors. The back of his box was the inside of the front wall. Through the glass ends and front he could see whoever entered or left, whoever used the main staircase and, at the same time, keep an eye on the lift doors. It was a strategic position which, if properly used, would enable any wideawake porter to know whether a senior member had come in or gone out, and this particular incumbent of the box was as beady-eyed as a falcon. Masters wondered why the man could

76

not give him a straight answer. Bloody-mindedness? Or was he acting on instructions?

"Please ring his set and enquire."

The man obviously didn't like being told what to do. "He's bound to be out at this time of night."

"Nevertheless, please ring."

"Who shall I say's calling?"

"Detective Chief Superintendent Masters of Scotland Yard."

The announcement changed the porter's attitude. "That'll be about his dead wife, I suppose?"

Masters was in no mood to discuss his business with the porter. But on the principle that you never know when you might want a bit of co-operation from a beady-eyed hall porter, Masters nodded. "Something like that."

The porter used the internal phone. When he put it down, he said: "The professor's got ten minutes before he goes out. Third floor. Opposite the lifts there's a passage. His door's half-way down on the right. His name's on the card."

"Thank you. You knew he was in, didn't you?"

"I knew he hadn't gone out since six when I came on. And I knew he hadn't come in since then, either. So you tell me how I could tell whether he was in or out. And if you don't scarper, he'll be out before you get to him."

"Going out at this time of night?"

"Often does. All togged up. It's either a woman or the tables."

Masters nodded his thanks and moved to the lifts. The door to Carvell's set opened as soon as he knocked.

"Chief Superintendent Masters? Come in. I've only got a few minutes. In fact you are lucky to get me at all."

"Oh yes, sir?"

"I had been invited out to a party, but because of what has happened today my hostess cancelled it. She's just giving me supper instead."

"It didn't happen today," said Masters, not in any way desirous of correcting Carvell but more to make sure that the man had not been misled by wrong information. Carvell, who was in his shirt sleeves, and obviously in the final stages of dressing, came to a halt as he headed towards what Masters assumed was the bedroom door leading off the study.

"I beg your pardon. I assumed you had come to talk to me about my late ex-wife."

"Late wife," agreed Masters, "but not ex."

"What are you attempting to do, Chief Superintendent? Put me through some sort of accuracy test?"

It was a question to which, Masters guessed, Carvell expected a hot denial. So Masters disappointed him. "That was my intention, professor."

"I see. In that case I'd better watch my p's and q's."

"Why?" Masters, who had been left standing in the middle of the room, glanced around while Carvell thought up his reply to what had been a startling question.

"So as not to disappoint you as well as myself," he replied tartly. "You obviously require facts and as for myself—well, I have been through many tests in my time. Oral as well as written, and I pride myself I haven't failed one yet. I shall try not to do so this time. So I will accept—for the sake of accuracy—that whatever happened to my late wife did not happen today, but was only discovered today or late last night. I will also agree that my late wife was not my ex-wife in so far as only a decree nisi had been granted and, as yet, no decree absolute."

"Thank you."

"Would you mind if I now put my jacket on?"

Masters shrugged. "I'll sit down while you fetch it."

"I would rather you didn't make yourself too comfortable. I'm just about to leave—with your permission, of course."

Masters sat down. "How did you get to know of your wife's death?"

By this time Carvell had passed into the bedroom. He shouted his answer back. "Your Assistant Commissioner was kind enough to telephone me." He reappeared at the door, shrugging his jacket on. "He told me that murder was suspected and that you would be in charge of the case. He also added that should I ever wish to speak to him about the matter..."

Masters looked up at him. "Yes?"

"I am at liberty to do so."

"Of course you are. I find it strange that he found it necessary to tell you. It is the prerogative of every citizen to approach the police. Not all of them get directly to Mr Anderson, of course, which is a pity. When we were entertaining him to dinner last week, my wife was counselling him to be a bit more available. He probably heeded her words, hence his offer to you."

Masters felt he had taken the sting out of Carvell's implied threat very nicely. He regarded the professor now he was fully dressed. Carvell was as Heddle had described him. A bronzed, muscular man. Good looking, with regular features and hair just greying at the temples. A lion in the menagerie of any hostess.

"Was Mrs Carvell a drinker, Professor?"

"If we are to play this game by your rules, you must be more precise, Chief Superintendent. Drinker is such a sloppy term as, in order to sustain life, we are all, perforce, drinkers."

"Did Mrs Carvell drink alcohol to excess?"

"There are gradations, even in excess. Certainly Rhoda drank alcohol. More than I cared for. So, to some degree, I will say she drank to excess. It was, perhaps, a hazard of her occupation. But if you wish to know whether she frequently got intoxicated, the answer is never, except..."

Masters waited.

"Except when she drank champagne. It had the most remarkable effect on her. Far more so than hard liquor. I can best describe it as inducing fits of the giggles, followed very shortly by childlike slumber. Quite an engaging experience for the onlooker."

"Actually, Professor, I asked the question because I have heard that Mrs Carvell was a fresh-air fiend."

"And you find it hard to imagine liquor and fresh-air fiendishness mixing, is that it?" asked Carvell with a short laugh. "The Royal Navy would smile at such ingenuousness, Mr Masters. Men who spend half their time on the open bridges of destroyers spend the rest of their waking hours in a wardroom drinking pink gins."

Masters inclined his head to acknowledge the point. "You mentioned gin, sir. Did Mrs Carvell drink gin?"

"Gin mostly."

"Every night?"

"Unfailingly. Are you telling me her drink was poisoned?"

"You don't know how she died?"

"The Assistant Commissioner mentioned poison, but said that as the pathologist's report was not ready at the time he spoke to me, he couldn't specify which substance." Carvell looked at his wristwatch. "Now, if you'll excuse me . . . ?"

"Arsine," said Masters laconically.

"Arsine? AsH$_3$! Arsenic in other words." Carvell banged a fist into the opposite palm. "That would be a messy death. Poor Rhoda! So chic and smart . . . to die in a mess of vomit." Carvell grimaced distastefully. "How she would have hated the idea of that! Must have hated it. Particularly with the two of them there together, ill, and incapable of helping each other."

"Have you any medical knowledge, Professor?"

"No."

"Yet you are familiar with the signs and symptoms of arsenical poisoning?"

"Everybody knows poisoning cases like that vomit abominably."

"But you are a scientist. You knew the formula for arsine."

"Of course I'm a scientist as you call it. I'm a geologist."

"Of course. That's a pure science isn't it?" Masters got to his feet. "You're obviously anxious to get away, but I shall have to speak to you again. I haven't really asked anything I came to ask."

"Chief Superintendent, I am sure you are a hardworking and conscientious man. The fact that you are still pursuing your enquiries at this time of night shows that. But please call on me during the normal working day. I attend almost full time at Disraeli College."

"I know it well," said Masters. "I was often there as a student."

Carvell was in the act of opening the door. He stopped with his hand on the knob. "You were a student? Here, in London?"

"Yes."

"You have a degree?"

"A first," confessed Masters. "Now I'll be on my way." As Carvell slowly opened the door and he passed through, he added, "In biological sciences. I've often found the knowledge useful. Goodnight, Professor."

As he walked along the narrow corridor towards the lifts, Masters wondered if the Cartwrights had gone. If not, he wanted a word with Cartwright. He began to hurry.

"They went soon after you telephoned," said Wanda, as she kissed him. "Really and truly, darling, they are a nuisance, but you shouldn't have gone out like that without your supper."

"It was unforgivable," confessed Masters, "but I'm not prepared to eat in front of a gawping audience of any sort, least of all one comprised solely of the genus Cartwright."

"They're not a genus," said Wanda softly. "They're a sub species."

"Whatever they are, I hope they don't get into the habit of descending on us at meal times."

"It was the first time," said Wanda quietly. "And, I think, the last."

"Oh?"

"I'm afraid I offended them."

"Not by design, my sweet. You would never do that to anybody."

Wanda didn't reply. She entered the dining room, crossed it and through the archway to the kitchen. Masters followed her. The smell from the oven was inviting.

She served up his food. He accepted it shamefacedly and carried it back to the relaid dining table. She sat with him while he ate. When he'd finished he had the grace to say he didn't know how she managed to hot it up without spoiling it.

With a knowing little smile she rose to get the coffee.

Thursday morning was again bright. The touch of overnight frost which had kept the air crisp and clear and had settled in circles on each of the paving stones was burning away by the time Masters left home, but its effects remained. The people he passed as he walked to the Yard seemed to him to be just that little bit livelier than the bleary-eyed, yawning crowd he usually encountered before nine in the morning. He, too, felt livelier. Happier, he supposed. Altogether more pleased with life than yesterday.

He went straight up to his office. There was an hour's paper work to be done. His report on yesterday and the odd bit to add to the brief entry on Carvell. Masters preferred to do as little clerical work as he could reasonably get away with. The AC Crime had frequently suggested that his reports could be fuller. Masters preferred brevity, and in view of his success rate, no serious complaint about his methods could genuinely be made. It was not that he actively disliked paper work. He found in it a sense of recording accomplishment that appealed to him. Besides this aspect, he regarded it as a refresher course. Having to marshal his thoughts for a precis of events, as opposed to a full account, concentrated his mind, aided recall and on occasion gave him the necessary alternative viewpoints. But he begrudged the time it took. DS Reed knew the routine, and never appeared till called for unless something out of the ordinary was happening.

It was ten past ten when Masters at last got round to using the internal phone to summon Green and the two sergeants. He asked Reed to have coffee sent in.

Green arrived first.

"What's on, George?"

"We're awa'oot after we've had a cup of coffee."

"You're sounding chirpier than you did yesterday."

"The Cartwrights called at the house just as we were sitting down to supper last night."

"And that has made you happier?"

"I believe it to have been their last visit."

"Ah! You saw them off."

"I didn't. Wanda did."

"Good girlie. But why let the lass do it when you've got a tongue in your head?"

"I went out. Chickened out, if you like. I gave them a bit of my mind and then left, without supper."

"Leaving Wanda to finish the demolition job? How did she do it?"

"She didn't say, and I thought it wiser not to ask. But when I got back, Wanda was alone, with supper re-prepared and literally exuding a sense of achievement."

"Good for her. Actually it was better to let her make the break. There'll be no feeling that you choked the Cartwrights off against her wishes." Green helped himself to a Kensitas from a crumpled packet. "What did you do? Walk the streets all evening?"

"I came here..."

"Whatever for?"

"...and then went to call on Carvell."

"You what?"

"I used the excuse that he might not have been told officially of his ex-wife's death. I said I'd forgotten to do it and I wanted to apologise if the first intimation he got of her death had been from a newspaper report."

"Humbug. Anderson was going to phone him."

83

"Quite. But I was at a loose end and I wanted a quick look at the professor."

"Have you arranged to see him again this morning?"

"He was on his way out last night when I called on him. He wasn't best pleased to see me."

"Came the old acid, did he?"

"Tried to treat me like a conscientious, hard-working copper slightly short on the grey matter and falling down sadly on my forelock-touching drill."

"He did that? To you?"

Masters grinned. "He told me that if I wanted to see him again it was to be in working hours at Disraeli College—presumably after ringing for an appointment."

"I like it," said Green. "Anybody who can put you in your place gets my vote."

"I didn't say he put me in my place."

Green stared at him for a moment. "I knew it was too good to be true. I suppose you disillusioned him."

"Not exactly. I think the honours were even. But I believe he will be expecting me to ring for an appointment this morning."

"Why?"

"Because I told him there were a few questions I needed to ask him."

"So. Do we go or not?"

"If I'm right and he is expecting me, wouldn't it be rather nice to disappoint him?"

Green grinned. "You're a devious bastard if somebody puts your back up. He'll be there thinking you're going to dance to his tune, and..."

Reed and Berger came in with the coffee. As Masters accepted his cup, he said to Reed: "Ring up Divorce and Admiralty and ask who represented Mrs Carvell in court last Tuesday."

"I did that, Chief. I thought you'd want to know her solicitor and what her will contained and if she had any property to leave. It's Vadil of Drawer and Vadil."

Masters nodded his thanks. He'd met Vadil and he was

of the opinion that he and the young solicitor were not each other's most fervent admirers. Vadil tended to act for a set which considered policemen should be permitted to nose into the business of everybody but themselves. He wasn't surprised to learn Rhoda Carvell had asked Vadil to accept service. As Carvell was divorcing her, it seemed likely that the professor's solicitor would not be available to her.

"Roger the dodger," said Green sourly. "You won't get much out of him."

"Maybe not," agreed Masters, "but I shall have to see him. I want to know the provisions before I see Carvell again."

"Vadil may not have her will—if he only acted in the divorce suit."

"True. But I should imagine that a good lawyer—and Vadil is a good lawyer—would go into the property side pretty closely when involved in a divorce suit. It could be that he knows something we should know."

Roger Vadil kept them waiting a few minutes, but it was a genuine wait. He was with a client. Green, with his eye to the partly-open door of the modern, well-heated waiting room, decorated with framed cartoons of eminent past and present advocates, saw a woman leave Vadil's office.

"He certainly gets the clients. That one's got Russian boots on."

"Russian boots?" queried Berger.

"That's right, lad. These tall boots women wear nowadays."

"What's Russian about them?"

"That's what they were always called in my day."

"I thought they were a modern fashion."

"Nothing's new, lad. You should know that. Only in the old days women wore Russian boots when the weather made them necessary. Now they're worn for fashion and god-awful most of them look."

Before Berger could reply, a secretary put her head

85

round the door. "Mr Vadil will see you now, gentlemen."

Vadil was on his feet behind his desk as they entered his office.

"I was going to ring you, Chief Superintendent."

This surprise announcement had no apparent effect on Masters who took the client chair opposite the solicitor. Green, however, said he liked to think of the Yard saving hard-up members of the legal profession the price of a phone call and pulled up, alongside Masters, a second chair upholstered in bright orange tweed.

Vadil, in his mid-thirties, smooth and impeccably dressed, with a gold fob in his waistcoat, remained standing until all four were seated. Masters waited to hear the reason why Vadil had intended to ring him.

"I should like to know when I can safely make arrangements for the funeral to be held."

"Just hers?"

"And his. I'd better do that for her. We can dispose of both at once."

"I shall make enquiries in Chichester and let you know. I don't think the coroner will want to hang on to the bodies too long after the forensic people have finished with them."

"Thank you. Now perhaps you will tell me what I can do for you?"

Masters paused for a moment before saying: "Mrs Carvell was divorced last Tuesday morning, I believe."

"Correct."

"She appeared in court?"

"No."

"No? That amazes me Mr Vadil."

"Why?"

"She was heard to state, in the *View* office last Monday, that she intended to be present."

"So she did—intend, I mean, but she didn't."

"You were expecting her and she didn't turn up? Weren't you surprised?"

"Not unduly. I had told Mrs Carvell there was no need for her to be there. There was no wrangle over the settlement. That had been fixed beforehand and she'd agreed. But she was a journalist, as you know. Every new experience provided good copy. She said she wanted to know, first-hand, how women were liberated—the actual mechanics of the business—so that she could tell her women readers there was nothing to be afraid of in the actual act of cutting loose. You know the line she usually took. Anything remotely reminiscent of Establishment was a target for her, and many readers lapped it up. She wrote for a number of women's magazines besides the *View* you know."

"So why weren't you surprised when she didn't turn up to take advantage of so unique and subjective an opportunity?"

"I simply took it that she had thought better of it and had followed my advice to stay away from what can be, even for a woman like her, an emotional experience."

Masters nodded his understanding. "When was the last time you actually saw her?"

"On the previous Friday. Here. A last minute conference to agree everything and so on. That's when she told me she would be in court."

There was a short silence. Then Vadil asked: "When did she die?"

Masters frowned. "After what you've just told me, my guess would be Monday night."

"On...you mean she was dead before...?"

"Before she was divorced? Yes."

"But that would invalidate the proceedings. Are you sure of your facts?"

"I'm not absolutely sure. We're trying to find out if anybody saw her after lunchtime on the Monday."

"But if she went down to Abbot's Hall with Woodruff..."

"On the Monday?"

"Yes. Say she had done that, there is the reason for her not turning up on Tuesday. It could just be that they were too wrapped up in themselves or just too idle to come back to London to attend the court. It's a long way to come when there is no urgent reason for doing so."

"Did Mrs Carvell tell you she was travelling to Abbot's Hall on the Monday?"

"I can't be sure. I knew she said she and Woodruff were going there, but exactly when it was to be...look here, Chief Superintendent, what makes you think she died on the Monday?"

"The gale."

"What the hell are you talking about now? What gale?" Vadil was getting slightly rattled. Masters guessed that he didn't like the idea that he had been instrumental in helping the divorce proceedings of a dead woman.

"Mrs Carvell was a fresh-air fiend, I've been told."

"Very much so."

"She always slept with her window open."

"I've had no first-hand experience, but I have heard it was a fetish of hers."

"In spite of that, my information is that when there was a southerly gale blowing straight into the front of Abbot's Hall, even Mrs Carvell—fetish or no fetish—had to shut her bedroom windows."

"That sounds more than reasonable. Please go on."

"She was found dead in a room with windows closed and fastened, which argues there was a gale when she went to bed."

"Yes."

"There was a howling gale last Monday night, but it had died down and backed away by noon on Tuesday."

"I can see why *you* are opting for Monday night, but what does the medical evidence say was the time of death?"

"So far, only that it was more than five days ago."

Vadil leaned back in his chair and played with the watch-chain across his slim stomach. "I hope you can do better than that, Mr Masters."

"Why?"

"Because all sorts of legal complications could arise. If you are right, the divorce could be invalid. Quite where that would leave Carvell in regard to the various dispositions and agreements that were made to come into effect when the decree became absolute ... but I needn't go into detail. I'm not at all sure that I know the answers, or anybody else for that matter, because it must be the only case on record where a divorce was granted after the death of one of the parties."

"If it was after death," said Green.

"Quite." Vadil turned again to Masters. "Was that all you came to see me about?"

Masters shook his head. "I suspected she died on Monday night on the evidence of the closed windows and the gale. But as I had been informed that she intended to be in court on Tuesday, I assumed she had been there, otherwise somebody would have wanted to know why not. So, in spite of my suspicions, I had expected to hear you say she had, in fact, been present to hear the decree granted. That is why I asked you when you had last seen her."

"I understand. So you really came to ask something else. The usual, I suppose? Who benefits?"

Masters nodded. "If marriage invalidates a former will, I suppose divorce does?"

"The new act complicates matters. I doubt if one would be able to cut out one's former spouse entirely, particularly if maintenance payments are to be made. But I don't think we need to discuss that particular point. Mrs Carvell had comparatively little to leave in the way of an estate."

"How little is comparatively?"

"Abbot's Hall was in joint ownership and though it was the only marital home that they actually owned, Mrs Carvell had contributed well over half the money towards it. She bought the fabric and he paid for the renovation. It was paid for. Carvell had no mortgage to pay, so he had agreed to her having it. As for other monies—well, I suppose you can guess that a journalist of her standing earned as much as a professor, so there was an agreement that no maintenance was to be paid."

"You agreed to that?"

"Mrs Carvell had announced her intention of marrying Woodruff as soon as the decree became absolute. To fight to obtain an order against an equal—probably smaller—earner would have cost more than would have been awarded for the three months or so which were to have elapsed before Mrs Carvell's second marriage. On her remarriage the order would have stopped."

"No proper marital home, you said?"

Vadil offered a cigarette box. Green and the two sergeants accepted, but the solicitor himself did not smoke. He offered them lights from a gold lighter.

"They used to live in a house owned by the college. They had furnished it, of course. Very attractively. It was my duty to see that Mrs Carvell received a fair share of the movable property, some of which she had contributed to the home."

"I see. But she had no money?"

"A few hundreds in cash. She had spent her capital on Abbot's, and a woman like Rhoda Carvell spends what she earns. She dressed with a capital D."

"The professor was amenable?"

"Entirely. All he wanted was his books, the bookcases and his desk."

"Not surprising, seeing he was moving into a set in Gladstone Hall."

"As soon as they broke up he left the house."

"That must have been fairly recently."

"He moved into Gladstone just before the beginning of this term. Towards the end of September, I believe. But he had rooms elsewhere before that."

"The professor's lawyer must have got the divorce through quicker than usual, Mr Vadil. They were still together in June."

"Whatever gave you that idea?"

"We have a witness—a colleague of Mrs Carvell—who called at Abbot's Hall in June, on a Sunday, on newspaper business, and met the professor there as well as his wife."

Vadil frowned. "You're sure of this?"

"We saw no reason to doubt it when we were told. Can you suggest a good reason why we should doubt it now?"

"Only because Carvell claimed he had not been cohabiting with his wife for some months previous to last June. And that claim, in a legal matter, is the equivalent of swearing on oath. So, to hear they were staying together at Abbot's more than surprises me. It astounds me. Are you sure your informant has not mistaken Woodruff for the professor?"

"Not a chance." Masters shook his head to emphasise the point. "Physical description correct as well as the fact that he was introduced to the professor by name. Besides, did Woodruff collect bits of stone and such like from the beach, using a geologist's hammer in the process?"

It was Vadil's turn to shake his head. Somewhat surprisingly, he said: "Woodruff was a lounge lizard. Or at any rate he was more at home with a cocktail in his hand than a geologist's hammer. And he'd be frightened to go on a beach lest he should get his suede shoes wet."

Masters didn't show his surprise. Green, however, grunted sceptically, and appeared so taken aback by this scathing description that his mental comment of 'hark who's talking' was almost audible. So much so that Vadil stared at him angrily. Masters coughed to break the constraint. "I have heard that you fence, Mr Vadil."

Vadil switched his gaze to Masters.

"That is one of the ways I use to keep myself fit."

"Only one of them?"

"I spend quite a few of my weekends parachuting with the Volunteer Reserve."

Green said: "I'd never have guessed it." But this time there was no scepticism, just genuine amazement. Vadil didn't look particularly like the archetypal paratrooper. "Just to keep fit?"

"Why not? I also happen to enjoy army life in limited dollops."

"You're not a married man, Mr Vadil, or you'd find taking weekends off a bit difficult."

"I'm not married. That's true. But my personal affairs are surely not the reason for your visit."

"We're finished," said Masters getting to his feet. "I'd appreciate it, Mr Vadil, if you did not start any legal procedures until we've established exactly when Mrs Carvell died."

"I shall think about it a great deal," replied Vadil. "But I shall do nothing until I have some facts to work on. It could well be that even then I shall not be required to take any action as I have no client on whose behalf I need take it."

Masters nodded his understanding and bade Vadil good morning.

When they were outside, Berger said to Green: "Are you thinking what I'm thinking?"

"Tell me, then I'll know."

"I'd always heard Vadil was a bit of a ladies' man. He's got a reputation as the solicitor all the dolls flock to."

"So?"

"So they wouldn't use him if he was a bit of a pouff."

"You trying to tell me he's not a Jessie Bell?"

"That's it. Besides, if he's a parachutist..."

"I can't see why you can't be a parachutist and effeminate. They're not mutually incompatible."

"He isn't married," asserted Berger. "Most heterosexual men are at his age. Particularly when they're as well-britched as he is."

"You think he's a homo?"

"I didn't say that. In fact I don't think he is."

"Then why go on about it lad?"

"I didn't. You did. I said he wasn't. You said..."

"I know what I said. I want to know what you're getting at."

"I've got a theory."

"Ah! He was pretty acid about Woodruff. You reckon it

92

could have been because he disliked him because Mrs Carvell had taken a shine to him. Right?"

"Something like that. She was an open-air type. Just the sort that a fitness buff like Vadil might fancy as a mate. And she was dishy enough for a bloke like Vadil, too. He could have had his eye on her for himself and then discovered she preferred the lounge-lizard type like Woodruff."

By this time they were entering the car, and Masters was close enough to catch the gist of the conversation.

"Go on, Berger," he encouraged the sergeant as they settled in their seats.

"Aye, spit it out lad," added Green.

"Vadil was the one who knew what her movements were to be. He was the one who did nothing about it when she didn't turn up in court. He could have kept her absence quiet on purpose."

"Why?" demanded Green.

"To stop any search for her starting too soon. The longer it was before anybody found her, the more difficult it would be for us to discover who killed her."

"Meaning Vadil killed her as well as Woodruff?"

"Why not?"

"Why not? Look lad, if you fancy a bit of capurtle you don't kill it off. The rival male, perhaps, but not the bit of goods herself."

"Answer, please, Berger," requested Masters.

"Jealousy, Chief. She wouldn't have Vadil, but she would have Woodruff. Vadil didn't like the idea of any woman preferring Woodruff to himself."

"So what are you suggesting? That he was affronted by her attitude and so killed them both? Or that he was determined to see that if he couldn't have her himself, nobody else would?"

"Something like that, Chief. Perhaps a mixture of both. He's a bit of a dark horse, that Vadil. Gives the impression of liking wine, women and high living, whereas he goes

in for fencing, parachuting and spending weekends eating
army rations."

"I don't get your drift."

"He's a hard man, Chief. Tough. Prepared to jump out
of aeroplanes to do a bit of killing, though that's not the
impression he gives."

"Meaning that he wouldn't hesitate to kill two people
who were—in his opinion—ripe for the killing?"

"Yes, Chief."

"It's a reasonable theory," agreed Masters at last.

"You mean you like it?" asked Green in surprise.

"I recognise it has some merit as a theory. You could
tear it to bits. So could I. As it now stands that is. But if
we were to establish that Vadil had been keen on Mrs
Carvell...if, say, they had been out and about in each
other's company and their friends had expected them to
set up together after the divorce...what then?"

"Different complexion," agreed Green. "What do we
do? Start asking questions?"

"I think so. Gently. Indirectly, that is. It would be entirely reasonable to seek to discover who her friends and
acquaintances were, but I don't want Vadil to learn that
we are asking questions about him and him alone."

"Frightened of him?"

"Not exactly. But smart solicitors can make life more
difficult for us if they want to, and I'd rather avoid that if
I can. There's Vadil himself to remember, as well. I
wouldn't want to sow the seeds of suspicion about an
entirely innocent man. A solicitor with his particular reputation could suffer if it got about that he was the subject
of a police enquiry."

Green grunted to show he appreciated these points. "As
it's young Berger's idea, I reckon that would be a good
job for the two lads."

"Basically, yes."

"Basically?"

"It occurred to me that one of the best people to ask

about Mrs Carvell's circle of friends would be her husband. I'd rather not subject the sergeants to his particular type of verbal arrogance."

"See what you mean, but I reckon it would be a smack in the eye for him if you sent only a detective constable to see him. That would show him we're not very impressed in spite of his high an' mighty attitude."

Masters laughed. "A good idea, Bill, but we'd better attend to him ourselves. Reed and Berger can see young Heddle again and that Lugano woman we've heard about."

"You said you'd be going down to Chichester today, Chief," reminded Reed.

"So I did. I'll ring from the office to ask whether the pathologist's report is ready. We'll make our plan after that."

— 4 —

When Masters rang DI Robson at Chichester, he was told
that the local man was out with DS Middleton, making
enquiries in the Climping area, but that he had left a
message to say that if Masters rang he was to be told that
the pathologist's report was expected at six o'clock that
evening. Masters thanked his informant and rang off.

"Are you going down to see it?" asked Green.

"What's the time now?"

"Half eleven."

Masters took out his pipe and tin of Warlock Flake. As
he rubbed the tobacco for the bowl, he said: "I want to
see it and to have a few words with the pathologist, but
six o'clock tonight...? That's a bit late for forensic men
to be available."

"And for us to be cavorting round the countryside, which
is what you really meant."

"True. So we'll not decide to go definitely until we see
what the day brings forth. Decision time four o'clock. How
does that suit?"

"Meaning that unless something crops up to send us
hurtling down there tonight we can go tomorrow morning
in the firm's time?"

"Yes."

"Fine."

Masters turned to the sergeants. "You know what we
want. Mrs Carvell's friends and acquaintances and all the
gossip you can pick up between now and four o'clock.
Report back here by that time."

"You'll be going to see the professor, Chief?"

"Yes. Leave him to us."

After the sergeants had gone, Green said: "What are we going to talk about?"

"What comes up. He was her husband and in any situation like this we have a duty to examine the victim's immediate family. We have to stick to that particular rule."

Green nodded his agreement.

"Ring down and ask for the duty car to take us to Disraeli College, please Bill. We can get a cab or a tube back here or to some pub for a bite of lunch."

While Green did as he was asked Masters took from his bookshelf the Yard central library list. He consulted it for a few moments and then, evidently dissatisfied with his search, returned it to its place.

"Something you want from Reference, George?"

"It occurred to me how little I know about arsenic. Where it comes from and so forth. I can look up the effects of the poisoning, of course, but I wanted to discover its availability. Not to worry. I'll find it later."

"It's used for a lot of things," said Green. "In agriculture as a pesticide, in paint, to colour glass, even in medicine."

"You're very knowledgeable, Bill."

"When I was a young copper, arsenic was popular with murderers. They got it from rat poisons, soaked it off fly papers and so on. You never see fly papers nowadays. In fact there's much less arsenic about."

"Thank you. That's more or less what I wanted to know. We shall also have to find out how it can murderously be turned into a gaseous state."

"You'll be doing some homework reading tonight."

Masters grinned. "That's the real reason why I'm not keen on going to Chichester." He got to his feet. "Did you get us the duty car, Bill?"

"Ready when you are."

The professor was lecturing his third year students. They were told they could wait outside the lecture theatre, and were directed to the geology department. They made their way down a long, wide corridor in one of the wings. They noted the name plates on the doors. Carvell's office. Geology tutor's office. Preparation Room. Finally, on the left the door to the theatre and at the end of the corridor, a door with a glass upper panel. This was the geology laboratory. Between the two doors was a small table carrying a ledger. On the wall above the ledger was a notice telling students that before entering the laboratory for private study they were to sign in, adding the time of entry. On leaving they were to sign out, again noting the time and the length of the study period in hours and minutes.

"Keeps tabs on them, doesn't he?" said Green.

"With good reason."

"Security?"

"That could be part of it. All geology laboratories have a tray of gems just as they have trays of samples of every rock there is. The gems may not be all that valuable individually, but together they could well be worth a few thousand. Diamond, sapphire, ruby and so on, besides the lesser ones."

"Just there to pick up?"

"The duty tutor will have a key to that particular drawer. It has to be asked for."

"I see. What else?"

"All these students are here on grants. Unlike a lot of the other disciplines, geology demands a lot of private study in the lab. Carvell will be able to see if any of his flock is being less than conscientious."

"If they tell the truth when they sign out."

"There's that possibility, but I imagine Carvell's tutors will be under orders to check the book whenever they pass by. Just to see that nobody has put down a time later than the time at which the check is made. Carvell is not the sort of man to allow any student to idle away his time at the expense of the public."

"I can imagine." Green turned. "Here comes one of his little lambs now, I suppose."

The youth approaching them along the corridor was weighed down with an armful of books and papers. He nodded to them and dumped his load on the little table, preparatory to signing in. The table was too small for so heterogeneous and untidy a heap. A number of items slid to the floor.

"Damn."

Green and Masters both stooped to help him retrieve his possessions.

"What's this, mate? Your kid sister's paint box?"

"No fear. It's mine. I'm just going to use it."

"In there?" asked Green in amazement, indicating the lab door.

"That's right. We have to draw the specimens and then colour them." He opened a thick A4 size book with plain leaves. "Here you are. I'm a rotten artist, but colour in minerals plays a great part in identification. In fact, colour is often its most striking property. As you can see, some of the damn things have different colours in the same species. Here are some quartzes, all pinkish-yellow, green, and even black. Here's fool's gold—yellow needles. Here's corundum, haematite...I could go on for ever about this because I've just written an essay on colour, lustre, opalescence, transparency and translucency, to say nothing of phosphorescence and fluorescence."

"Stick with it lad. What are the little line drawings?"

"Crystals. Crystallography is a bastard if I may be allowed the term. It's so complicated..."

"This is your book on the elements of mineralogy," said Masters. "I just looked at one or two pages..."

"Help yourself if you're interested."

"I am actually. I'd like to get hold of a copy for an hour or two."

"Well...I don't know about lending you mine..."

"I'm a policeman," said Masters. "A detective chief superintendent. If you would trust me with the book until tomorrow...against a deposit of a fiver, of course..."

The student grinned. "You're on," he said. "It's only

the beginning of term you see, and my grant hasn't arrived, so I'm stuck for a bit of ready. If you keep the book for a day or two, I should be able to redeem it by the time you return it."

"Keep it," said Masters, giving him the note. "As a hiring fee. I'll give you a receipt for the book, too, though I shall certainly return it to you, Mr..."

"Finmore. Harry Finmore. It's written in the front of the book. Just leave it at the union office when you bring it back. I can pick it up from there. Now, if you'll excuse me, I'd better sign in and start work otherwise the prof will be out of the theatre before I get going, and I'd rather that didn't happen."

"Understood, lad," said Green. "Good luck."

Finmore grinned. "Thanks. I'll need it."

When the young man had left them, Green turned to Masters. "What's your little game now?"

"No game at all."

"You're up to something."

Masters opened the chunky mineralogy book at the back. "I merely looked at the index. I was looking for a reference to arsine or arsenic."

"And?"

Masters pointed to the index. "I saw these—arsenical nickel, arsenical pyrites, arsenic minerals, arsenious acid, arsenolite and arsenopyrite. It seemed those entries might give me the information I couldn't find in the library catalogue."

Green grunted. "You didn't give that lad a fiver just to..."

Masters laughed. "As a matter of fact, I wasn't proposing to give it to him, but his attitude made me change my mind. He struck me as a thoroughly nice chap, suffering from the shortcomings of local government bureaucracy, so I decided to help. Some of these kids must find it hard going."

Green nodded to show his agreement. Masters busied

himself with the book, forcing it gently, despite its bulk, into one of his coat pockets.

"Don't want the prof to see it?"

"I should hate him to jump to the conclusion that I had been suborning one of his students. Besides, if he got to know where it came from he might take it out on young Master Finmore."

"He's that type is he?"

"You'll be able to judge for yourself. It looks as though the lecture is over."

The theatre door had opened and a dozen or so students came out. Both sexes, in all manner of dress, some looking bright and cheerful, others pasty-faced and intense.

Masters let the last one pass him before he entered the theatre. The tiered seats were empty, but Carvell stood behind the laboratory bench on the floor at the front. He was re-assembling his lecture notes. One point on each piece of paper about three inches by four in size. Masters guessed they had probably served him for several years and would do so for several more. They would be filed away for an exactly similar lecture a year hence.

"Good morning, Professor."

Carvell looked up. "Good morning, Chief Superintendent."

"May I introduce my colleague, Detective Chief Inspector Green, currently acting as Senior Scene of Crime Officer at the Yard?"

"Morning," grunted Green. "Been teaching the young how old the world is?"

"That doesn't take long, Mr Green. I just draw a chalk line from one end of the blackboard to the other and tell them that is the age of the earth."

Masters was looking at some of the drawings on the board. "Palaeontology?" he asked politely.

"Of course, I was forgetting you are a senior member of the university. Perhaps you had to study something of this sort."

101

"The odd fossilized plant. Nothing quite as technical as this."

Carvell finished putting his notes in order and fastened them with a small bulldog clip. "What can I do for you?"

"I thought I ought to come to forewarn you that you may be in for an unpleasant shock."

Carvel frowned. "The lab assistant will be wanting to clear up in here and prepare for this afternoon's lecture. I suggest we talk in my office."

"Just down the corridor, is it?" asked Green.

"Quite correct. If you would follow me..."

The office was book-lined, but had a number of chairs, obviously needed when Carvell held his tutorials in it. Only when all three were seated did the professor say to Masters, "I'm in for an unpleasant shock, you say?"

"In so far as we believe that Mrs Carvell was dead before the divorce came up in court. I imagine it is an unpleasant thought to a sensitive man to know his wife had died the night before the hearing. If that is not a shock in itself, then the knowledge that you are still Mrs Carvell's next-of-kin and that all the arrangements you both made before the hearing are null and void must be slightly bemusing."

Carvell said nothing for some moments. Then he asked: "You only believe this? You are not sure?"

"Not one hundred per cent sure. But we have strong reasons to suppose so. Not the least important reason is that Mrs Carvell did not attend the court on Tuesday morning, despite having announced her intention of doing so."

"And your other reasons?"

"I would prefer not to enumerate those, sir, until we can establish them more firmly. But I should like to know if you were expecting to see your wife in court."

"I was there myself, but I did not know Rhoda's intended movements."

"When did you last see Mrs Carvell?"

"We haven't met...hadn't met for at least two months before her death. All our communication was through our respective solicitors."

"Usual form," grunted Green.

"I'm afraid so. An unsavoury business."

"All for nothing, apparently," said Masters. "You will understand, Professor, that I expect to establish that you were still her husband when she died. That, I suppose, will mean that Mrs Carvell's not inconsiderable estate will revert to you by a former will?"

"Not inconsiderable estate, Mr Masters? Rhoda hadn't that much to dispose of."

"Abbot's Hall? I understand you agreed to her having that."

"She put up most of the money."

"And you the rest. And, I suspect, you also paid for the improvements which must have cost a great deal of money but which will have added a lot to its value."

"I was her husband. Naturally, I paid the bills."

"And the furniture at Abbot's. Some of the pieces there are valuable. I know nothing, of course, of the furniture in your former home here in London, but all-in-all I would say you made a more than generous settlement on Mrs Carvell as a prelude to divorce."

"What are you trying to say, Chief Superintendent?"

"Nothing more than I have stated."

"My generosity, as you call it, was based on the fact that I should not be paying my wife the usual maintenance and, as I said, she virtually bought Abbot's Hall."

"Still," grunted Green, "I've heard of couples who've fought over possession of a clothes line. Literally."

Carvell shrugged. "Is that all, gentlemen?"

"Not quite, sir. I shall want to see Mrs Carvell's friends and acquaintances. Perhaps you could let me know who they were."

"I know very little of her friends, Mr Masters."

"But surely, Professor, you entertained and were entertained? Had a social life together?"

"Not for some years now. We did some duty entertaining, of course..."

"But you had been going your separate ways for some time?"

"Rhoda knew a lot of newspaper people and the like. They were not exactly..."

"Your cup of tea?"

"Precisely."

"Relatives?" asked Green.

"Rhoda was an only child. Her parents are both dead, though I believe there are some aunts and cousins whom I've not met since we were married over thirteen years ago."

Masters got to his feet. "In that case, sir, we shall leave you to have your lunch."

"And come back another day, I suppose?"

"Should it seem necessary. But we shall not hound you. I have no desire to do so and I daresay you would resent it."

"Most emphatically."

"That being so, Professor..."

"Yes?"

"Would you be so kind as to write out an account of your movements for last Sunday, Monday and Tuesday? It would save us having to question you on the matter."

"By God, you suspect me of killing Rhoda."

"Not really," said Green wearily. "But you must know that we always have to look closely at the immediate family of any victim. Statistics prove we're right. Most killings are domestic."

"That's not very reassuring."

"It wasn't meant to be. But you can be reassured..."

"What by?"

"If the DCS suspected you of killing your wife, he'd have you at the Yard and your statements would be taken down by a shorthand writer for typing out. We've just asked you to write your own list."

"For Sunday, Monday and Tuesday! Some list."

"We have to leave ourselves a good time bracket," said Masters.

"You mean Rhoda was not seen alive later than Sunday?"

"Oh, she was. On Monday morning, in fact."

"Then I can see no reason for you wanting to know my movements on Sunday. And all day Tuesday I was either in the court or here in the college."

Masters seemed to make a sudden decision. "Right, Professor. Make it Monday, then. Should I need more, I'll come back and ask. I don't want to waste your time."

"Thanks."

"Nor my own."

Reed and Berger were again talking to Derek Heddle in the *View* interview room. The young man looked better for a night's sleep, and he was noticeably less keyed up than on the previous day.

"I told Mr Masters everything I knew."

"Not quite," said Reed.

"What didn't I say?"

"You didn't tell us that bedroom smelt of garlic."

"Garlic? It ponged like hell of...wait a minute. I've been wondering about that stink. I've had it in my nostrils ever since. I tried sluicing my nose out last night with salt and water. All I did was nearly drown myself."

"Skip the gory details. You were wondering about the stink, you said."

"Yes. Although it was so god awful, I thought I seemed to recognize some of it."

"Some of it?"

"Yes. As though it had been made up of two or three different stenches. The smell of death...and now you've mentioned it, yes, garlic." He looked across at Reed. "What's so important about garlic?"

105

"It only told the pathologist straight away that they'd been killed by arsenic. If you'd told my boss, he'd have known, too."

"Sorry."

"Any other smells you can recall now?"

"Yes. Booze."

"Drink? Alcohol?"

"Yes. At least I think so. It was one of the stenches I told you about. Stale booze. But honestly, I didn't think of it at the time. It's really only just come to me that that is what it was."

"So you think those two had been drinking heavily?"

"I suppose they must have been."

"Did you see any bottles and glasses in the room?"

Heddle shook his head. "I can't remember any, but I didn't really look."

"In the sitting room?"

Again Heddle shook his head, but stopped in mid-gesture and frowned.

"What's up?" asked Berger. "Remembered something?"

Heddle looked shamefaced. "I'm sorry. I think I could have misled you."

"How?"

"I've been so obsessed with the stink of that room ... look, the whole place smelt frowsty ..."

"So?"

"I think that the place where I really smelt the stale booze, worst of all that is, and to recognize it properly, was the sitting room." He frowned. "And that's strange, isn't it, seeing there's a fireplace in there. Wouldn't that air the room? Let the fumes disperse?"

"Maybe," said Reed. "But we've got it right now, have we? Think before you say."

"Yes," said Heddle after a moment's pause.

"So," said Berger, "it would seem from what you've told us that there was some really heavy drinking that evening in the sitting room. Then, somehow or another those two staggered up to bed, got in and breathed out enough al-

106

cohol fumes to make the bedroom smell, and at the same time breathed in enough arsine fumes to kill them."

"Arsine?"

"Arsenical gas."

"Oh, I see. Well, yes, I suppose that's what must have happened, but I can't say for certain."

"Of course not, Mr Heddle. In fact there could have been a party downstairs. You know, a few people in for a celebration. A group of drinkers would make that room smell even if it wasn't a real boozy affair. Quite a lot drunk and spilled by a number of people rather than a hell of a lot drunk and spilled by just two. See what I mean?"

"Yes."

"Good. So who would be at the party?"

"I don't know what you mean?"

"Friends and acquaintances, Mr Heddle. Who was Mrs Carvell friendly enough with to invite to a party?"

"Don't ask me."

"Why not?"

"Because I wasn't in her league."

"Maybe not, but you can overhear every word she says when she comes into the editorial office or whatever you call it. She must have mentioned people—her pals and others—when she was talking to the Lugano woman."

"Well, yes. She named names, but they never meant anything to me, because I didn't know them, see. If she mentioned somebody whose name I knew..."

"Like who?"

"The Prime Minister or the leader of the GLC or the Archbishop."

"No private friends?"

Heddle shrugged. "The odd socialite, I suppose, but nobody of interest to me."

"So you reckon we should see this Golly dame?"

"She won't like it, but yes, she's the one. Though to be honest, I don't think Rhoda was ever friendly with Golly. I mean they worked together and that was it."

"Okay," said Reed. "How do we get hold of her? Do

you take us up there, or do you send her down here?"

"I'll ask her to come down."

"Tell her," corrected Reed. "And leave her in no doubt about coming straight away. Our time's valuable."

Heddle grinned. "It'll give me great pleasure to give Golly a few orders. As I said, she won't like it. In fact, she'll snap like an alligator, but she's a nosey old besom..."

"Most alligators are. All nosey."

"Oh, yes. Of course. What I mean is, her curiosity will overcome her objections."

Heddle was right in his forecast. In less than five minutes Golly Lugano entered the interview room breathing fire—almost literally, judging by the aura of smoke from the inevitable cigarette that surrounded her.

"Mizz Lugano?"

"That's me." She sat down heavily in the chair formerly used by Heddle, stubbed out her cigarette and opened the packet she had in her hand to take another one. "I'm a busy person. I've got a page to edit."

"Your colleague Rhoda Carvell was found dead in her cottage two nights ago."

"I know." She flicked the lighter for her cigarette. "What's it got to do with me?" She peered challengingly at Reed through the haze of smoke that surrounded her head.

Reed strove to keep his temper in check. He wasn't sure which irritated him the more. The callous attitude, with no sign or word of regret, or the repulsive raddled appearance of the woman. The black nostrils, the over-painted and powdered face, the coarse skin, the short-cropped wig of hair that didn't know whether it was black or ginger...

"To do with you? We believe her to have been murdered. Aren't you anxious for us to find her killer?"

"Anxious? It was probably her own fault. Taking on that wet hen, Woodruff."

"Are you suggesting Ralph Woodruff killed her and himself?"

"Not just like that. Woodruff hadn't the guts to hurt himself."

"What are you suggesting then, Mizz Lugano?"

"Rhoda was a fool. She knew what men are like. Carvell had treated her like dirt. Woodruff smarmed over her so much he was like a snail leaving a trail whenever he touched her. She should have steered clear of men: should have learned from experience."

"Instead she went off with Woodruff as soon as she was free from her husband."

Golly barked a laugh. "As soon as? She'd been going around with that gigolo for years."

"Years?"

"Of course, Carvell didn't know. He only realized it about a year ago—probably eighteen months."

"Why had she been fooling about with Woodruff?"

Again Golly cackled. "You men! Have you met Carvell? No? Well, when you do, you'll see he's a lusty man. You can sense it."

"What are you driving at?"

"All I'm saying is that Carvell and Rhoda weren't equally matched. He demanded more than she was prepared to give."

"In bed, you mean?" asked Berger.

"Of course I mean in bed. Where the hell do you think I mean? On the top of the Matterhorn?"

"So why link up with Woodruff as well?"

"Because that piece of soft soap didn't make the same demands on her as Carvell."

"But if he...in addition to her husband...that would make it worse for her."

"Not in addition to. Instead of."

"You mean she and Carvell didn't...?"

"That's it, dearie. He took up gambling instead. And he wasn't above giving a few private tutorials to female stu-

109

dents, I dare say, but I think mostly he got his fun with all those social hostesses who entertained him. He was bloody discreet. For a man of his drive to avoid a bit of scandal must have taken some doing."

Reed nodded and rose to offer Golly a light for her next cigarette. "So he was reconciled to the fact that he and his wife didn't live as a normally married couple?"

"Normal? What's normal? And as for reconciled...believe me, dearie, when you meet Professor Ernest Carvell you'll realize he'd never be reconciled to anything."

"Are you saying that when the Professor got to know of Woodruff's relationship with Mrs Carvell he threatened the man?"

Golly didn't answer for a moment or two. Then: "Apparently not. And that surprised me. Carvell's built like a hammer-thrower and he's not short on temper. He could have eaten Woodruff—literally—as well as being a man with more academic and establishment clout than him. I expected daily to hear there'd been some sort of rumpus after Carvell found out about Woodruff and Rhoda. But it never came."

"Why do you suppose that was?"

"I don't suppose anything, except perhaps that Carvell, despite his appearance and reputation, was as big a bladder of lard as Woodruff. It could be, you know. There's a strongly held belief that a man who takes a second wife often chooses a woman of like character to the first."

"Meaning?"

"If you know the character of the second wife, you know the character of the first."

"I get it. The same could apply to women. Mrs Carvell chose an obvious weakling in Woodruff, so it could be that underneath his hard exterior Professor Carvell is just as weak."

Golly nodded. "With a worse temper and more sex drive."

"That could mean that in spite of your less than flat-

110

tering remarks about Woodruff, Mrs Carvell could have been happier with him than with her first husband."

"She obviously thought so."

"But you don't?"

"I just think she was a bad picker altogether."

"You said that her death was probably her own fault. And then added that it was because she had taken on that wet hen, Woodruff. What did you mean by those two comments?"

"You don't give up, do you?"

Reed didn't reply. He rose to light her next cigarette.

"Her own fault," reminded Berger.

Golly snorted and removed a scrap of tobacco from a lower lip gleaming with dark lipstick. "Rhoda Carvell was a good looking woman with a superlative figure."

"So young Mr Heddle has told us."

"Men, and by men, I mean all men, think that such women are highly bedworthy. Let me tell you, they're not. Not all of them. Rhoda wasn't. But women who look like her want men around them, and Rhoda was no exception. The most forceful of the men who flock round them are naturally men with drive."

"Like Carvell?"

"Like Carvell. And they are the men who hound these girls into marrying them. Mistakenly. Men like that want women of equal appetites—whether they're marvellous lookers or not. Otherwise the options open to them are limited. The two either have to adjust or go their separate ways. Carvell and Rhoda couldn't adjust. So Carvell went off his way and left Rhoda to do very much as she pleased.

"Now this is where her fault lay. Instead of being content..."

"In the knowledge that her husband was consorting with other women?"

"Not in the knowledge. I told you he was discreet. It would be a fair assumption on her part, knowing his proclivities, but not in the knowledge. And ignorance is bliss. Or should be. But not for Rhoda." Golly sounded bitter.

"She was a pretty woman, and pretty women like to have a man in tow. It's as important to have a man as to have the right bag. And that's why I say it was her own fault. She didn't play it right. She could have done, but she didn't, and because of that Carvell divorced her and she's dead."

"Without the divorce she'd still be alive?"

"That's what my guts tell me. I can't separate the two, even if the divorce action only caused her to be in the wrong place at the wrong time with the wrong man."

"And that's why you say that if she hadn't taken up with Woodruff she'd still have been alive?"

"Yes." She was emphatic. Suddenly the façade seemed to give way. "I know what you two think. You think I've no feelings at all. But I have, damn you, I have. I liked Rhoda. Admired her. She was everything I wasn't, had everything I hadn't, so you could expect me to be as jealous as hell of her. But I wasn't. And I'm already missing her...look, blast you, since I heard she was dead I've been about as much good as...as a colour-blind snooker professional. So now you've heard what you wanted, get out."

She reached for her cigarette packet. It was empty. In silence Reed put his own packet in front of her.

"Keep those," he said quietly. "And before you go back to your office, slip into the ladies. Your mascara is a bit blotched."

"He's a ripe bastard," said Green as they left the college, "but not quite as bad as you'd led me to believe."

"He'd toned it down a bit from last night."

"When he realized you weren't your average Mister Plod?"

"Maybe."

"Meaning you don't think so?"

"Meaning that finding we are not, in his eyes, numbskulls, could be one explanation or part of it."

"He's shrewd, you reckon?"

112

"No."

"A bloke like him, a professor, not shrewd?"

"That's why I said it could be one explanation or part of it. If he was all that shrewd, his tactics last night would never have been employed—until he knew the lie of the land—or they would have been carried over this morning."

"Consistency?"

"Exactly. There's a cab, Bill ..." Masters raised an arm. "Scotland Yard, please."

"So he's not consistent. But he's clever, astute even."

"Agreed. But is he wise? Sagacious? Gifted with acuteness of mental discernment? I think a lack of consistency in attitude would argue against that."

"So what is he?"

"A bit of a paradox, I'd have said. He appears to be a muscular, practical man. But he's an academic."

"A muscular academic."

"There was a bit of bluster about him."

"Okay, full of academic bluster."

Masters grinned. "That's about as close as we shall get for the moment, I suppose. Smacks a bit of muscular Christianity, doesn't it?"

"Except that I don't suppose he ever goes to church."

The cab deposited them at the Yard.

As they went to the senior mess bar, Green asked: "Now what about this afternoon, George?"

"I want to do a bit of reading, Bill. I also want to hear from the sergeants."

"Before you decide whether to go to Chichester?"

"Yes. Come on, I'll stand you a drink."

While Masters was buying, Green went to the gents. When he came back he told Masters he had seen the sergeants, who wanted to report on their meetings with Heddle and Golly Lugano.

"In that case we'd better confer immediately after lunch. What they have to say may determine what we do later. I am assuming that they wouldn't have asked to speak to us before four unless they've got something they think is important?"

Green took a large gulp from his tankard before replying. "They seemed a bit agog."

"Ah! All excited like?"

"Actually, a bit subdued. Reed was grumbling about having lost a packet of fags."

Masters and Green listened carefully to the report from Reed and Berger, both of whom had emulated Green in mastering the habit of almost total recall when aided by the notes they had made. So Masters got a fair picture of the interviews.

"Drink," he said when the sergeants had finished. "We didn't notice it. The smell I mean."

"Dissipated," grunted Green. "Up that dirty great chimney in the sitting room."

"Did any of you notice signs in the sitting room—or the bedroom?"

"Signs, Chief?"

"Empty glasses, bottles . . . the usual end of party mess."

All stated they had seen no such signs.

"The kitchen, Chief. We didn't go out there. She could have cleared away."

"Not likely," grunted Green. "If the stink of booze was so strong, it meant those characters would be half-seas over by the time they staggered upstairs. Too far gone, at any rate, to fancy clearing up a mess."

Masters sat thoughtful for a moment or two. Then Reed asked: "The drink, Chief? It's important?"

Masters came back with a jerk. "Their alcoholic state? Very important. Very important indeed."

"Can we know why?" asked Green. "Or would that be telling?"

"What? Oh, I see. These two were killed by a noxious gas."

"We don't know that for sure, do we? Couldn't they have eaten some arsenic."

114

"The medics think not. I'll tell you why they think so. Had they ingested arsenic—in any form taken through the mouth—it would have gone straight down and irritated their stomachs and guts so much that they would have vomited to glory."

"Which they didn't," admitted Green. "But that begs another question. Drunks usually puke, too. Which again they didn't. So my guess is they weren't kalied either."

"I'm going to disagree, Bill. I think they were drunk. Dead drunk, almost. They had to be for all this to work as it did."

"We're not with you, Chief."

"How do drunks breathe?"

"The same as anybody else," retorted Green.

"The pattern of their breathing," insisted Masters. "Initially—when they first become blotto—their breathing is very deep and stertorous."

"Got it!" shouted Green. "If they were killed by a gas, they had to take it in in great gulps for it to kill them."

"Right."

"And they'd have to be blotto not to be wakened up or become aware of the stink of the gas."

"Right again. Go on."

"If they breathed deep, and took in a lot of gas, it would kill them by attacking their...what? Their lungs?"

"Yes."

"It would attack their lungs and stop them breathing before it could get down to attacking their guts to make them puke."

"Admirably put, Bill. It means there was a high enough concentration of gas to kill them quickly so long as they were unaware they were being gassed and so long as they breathed deeply. Because, once they were approaching death—and this applies to drunks as well as, or so I should imagine, people who have been poisoned—their breathing becomes shallow."

"You've got it, George," congratulated Green.

"Steady, steady. We've got one little point. There's a

115

hell of a lot more to ferret out yet."

"When you know how it happened..."

Masters shook his head. "All we've got is one small medical fact—a mechanical fact, if you like. We don't know how the gas got into the room, where it came from or who introduced it."

"A pipe through the keyhole," grunted Green. "It's been done before. A canister of gas and..."

"Where does one get canisters of arsine?"

Green looked surprised. "Can't it be made and caught in a container? Most gases can—with retorts and what not?"

"I'm sure most gases can be collected with suitable chemistry apparatus."

"Carvell. He's got a laboratory."

"True. But it's ten to one he has none of the apparatus you're talking about. Scads of microscopes for examining slides, bunsen burners for doing borax bead tests, charcoal blocks..."

"I don't know what you're talking about."

"Simple tests for identifying minerals. All to do with colour and streaking and such like. It's not a stinks lab."

"I see. Or at least I think I do. So the prof didn't make a nice bottle of gas there." He stopped suddenly. "Bottle gas...?"

"Not arsenical. And none there."

"No, I suppose not."

Reed asked: "So what now, Chief? We know they were blotto when they bought it."

Masters stocked his pipe, every movement deliberate. "It doesn't hang together," he said at last. "If they got as drunk as we imagine they did, where did they do the actual drinking?"

"Meaning it needn't have been at the house at all?" queried Green. "At the local pub, perhaps?"

"I think not."

"So do I," agreed Green. "For one thing, if they'd been supping up in the local boozer, Bert Robson would have discovered it by now, and if he turned anything up at all about their movements he'd have been on the blower to tell us—just to show how good he is. And..." Green looked round triumphantly, "...they wouldn't have been able to drive the car back along the lane, get between those two huts at the gate and then put the barouche safely in the garage."

"Do we know it was safe?" asked Berger. "We didn't examine it to see if it had been pranged."

"The locals did," retorted Green. "If there'd have been a mark on it they'd have told us."

"All good points, Bill," admitted Masters. "And they apply to any suggestion that they might have had a drinking bout further afield, only more so, because they'd have had an even longer drive back."

"So they drank at home, Chief?"

"We none of us saw any signs in the sitting room, and I can't think that if they were so drunk they would have cleared up."

"In the dining room, perhaps then?"

"The fire had been in the sitting room. The ashes were still there. But I must admit, the dining room sounds a possibility. We must check. We must check this whole business of drink, in fact."

"It's bothering you, isn't it?" asked Green.

"Yes. How did they manage to get upstairs, to undress and then get into bed if they were really *stinko profundo*? Did anybody notice any clothes lying on the floor in the bedroom?"

Everybody agreed they had seen no signs of disarray in the bedroom.

"Perhaps Heddle was wrong, Chief," said Berger.

"If he was," said Green, "how are we going to explain the business of them just lying there and dying. Arsine would distress them so much they'd have wakened up, wouldn't they, George?"

"I would have thought so. Sleep is a funny thing. Anything out of the ordinary can disturb it. I know that after

117

Wanda has put young Michael to bed she insists that we talk in normal tones, have people in or the telly on. No whispering. She thinks—and I believe she's right—that a totally quiet house would waken him."

"She must be right," said Green. "In a house the size of yours nobody can get away from any noise that's made and yet the young choker sleeps through it. Strong fumes and the stink of garlic would make anybody cough and sit up."

"And," said Masters, "I'm inclined to believe young Heddle. Everything he has told us, and we have checked, has been proved true, so I can see no earthly reason why he should make up this story about the strong smell of drink."

"That's what we think, too, Chief," said Reed.

"So," said Masters, decisively, "we'll go down to Abbot's Hall and Chichester and try to sort the business out."

"Now?"

"In half an hour's time. Bill, will you try to contact Robson and let him know we hope to be at the house at about four thirty?"

"And back to Chichester for six?"

Masters nodded and turned to the sergeants. "I'll be ready at three. Get your report written up while it's still fresh in your mind. There are some bits of it we haven't discussed, but we may well have to later."

"Right, Chief."

When he was alone, Masters went to his coat and took the mineralogy book from the pocket. He sat at his desk to consult it. Then he rose to take another book from the shelf. A few minutes later he was leaning back in his chair, smoke rising from his pipe while he dealt with the mental problem he had set himself.

As the car made good time west, Green grew restive at the lack of conversation.

118

"What's up?" he demanded at last. "Or has the cat got everybody's tongues?"

Masters turned to him, where he sat, in the nearside rear seat. "Thoughts, Bill," he said quietly.

"Yours or mine?"

"My own, naturally, but I should be pleased to listen to any relevant ones from you."

"Fine. Normally...and I say that in the full knowledge that we never proceed normally...we try to get the three usual needs of a case. Means, opportunity and motive. So far we've got none of them."

"We know the means," protested Berger. "Arsine."

"Don't let's play clever beggars, lad. We don't know where the arsine came from nor how it got into that bedroom. We don't even know whether it got there by accident or design. And what's more, there's nothing so far to give us any hint."

Masters asked: "You do agree they were gassed in the bedroom, and not somewhere else?"

"I'm banking on it."

"Why?" asked Berger.

"Because the bedroom stank of garlic. Because if they'd been gassed somewhere else they wouldn't have been able to get upstairs to bed in good order. And if his nibs is right about the drunken breathing..."

"I think we can rely on that, Bill."

"Right. So don't let's start unnecessary hares about them being gassed in some other place."

"I agree. Please go on."

"No means," grunted Green. "No opportunity for anybody to have killed them either—so far, that is. Two people alone in an isolated house on a wild night? Who's going out there to do them in? And don't say it could be some tramp, because the job is obviously too sophisticated for a spur of the moment job. And there's another thing. As far as we know, nobody expected those two to be down at Abbot's Hall that Monday night. Everybody expected

119

them to go there on Tuesday, after the divorce."

"All that is true, Bill. So what is your answer?"

"I haven't one. The thing just doesn't hold together. Either we're on the wrong track or..."

"Or what?"

"It's a damn good job that Carvell dame was an open-air fiend, otherwise she might not have lived as long as she did."

"How's that?" asked Berger.

"Meaning she could have been poisoned in that room any night she went to bed with the windows closed. The first time she did, she died."

"You reckon it was an accident, and that there's something in the plaster or under the floorboards that gives off arsine?" Berger sounded highly sceptical as he asked the question.

"Why not lad? Some paints have arsenic in them. Has there been any painting done there recently?"

"Using paint that was a bad mix, you mean?"

"Mistakes have been made before, lad."

"It's a thought," agreed Masters.

Green turned to him. "George, you're not the only one who can read a book, you know. After I rang Chichester I did a bit of research myself. Not much, because there wasn't time. But I found an American book in the library, and it said that many colouring materials, mordants..."

"Who?" demanded Berger.

"Mordants." Green turned again to Masters. "I had to look that up myself, that's why I didn't get very far with my research. Apparently mordants are substances used for fixing colours in dyeing materials and in adhesive compounds for fixing gold leaf."

"I didn't know that, Bill."

"No? Well, besides colouring materials and mordants, this chap mentioned rodent poisons and insecticides. So you see there could be any amount of arsenic about that house that we don't know about. And if there's arsenic, there could be arsine, I reckon, because gases can be given off quite easily, can't they?"

"Under certain conditions," agreed Masters.

"Shall I tell you one I know about?"

"Please do."

"Fungi," said Green cryptically.

"Poisonous toadstools?" asked Berger.

"No, you berk. The book I was reading said that ethyl arsine and similar vapours are released from arsenic compounds by the action of various fungi."

"Again something I didn't know," admitted Masters.

"So," said Green triumphantly, "perhaps what we're looking for is still there and has been for some time. What I mean is, it could be something like dry rot that has gradually crept into the floor joists and started releasing the poison and the stink of garlic. If damp has got in. After all, it's an old house."

"Those fungi that grow on timber give me the creeps," said Reed from the driving seat. "Dirty great things as big as dinner plates. I had some on one of the trees at home. I wouldn't touch them, even with gloves on. I hacked them off with a spade and put them on a bonfire."

"Quite right, too, lad. As I've just said, they can be killers." Green turned back to Masters. "Makes you think, doesn't it?"

"It certainly does. Have you finished demolishing what little bit we have of a case?"

"Not quite. Besides having no means and no opportunity, we have no known motive."

"And no suspect," added Berger.

Green helped himself to a crumpled Kensitas.

"You did ask for my thoughts," he said. "Have they given you something to think about?"

"They have, indeed. It's a pity you couldn't tell us where the arsenic compound is, or what it is."

"You're expecting me to do all the work?"

"That'll be the day," said Reed.

"You shut your trap, lad, and get us to where we're going in one piece or I'll start shoving fungus spores in your woodwork. I've often wondered why timber pests don't affect blockheads, so I'll be glad of a chance to experiment."

"All this because you had a look at a book! Heaven help us if you ever learn to read."

"Can it, son," growled Green who then turned to Masters.

"Upset your applecart, have I?"

"No, Bill. What you have said has been most valuable."

"You mean you can use it?"

"To lead up to something I was going to say."

"You said you didn't know anything about mordants and fungi and so on."

"Quite right, I didn't. What I have to say is far more mundane."

"I thought there'd be something a bit more down to earth," said Reed. "Keep it simple, Chief. I'm no science buff."

"I shall try. Arsine gas is produced wherever a reducing agent, such as an active metal like iron, zinc or tin..."

"Hold it. What's this reducing agent business?"

"Don't let that baffle you. For the sake of simplicity, I'll just say that it means removing oxygen from a compound or, in other words, the action or process of reducing one substance to another, usually simpler, form."

Green grunted. "So if I reduced water by taking the oxygen out I'd be left with hydrogen. Is that it?"

"Correct. But in most reducing processes you need an agent. A sort of catalyst if you like. So wherever a reducing agent—in this case, metal—reacts with water or an acid in the presence of a compound of arsenic, you get arsine."

"I think I'm with you."

"Good. But the trouble again is, where does the compound of arsenic come from?"

"Are you going to give us the answer?"

"By asking a further question, yes."

"Here we go."

"It's the obvious question, Bill. Where do we find a compound of arsenic? But even more so, where do we find a compound of arsenic in the presence of a reducing agent such as iron, zinc or tin?"

"I suppose you're going to tell us."

"I'd better, otherwise you'd accuse me of withholding information."

"Or even of clamming up on us," said Reed. "Like you did about that eskimo yesterday."

"You mind your barrow, lad. And if you can't push it, shove it."

"Rude."

"It was meant to be."

"What I'm going to tell you," said Masters, "came from a few minutes spent in studying young Harry Finmore's mineralogy text book. I hope when you've heard what I have to say you'll agree that the fiver I gave him was money well-spent."

"We're listening."

And they did listen, intently, while Masters spoke for a long ten minutes. When he came to the end of his report, there was a pause before anybody decided to comment. Then—

"You haven't got it sewn up, George," said Green quietly, "but you've discovered where that blasted arsine came from."

"Could have come from."

"Did come from," asserted Green. "They were killed by a gas that not one in a million people would be able to get hold of or know where to find. Now you've discovered a source right bang on the doorstep of Abbot's Hall and you're not willing to go nap. You've even suggested how the blasted stuff could be introduced into the bedroom. And for my money it was a practical, easy way."

"Thank you for the vote of confidence, Bill. At any rate we can proceed with my suggestion as a possibility that helps us forward. All we have to hope now is that the forensic boys confirm arsine as the cause of death."

"Is there any doubt about that, Chief?" asked Reed.

"None that I know of. But the pathologist gave it as an instant and immediate diagnosis, based, I should think, on the odour of garlic in the bedroom."

"And the oedema round the eyes."

"True. But any arsenical compound would cause that. If they'd ingested arsenic..."

"Don't start hares, George," said Green. "If they'd eaten the stuff it would have gone down into their guts, damaged the intestines and caused them to puke. We've been over this. What killed them did its dirty work in the lungs. In other words they inhaled it, and they could only do that with a gas."

Masters grinned. "You're determined we are right, Bill."

"Feel it," grunted Green. "I know I was raising all sorts of hurdles a short time ago, but having heard what you said, I've changed my mind." As he finished speaking, the car turned on to the track leading to Abbot's Hall. Green was swayed in his seat by the transfer from smooth tarmac to unmade-up surface. "Watch it, young Reed," he grated. "This isn't a whippet tank. Now we've heard from his nibs, we've all got something to live for."

— 5 —

Robson and Middleton were waiting for them.

Robson approached Masters as the four Yard men left the car. Green said to Middleton: "Had a good day, lad?"

"Not so's you'd notice, sir. Everybody round here is blind."

"Don't you believe it, son. If you haven't found anybody who saw those two cavorting about, it tells you something."

"What?"

"That they weren't cavorting about."

Middleton wasn't impressed with this thought, and said so.

"You're wrong, lad. It's important. If those two died Tuesday night—having come down on Monday—they would have had more time in which to be seen. But they weren't seen. That supports the Monday theory."

"If you say so."

"I do, lad, I do. Now then, have you examined that car in the garage?"

"Not examined it exactly. I've looked at it."

"Right. You and Sergeant Berger examine it closely. And the gateposts. We want to know if it had a bump on the way in. Berger will tell you why as you have a look."

"I'll go round the house looking for bottles," said Reed.

"Don't forget the bin," warned Green. "And I don't suppose the dust cart comes out here, so look about for a rubbish sack or a dump."

Green moved across to join Masters and Robson. It was

still light, the westering sun glowing red above the horizon.

"I've set the lads on," said Green. "They might as well start to earn their keep."

Robson said: "Mr Masters has been telling me a few things."

Green grinned. "Little points you never thought he'd come up with, were they?"

Robson looked slightly uncomfortable. "I can't say that, seeing I didn't know anything about them, but... well, yes, I don't reckon Sergeant Middleton and I would have been able to..."

"Forget it," said Masters. "Now about the drink."

"What drink?" demanded Robson.

"Didn't he get as far as telling you they must have been kalied when they went to bed?"

"No. Just about the source of the arsine."

"Well, I'll tell you how we know." Green gave Robson the gist of the matter and ended by saying the object now was to find the evidence.

"There's nothing of that sort," said Robson. "Nothing at all except a nearly empty gin bottle and some white wine, unopened."

"No empty bottles of any sort?"

"No."

"Nor dirty glasses?"

"No."

"Odd," murmured Masters.

Robson looked from one to the other of the Yard men. His voice sounded sceptical as he said: "You couldn't have made a mistake about the source of the arsine as well as about the drink, by any chance?"

Masters said mildly: "Shall we wait to see what the forensic report tells us before we get into any arguments about whether we're right or wrong?"

"I'm more than willing to do that," said Robson sourly.

"Good. Now, I'd like to look round the house while

there's still light enough. Bill, would you take the upstairs? I'm not expecting you to find much up there, so
you can make it very cursory. I shall be downstairs."

"What about me?" demanded Robson.

"Please join me," said Masters. "We'll look round downstairs."

"There's nothing," declared Robson.

"You've looked? But of course you have. However..."
Green left them.

"If I knew what you were looking for..." began Robson.

"Trays," said Masters.

"Trays?" Robson sounded as if he thought Masters had
taken leave of his senses. All the local man's worst fears
seemed to be confirmed.

There was no tray in the sitting room. The sideboard
in the dining room carried a silver tray with a fretted
gallery. On it were a water jug, an empty sherry decanter
and two heavy tumblers. Masters removed the ground-
glass stopper and sniffed the decanter. "There's been no
alcohol in this recently. In fact, I would say it was washed
some time ago and not been used since."

"I told you what alcohol there is in the house. A few
tots of gin and several bottles of white wine in a rack in
the kitchen."

"Ah, yes! The kitchen! We'll have a look round there."

It was stone flagged, rough and uneven, cold to the feet,
but—in Masters' eyes—pleasant to the eyes. Squarish in
shape, it had a scrubbed wooden-topped table in the centre
of the floor. All the rest of the equipment was modern.
Stainless steel sink with two draining boards; a whole run
of cupboards with a melamine working top made to re-
semble marble; a tiled recess where the old fire had once
been, now occupied by a small, modern anthracite stove,
presumably for heating water; an electric cooker, presumably powered by the generator; and finally a refrigerator.

"Clean," grunted Robson. "As I told you." He pulled
open a couple of drawers. "All the cooking stuff in here—

127

cutlery and so on, and tea towels etcetera here. The cupboards have all the bits and pieces: tinned foods, salt drum, pepper and what not."

Masters nodded. Reared against the wall was a chopping board, a cheese board, and a small white-metal tray. He examined the last closely.

"Any good?"

Masters didn't reply. He stood near the table looking about him, then he went to the cupboards, opening each in turn until he came to the one containing the ovenware dishes. He considered these for a moment or two.

"There seem to be complete sets here," he murmured. "And there doesn't appear to be any gap from which dishes have gone missing." As he straightened up, Robson asked: "You're looking for something that should be here, but isn't? Is that it?"

Masters nodded.

"Trays, you said."

"Receptacles, like trays, with a large surface area, but not necessarily a great deal of depth. Not deep casseroles for instance, but their shallow lids would do, if they were big enough. But all the lids are there." Masters again looked about him and then moved to the cooker. He squatted to undo the oven door. His grunt of satisfaction brought Robson to squat beside him.

"Found something?"

"A space where something should be."

"What?"

"Think of Mrs Robson's oven—I take it there is a Mrs Robson?"

"There is."

"Excellent. What would you see if you opened her oven door?"

"A dripping tin—two actually. One for roasting something big."

"Anything else?"

"Yes. Baking trays. And somewhere there'd be a big

128

grill pan." Robson looked at Masters. "Nothing at all here. But she must have used the oven. You can see by all the burnt-on splash marks and grease...wait a minute, though. She could have used all that Pyrex we saw."

Masters closed the oven door. "She could have used that a lot, I agree." He straightened up. "But all ovens are sold with a complement of roasting tins and a grill pan of the correct size. They last a long time. This oven seems fairly new, so the bits and pieces couldn't have worn out by now. And I don't think any woman would throw them away. Besides, I should imagine that Mrs Carvell was the type to rely heavily on the grill pan, and that isn't here."

"I'll look round to see they're not hidden under the sink or in that old wall cupboard just inside the back door."

"Please do. And, Mr Robson..."

"Something else?"

"Just a word of advice. Don't be too sceptical of other people's ideas. Or at any rate, try not to show it. Here is an illustration of why you shouldn't do so. I surmised, in London, that these trays, or something like them, would be missing. Yet you have examined the house and not noted their absence as being out of the ordinary."

"You could still be on the wrong track."

"Admittedly, but at least I am testing my theory, and the absence of the trays fits. Have you any theory you can test in a similar way?"

"No. And I'll be honest, sir. I've been thinking you're floundering."

Masters grinned. "You're right. But it would be more diplomatic to suggest I am casting about for leads. But you will be able to decide for yourself whether or not I have been successful after we have seen the forensic report."

Robson shrugged and set about trying to locate the missing oven trays.

Green and Reed came into the kitchen together.

"Any luck?" asked Green.

129

Masters told him of the possibility that the oven trays were missing and that Robson was conducting a search to ascertain if they were stored elsewhere.

"They'd be in the oven," said Green dogmatically. "My missus always puts them in upside down because if they're put in right way up there's a possibility that a drop of moisture will gather in the bottoms and rust the tins."

"My old mum has a big one for a turkey," said Reed. "It's mottled grey. Some sort of enamel, I suppose. About an inch deep. It's always kept in the oven because she uses it for these new chips we get these days. She spreads them out on it to heat up."

Masters acknowledged this support for his supposition and asked Reed if he had anything to report.

"Not a sausage, Chief. I'm too old a hand to say you're wrong, but there is no sign of any drinking having taken place here. Not even an empty tonic bottle. Sergeant Berger may have found something outside, of course..."

"Bill?"

"Something odd, George."

"What?"

"Did you see the corner wine cabinet in the dining room?"

"Yes, but I didn't open it. Ought I to have done so?"

"Not you. Robson. All the usual sets of glasses are in there, in half dozens. You know the sort of thing—and all the sets are complete. Even six shallow champagne bowls."

"Thanks, Bill. Champagne, you said?"

"And general purpose stemmed goblets."

"It helps, Bill. But why are they all in there and not on the draining board?"

Green grinned. "Another bit for you, George."

"What's that?"

"There's a new pack of two dozen tonics under the stairs. One of those that has a cardboard tray and a sheet of plastic over the top."

"I know the sort."

"When I said new, I meant it looks new. No dust on it

or anything like that, but the plastic top has been torn and three bottles are missing."

"Go on. You've got something else, obviously."

"There's the price sticker still there on the plastic. It's got the shop name on it."

"Local?"

"I reckon so. We should be able to trace it and discover when it was bought."

"Thanks, Bill." Masters turned as Robson came back. "Any finds?"

"No sign of anything like baking trays."

"Thank you. Now, just one more thing. Has the gin bottle you found got a price label on it by any chance?"

"I honestly can't remember. But I'll look."

"Please do."

As Robson left to do his checking, Berger and Middleton came into the kitchen. "There's a rubbish sack in a bin just outside, Chief. We turned it out. There's some torn-up paper, three or four empty tins—lobster bisque, one of those oval ham tins, and a potato can—some remnants of a lettuce wrapped up in paper and not much else. No bottles at all."

"Thank you." Masters looked at Green. "Did you see any newspapers, Bill?"

Green stared back. "Dated a week last Monday, you mean?"

Masters nodded.

"No, I didn't. But it doesn't signify. They could have used it for lighting the fire, unless..."

"I know," said Berger. "I've got to unroll those lettuce leaves again and check the date on the paper."

"And check the tins for price labels, please."

Robson came back. "The gin was bought locally," he said. "I know the shop."

"And the tonic for a bet," added Green. "A full tray of it. The shopkeeper should remember the sale. Get your lad to check."

"And the groceries Berger mentioned," added Masters.

"They could have been bought at the same time."

Green lit a crumpled Kensitas without offering the packet round. Masters stood in thought. Reed and Robson chatted quietly. They all looked round as Berger returned with three empty tins and the parcel of vegetable waste half unwrapped. "It's the Monday edition, Chief," said Berger quietly.

"Proving nothing," asserted Robson. "They could have had a yesterday's paper in the car if they arrived on Tuesday. We've got papers in my house that are months old."

"Quite right," said Masters. "It proves nothing. Neither does it disprove anything, as it would have done had it been the Tuesday paper."

"Prove or disprove," snorted Green, "is neither here nor there. And we all know it. That paper is a hell of a pointer."

"We have to bear it in mind," admitted Robson, "but I still think it doesn't prove they were here on the Monday, still less that they died that night."

"I think we should get going," said Masters. "It's almost dark now and I'd like to see the forensic report."

Green said to Robson, "You travel with us, mate. Your sergeant can take Berger with him and check that shop on the way. You never know, we might get another pointer."

Masters appeared to agree with this arrangement for a moment and then amended Green's order. "I'd like Reed to stay with Middleton. He can dust those sets of glasses you saw in the wine cupboard. I want to know if any of them have been used recently and then washed."

Green turned to Reed. "Get your gear out of the boot."

Dr Peter Fisk, the forensic pathologist, brought his report in person to the Chichester police station. He was a man in his fifties, with a lugubrious face, sparse grey hair and—when he was reading—a pair of half-moon spectacles which he wore low on his nose. When not using the lenses, he peered over their tops in a way which Green later described as reminiscent of an ageing Egyptian belly-dancer having trouble with her yashmak.

"I came myself," he explained to Masters, "because you have here a problem which I myself would not like to have to sort out."

"It has presented you with difficulties, has it, sir?"

Fisk nodded. "Quite a problem. Quite a problem." He paused for a moment and then continued. "You see, Chief Superintendent, I think it safe to say that the fundamental effects of arsenic—and arsine is only gaseous arsenic, after all—on the body tissues, have been elucidated... er...but slightly." He leaned forward to make his next point. "One of the major observations that has been made is that arsenite inhibits lactate utilization in liver slices, of course, but..." he shook his head, "...but in a case of acute poisoning such as this..." He looked at Green who seemed completely lost. "Death, you see, occurred within a very few hours. Certainly during the first twenty-four, but the usual course runs from three days to a week..."

Masters stepped in. "What you are saying, sir, is that death occurred so quickly that the usual pathological signs in the body had not developed."

"Quite. Normally, with acute arsenical poisoning, the digestive tract becomes inflamed and, indeed, may show ulceration."

"That's why they vomit, isn't it?" asked Green, determined to show he was keeping up.

"Oh, yes, quite. And the mucus of the intestinal tract shreds into an oedematous fluid. And, as you no doubt know, when death is delayed for a few days, there is fatty degeneration of the liver, or even acute yellow atrophy."

"So you presume they died very quickly?" asked Masters.

"That is my point."

"So they were subjected to a really high concentration of arsine?"

"Yes, yes," said Fisk a little testily. "That is the point I was about to make. The estimated safe concentration of arsine in air is just one-twentieth of one part per million. After a few hours in air containing as little as ten parts per million, one would get symptoms."

"Serious symptoms?"

"Not to say serious, exactly, but nasty. For serious symptoms to emerge, I would estimate forty parts per million."

"One part in twenty-five thousand! Is that what these two were subjected to?"

Fisk shook his head. "Oh, no. Far more than that. Far more. Though where it came from ... but that is your problem. As I said, I would not like to tackle it myself."

"So how exactly did they die?" asked Robson.

"Arsine produces poison by inhalation. The gas diffuses through the pulmonary sac. The symptoms would develop inside thirty minutes ... yes, inside thirty minutes. Early respiratory irritation, you might say. Due to haemolysis ... yes, arsine death is caused by respiratory collapse in cases like this, due to haemolytic action, though one would expect to find also excretion of blood cell debris by the kidney."

"Haemolytic action, Doc?" asked Green. "What's that in words blokes like me might understand?"

Fisk peered at him. "The destruction of the red blood cells and the resultant escape from them of haemoglobin. And haemoglobin is the respiratory pigment of the red blood cells. So you see they were killed by respiratory failure."

"Got it. Thanks."

"Why did they die so quickly?" asked Masters.

"Why? Because of the high concentration of arsine to which they were subjected and ..."

"Yes?"

"Because, Mr Masters, they had been drinking heavily."

"Ah!"

The doctor looked over his spectacles. "They had a great amount of alcohol inside them. In fact, they were drunk. Had they not been intoxicated it is my guess that so heavy a concentration of arsine would have caused them so much irritation that they would have awakened and so saved their lives. But I believe that they were dead to the world in a drunken stupor, breathing heavily and oblivious to any irritation. That is why all the usual pathological indications were not present. The one good thing is that they died quickly, without pain or distress."

"There you are, lad," said Green to Robson. He then turned to Fisk. "Gin, was it, Doc?"

Fisk considered the point. At length he replied: "   · ık the foundation was gin." He consulted his report. "Yes, definitely gin. I estimate that they had taken some twenty-five centilitres each."

"That would be a third of a bottle each?"

"Just so."

"Foundation, you said, Doc. Do you mean they built on it?"

"Most assuredly."

"What did they use for bricks?"

"Ah! There I cannot be quite so precise as to the true nature of the liquor. Suffice it to say that it was a white wine. No sign of red anywhere. But I am unable to identify it further." He peered at them. "There were very definite indications of a gaseous liquid—aerated if you like. But I should remind you that the gin had been accompanied by tonic water which is, as you know, gaseous."

"Meaning that you are unable to say whether the wine was gaseous or not, doctor?" asked Masters.

"That is my point. The wine could have been, for example, sparkling Niersteiner. In the mix-up within the body organs, I could only establish that there was something of a gaseous nature there."

"But you incline to the view that it could have been a sparkling wine."

"I merely admit the possibility."

"Thank you. Can you give us some idea of how much wine each had drunk?"

"To be sure. I had to do some comparative calculations between blood and urine and other organ contents, of course, but my estimate—a conservative one—is that those sorry people had taken almost a litre each."

"Good heavens!"

"It is certainly astounding. Not only the amounts imbibed, but the fact that the woman kept pace with the man."

"Even Steven," grunted Green.

"A litre each," murmured Masters. "That's the equivalent of three bottles between them." He turned to Fisk. "An unhealthy combination, gin and wine, in those amounts, sir?"

"Without a doubt. But my observations show that the gin was drunk before a meal of..." The pathologist again consulted his notes. "Soup, potatoes, ham and lettuce, whereas the wine came later."

"Later?" asked Masters. "Not with the meal?"

"I cannot be entirely specific on the point because there has been a great deal of activity within the organs, but yes, I believe the wine to have been taken sometime after the meal. And that, gentlemen, is about all I can tell you. The technical details are all here, of course, in the Coroner's report."

"Can I ask you a further question, sir?"

Fisk removed his spectacles. "Please do, Chief Superintendent."

"When you inspected the bodies, they were in every way clothed for bed?"

"Yes."

"And there were no bottles or glasses in the bedroom they were occupying?"

"None of either. When I am called to these cases I make a point of looking for such things."

"Can you then suggest how two people, obviously very much under the influence of drink when they died, managed to clear up all traces of their drinking spree, get upstairs, undress, and then get into bed without leaving a heap of discarded clothing on the floor?"

Fisk shook his head. "This is one of the facets of the

136

case which has defeated me. I can only assume that they retired to bed soon after their meal and then lay in bed drinking until they were...well, in my day we referred to it as paralytic."

Masters looked at Fisk. "Had they indulged in sexual intercourse, sir?"

"I believe so, but the traces decay so rapidly that it is difficult indeed to say that intercourse took place after supper."

"Early bed-time," said Green laconically. "She was about to get divorced. She was in bed with a man other than her husband."

"Quite, quite. You should take these things into consideration, but I cannot swear to them. One thing, however, does lead me to support your supposition. And that is that physical tiredness, if allied to heavy intoxication, would help to further explain the fact that they were stuporous beyond the point at which they would have reacted to the irritation caused by the arsine."

"Good point, that," applauded Green. "But it doesn't answer the question of what became of the glasses and bottles." He turned to Masters. "Or does it?"

"It seems to indicate very strongly the presence of a third person at Abbot's Hall that night. And that, I suppose, merely adds confirmation to what we have all assumed."

"That there was a murderer there?" asked Robson.

Masters nodded. "A murderer present who decided to tidy up the house. The point is, why?"

Fisk got to his feet. "I cannot help you there, gentlemen, so if there are no more questions...dear me, how time flies! I promised my wife..."

They saw Fisk away, and almost immediately thereafter were joined by Reed and Robson.

Reed reported.

"Two of the stemmed goblets have been washed recently, Chief. Not a print on them. Whoever did it was careful not to leave his dhobi marks for us to find. The other four were clean, too. Slightly dusty as though they hadn't been used for a week or two, but they carried prints."

"And?"

"You're expecting an and, too, Chief?"

"You wouldn't surprise me if much the same could be said about a couple of glasses suitable for drinking white wine."

Reed grinned. "Well, Chief, you were the one who said I had to dust the glasses, so I can't claim that I've really caught you out, but the wine glasses were all okay except..."

"Come on, lad," grated Green. "Don't keep us in suspense, standing there looking pleased with yourself. Your face is like a riven dish, cracked across from ear to ear."

"Champagne glasses," suggested Masters. "Three of them, perhaps.

"How the hell did you know that, Chief?"

"Got it," grunted Green. "Sparkling Niersteiner, the man suggested. It wasn't. It was shampers. Bubbly!"

Reed looked crestfallen. "How did you know, Chief? And that there'd be three that had been washed and polished?"

"As you heard the DCI say, the pathologist thought he had detected signs of sparkling white wine. He hadn't been able to identify it, of course, and he wasn't absolutely sure that it was a sparkling wine because there was tonic water there, too. As you know, tonic bubbles, though for a different reason, perhaps. However, that is immaterial. We know they were drunk on gin and champagne."

"But you guessed there would be three glasses, Chief."

"That was easy, I'm afraid."

"Not to me," said Robson.

"After we reckoned we had proof there was a third person present?"

"No. At least not why whoever it was should clear up and wash a lot of glasses."

Masters looked closely at him. "No?"

138

"Well...I suppose his own prints...Christ! Are you suggesting he was actually here, drinking with them?"

"Go on."

"That he was somebody they knew and were matey enough with to ask him in for a drink?"

"Basically, yes. But I would go even further than that."

"Think, lad," said Green. "Before this joker arrived they were drinking gin and tonic. The gin bottle's still there, and so is the crate of tonic. After he arrived, they drank champagne, and the champagne bottles have disappeared. Why? Because the joker brought them with him, so he had to get rid of them in case we could trace them to him. In fact, I reckon he was hoping or expecting we'd never get to know they'd had champagne. And he had to wash the glasses because he'd handled them—or at least one of them, and I don't suppose he could remember which one or they got mixed up somehow."

"In that case, why wash the goblets they'd drunk the gin from? If he was wanting to mislead us, he'd have left those."

Green looked across at Masters. "There's a point, George."

"A point, certainly, but it happened, so we ought to try and make use of the fact."

"Meaning?" asked Robson.

"Our third person—the murderer—was obviously known to Mrs Carvell and Ralph Woodruff. We've already agreed that. He brought the champagne. A friendly gesture, you might say. But friends don't come to a party wearing gloves. I suspect that in the normal course of events, while he was serving champagne, he had to touch the other glasses. What I mean is this. He offers a glass of champagne to Rhoda Carvell who is sitting by the fire. She accepts it, says thank you, and then hands him her empty gin glass, asking if he would mind putting it on the drinks tray. He has to do as she asks. So he knows he has to wash that glass, at least. Perhaps the same thing

139

was repeated with Woodruff or—worse from our murderer's point of view—Woodruff gets up and puts his own empty gin glass on the tray. As he does so, his body hides his movements. Which glass is which? Our murderer can't be sure, so he has to wash both."

"So he had to wash all five glasses? Right," acknowledged Robson. "Then what?"

Masters grinned. "You wouldn't want me to speculate, would you, Mr Robson?"

Robson raised his eyes. "Oh, no, sir! I wouldn't want you to do anything like that. Not you! You've only guessed when they died. You've only guessed they were drunk. You've only guessed this, that and the other."

"Not guessed, surely?"

"It seems like it to me."

"Do you reckon we're getting anywhere, lad?" Green asked him.

Robson shrugged.

"You reckon not?"

"There's all this business about missing dripping tins and missing champagne bottles. How do we find those? There's the English Channel not two hundred yards from the doorstep of Abbot's Hall."

"That's what I'm afraid of," conceded Masters. "However, we haven't heard, from Sergeant Middleton, how he got on with his enquiries at the shop."

The local DS said: "You got it right, sir. They bought all the provisions as well as the gin and the tray of tonics on the Monday evening, just before closing time. From the grocer's shop."

"The shopkeeper is sure it was Monday?"

"Yes, sir. You see, I thought it a bit funny they should buy a whole tray of tonics and only one bottle of gin. It seemed a bit lopsided like. So I mentioned this in the shop and they said that Mrs Carvell had actually asked for three bottles of Gordon's. But he'd only got the one of those. He'd offered her some other sort, but she turned them down when he told her the new lot of Gordon's

140

would be in next day. He always gets his booze delivered on Tuesdays."

Masters murmured his appreciation of this piece of sagacity on the part of Middleton who continued: "And I don't think they sell champagne there, sir, so I don't think the three bottles could have been bought locally."

"Thank you. That is most useful information." He got to his feet. "Would you mind ringing Mrs Masters again, please, Sergeant, to tell her I shall be back by eight o'clock?"

As Middleton left them, Masters said to Robson: "We'll get off now. I think we could all do with a few hours away from our problem. We shall be in touch tomorrow."

As they sped towards London, Green asked: "What's the form, George? Young Robson wasn't kidding, you know. We've got a hell of a lot of fact, but we don't know who we're after, do we? Or if we do, we can't pin it on him."

Masters, packing his large-bowled cadger's pipe with freshly rubbed Warlock Flake, didn't reply immediately. He put the stem in his mouth and tested the draw before answering.

"The title of an essay written by Thomas de Quincey was 'Murder Considered as One of the Fine Arts'."

"I'm not familiar with it. Are you trying to say we've got something here done by an old master? Something that's beyond us?"

"Preparing you for it, shall we say."

"Oh, come on, Chief," expostulated Berger. "We've been at it for two days and we ... that is you ... have got no end of fact to work on."

"Not all that much. True, we know when, we know where and we reckon we know how. But we don't know why and who."

"I'll go along with that," said Green. "I don't have to remind you of the quote that every detective constable learns on his first day in civvies, but I'm going to. 'Murder, like talent, seems occasionally to run in families'."

141

Masters lit his pipe, waiting for the tobacco to glow evenly before asking: "You would go nap on Professor Ernest Carvell?"

"He's my bet."

"On what evidence specifically?"

Green thought for a moment. "He seems the most likely."

"Not good enough really, is it?"

"No," grunted Green. "He was getting rid of his wife on advantageous terms anyway. He wasn't going to lose a penny by it."

"Quite. And we haven't a single fact or clue to hang on him except, perhaps, that being of a scientific mind, he could be said to know about arsenic. But that's like saying I could be judged to have killed somebody because I know a lot about murder."

"You're waffling."

"Perhaps. However, in spite of what I've just said..."

"Don't be shy. We shan't laugh."

"We're going to look hard and long at the Professor."

"That's about all we can do, and I must say I'm backing you."

"Thanks."

"Tomorrow?"

"Certainly not tonight. I expect Wanda will be hoping I can see my way clear to staying at home with her."

"I should bloody well hope so."

Masters was right. His wife never tried to interfere with his comings and goings, but there was no hiding her pleasure when he announced his intention of not turning out again. While in no way wishing to involve her in the case, he did, however, attempt to satisfy her unspoken but natural curiosity. She said very little as she listened, curled up in a huge armchair, with her shoes off. But when he had finished she made one remark.

"If you want to know about her cooking utensils, darling, find a woman who visited her at Abbot's Hall. Men— and probably some women—don't notice these things. But women—well, quite a lot of them could tell you every

142

item you have in your sitting room within two minutes of being shown in."

"Thank you, sweetheart. Though whether she ever invited women there..."

"She must have done. Married couples to stay for a few days. That sort of thing."

He rose to pour her a drink. "I'll take the hint. Would you like the brandy straight or a Horse's Neck?"

She smiled up at him. "Long and weak, please."

"That sounds a bit like my case."

"I don't think so. To me it sounds very neat."

He grinned at her little play on words. The world, to him, seemed to be back on its course.

— 6 —

"Bill," said Masters, when he and Green met next morning, "there's one little job I would like you to do for me."

"Alone, you mean?"

"You and Berger."

"What's that?"

"Interview the night porter at Gladstone Hall. I want to know what time Carvell got in a week last Monday night, or Tuesday morning as the case may be."

"Why me? Is he liable to be difficult or something?"

"Yes."

"Just like that."

"Yes."

Green grunted. "If he's the night porter, he won't be on duty now."

"Not until six tonight I suppose. I was just giving you fair warning."

Green nodded, sat down and—for once—produced a pristine, unbattered packet of cigarettes. As he unwrapped it, he said: "If this chap is going to clam up on me..."

"Out of loyalty, perhaps, or because he just dislikes policemen."

"Right. I'm pleased you told me now. Just so's I can think about it."

"Good. Now, what time will our friends on the *Daily View* reach the office, do you suppose?"

"Not before ten."

"And Roger Vadil?"

Green grimaced. "He's the sort that could surprise you. Looks as if he would stroll into his office at eleven, whereas, in fact, he probably beavers away from half-past eight every morning."

"In that case, I think we should try him first."

"And Carvell himself?"

"We shall have to speak to him again, of course, but I'd rather leave it until we've got all we can from the others."

"To go into battle fully armed?"

"Fully armed, and with as big a supply train of spare ammunition as possible."

"And the lads?"

"We shan't need them when we visit Vadil. But I would like them to get in touch with Robson. I want the locals to comb that area for three champagne bottles—whole or in pieces—and a number of oven-trays."

"Robson won't like that."

"Perhaps not, and I must admit it's a forlorn hope. They could have been ditched in the sea, as Robson said yesterday, though I think not."

"No?"

"With a howling gale blowing? Why struggle against it across that heathland to throw stuff away when you can dispose of it anywhere between West Sussex and Inner London?"

"Miles from anywhere."

"Quite. Disposed of piece by piece in overgrown ditches."

"Or bottle banks for the champagne bottles."

"I'd forgotten those."

Green got to his feet. "Ready to go in about ten minutes?"

"Fine."

"I'm pleased to see you, gentlemen," said Vadil. He waved them to take the two modern chairs drawn up before his desk. "Though I had not expected a second visit quite so soon."

"*Pleased* to see us?" asked Green.

"Why not? You have presented me with the possibilit of an unusual, if not unique legal problem. I'm interested Am I to know whether the court divorced a dead woma last Tuesday morning?"

"It did," replied Masters.

"Without any shadow of doubt?"

"The merest shadow, perhaps, but I think not."

"Forensic examination puts the deaths as occurring o the Monday night?"

"Not precisely. You know that the medical professio is never willing to commit itself exactly. But the pathol ogist has given us a time bracket which includes the Mon day."

"But you know Mrs Carvell was alive on Monday—i the morning at least."

"We know she was alive in the early evening of tha day, too. She visited a local shop close to Abbot's Ha just before closing time that day."

"So you have established that she went there that da instead of Tuesday, which was her original intention?"

"That is so. And such information, linked with the tim ing of the storm and the closed windows we spoke of th last time we were here, has satisfied us that Mrs Carve and Mr Woodruff died on the Monday night. There ar other bits of evidence to support our belief. For instance the shop could not supply the three bottles of gin Mr Carvell wanted. She said she would return the next da when the fresh supplies were in. She didn't go for them."

Vadil laughed. "That is the most telling bit of evidenc you've produced so far. Rhoda Carvell would not hav missed her gin, had she been alive."

Masters nodded. "So we are led to believe." He hel up his pipe. "Do you mind if I . . . ?"

"Go ahead. There'll be some coffee here in a minute I was in soon after eight this morning, so I asked for it be sent in early."

146

"Thank you. So, Mr Vadil, you have your legal problem. How do you propose to resolve it?"

"I've given it some thought. I feel sure the answer will be the easy one. Facts count. If Carvell was a widower before the court sat a week last Tuesday morning, he could not be granted a divorce. The petition and subsequent ruling will be declared null and void. The agreed settlements will not be valid. Carvell will still be deemed to have been Rhoda's next-of-kin at the time she died. Her previous will is legal and as he was her sole heir, he will get everything with—as you know—no death duty to pay—as between man and wife."

"Could be a motive there," grunted Green.

Vadil considered this for a moment. "It could be regarded as such, I suppose, but I would have said it was a slim one."

"I think so, too," agreed Masters.

"I've known slimmer ones," asserted Green.

"So have I, Bill. But in view of Mrs Carvell's expressed intention of attending court on Tuesday morning, we must assume that she did not propose to go to Abbot's Hall until Tuesday afternoon at the earliest. So we must also assume that she was killed twenty-four hours earlier than her murderer had planned."

"Got it," said Green. "By that time she would no longer have been Missus Professor, so Carvell would not be her heir, so the motive of gain disappears."

"That's how I see it."

Vadil smiled. "You two think it all out, don't you?" He got to his feet as the door opened and a typist backed in, drawing a trolley behind her. "I must say it is most reassuring to hear you do it. Thank you, Brenda, we'll manage for ourselves."

Masters waited till the door closed behind the girl. "Reassuring?" he asked.

"I used the word advisedly," replied Vadil, pouring black coffee from a flask. "Milk? Sugar if you would like it." He stood by the trolley. "I have confidence in the police, Mr Masters. I've met the odd exception within your ranks, of course, but there are slightly bruised apples in every professional barrel. Reassurance merely means a bolstering of that confidence—in a practical way—after hearing you think aloud."

"Thank you. Now, Mr Vadil..."

"That sounds as if you were going to question me." Vadil moved round the desk to his chair. "I don't know whether I shall take kindly to that."

Masters grinned: "Let me reassure you..." he began.

Vadil had the grace to laugh.

"That's it, lad," said Green approvingly. "Nip your nose and take the plunge like you do when you do your parachuting. You'll find it's not too bad."

"Confidences," reminded Vadil.

"Won't be probed," promised Masters.

"In that case, please ask your questions."

"When we were last here, you expressed surprise that we had a witness to a meeting last June, at Abbot's Hall between Rhoda Carvell and her husband. You said that the Professor claimed in his application that he had not cohabited with his wife for some months previous to last June."

"Quite right. I did."

"May I know if Mrs Carvell made substantially the same admission?"

"She did."

"Theirs was, I believe, what one may call an amicable divorce. There was no quarrelling over settlements and so on, so I can assume, can I not, that there was a large measure of agreement about the whole business?"

"You can."

"In your experience, does agreement in such matters amount to collusion?"

"I had no cause to think so in this case."

"Thank you. So I am at liberty to presume that the meeting last June was fortuitous."

"I don't follow your reasoning."

"If Mrs Carvell had known that her husband—a mistrustful and powerful man—was in the vicinity of Abbot's Hall, would she have allowed a much less physically powerful man to stay there, sunbathing with her most of the day?"

"If you are asking whether she would allow this third person to run the risk of being subjected to Carvell's anger, the answer is no. Rhoda Carvell had her faults, but sadism of that sort was not one of them."

"So if I believe your assessment of her character—and I do—I can suppose that she was unaware of her husband's presence in the area?"

"That is my belief."

"Now, Carvell himself. Do you suppose he was there spying on her at that time?"

"I think that would be unlikely. I don't know much about him, but he strikes me as being too direct and forceful a character to act the part of a divorce snoop."

Masters inclined his head to acknowledge this assessment. Then he said: "We have been told that Carvell was carrying a geological specimen bag partly filled, and a geologist's hammer. That part of the coast is, I am told, rich in pickings for a geologist. So I assume Carvell went there to find specimens, not knowing that his wife was in residence at Abbot's Hall. But he visited the house to see that all was well and found his wife there with another man."

"That would seem a logical assumption to me, because I cannot believe that both would claim not to have been living together when, had they been doing so, both knew there was a witness to their meeting at Abbot's Hall in June. I could put up a very strong argument to support your assumption, Mr Masters, without relying too heavily on the fact that I believed my client."

"Thank you. I think I am further borne out by the fact that Carvell was not antagonistic to our witness. In fact I believe they chatted amicably for a while."

Vadil spread his hands. "I believe you have answered your own questions. More coffee, anyone?"

Green said: "Ta! Don't get up. I can help myself." As he poured, he said: "There's just one thing."

"What's that?" asked Vadil.

"If the Prof was thinking of doing his wife a bit of mischief, he would not want to appear unfriendly to her or third party. It would be remembered later. So he could have been nice on purpose."

"I refuse to comment on that," said Vadil. "It is no part of my business to speculate as to whether Carvell did or did not murder his wife."

"Apologies," said Green, totally unabashed by the implied rebuke. "It slipped out."

Masters said: "You will appreciate, Mr Vadil, that we are bearing in mind a number of people. One of them is Carvell. We have, however, no basis for supposing that he killed his wife."

"Understood."

Masters got to his feet. "Thank you for talking to us."

Vadil also rose. "I shall watch the progress of the case with interest."

Green slurped the last of his coffee and put the cup down so that it rattled in the saucer to announce that he too, was ready to go.

"A nice point you made there at the end, Bill," said Masters after they had left the solicitor's office.

"Apart from the fact that it got Vadil jumpy, you mean?"

"Yes. Of itself it was pertinent."

"Thanks. Where now?"

"Fleet Street." They entered the car. These days Green was beginning to sit in the front when Masters drove. Seat belts at last seemed to be having a reassuring effect on him.

"Who're we going to see this time? Young Heddle again?"

Masters shook his head while concentrating on missing a taxi doing a right turn ahead of him.

"The Lugano dame?"

"Yes. On her own. If I drop you outside the office, Bill, would you get her down to that interview room while I'm parking the car?"

Golly had already accepted and smoked half of one of Green's Kensitas by the time Masters joined them.

"Mizz Lugano isn't very happy at being here," announced Green.

"She is a busy...er...person," said Masters, "so we'll try not to keep her long."

"Got your eye on anybody?" demanded Golly as she stubbed out the cigarette and opened a large handbag to take out her own packet.

"We're getting along," replied Masters.

"Meaning you haven't a clue, I suppose."

"Not quite. In fact we have lots of clues. You, I hope, can give us a few more."

"Me? Not a hope. What can I know about Rhoda's murder?" She lit up, sat back, and blew smoke from her nostrils.

"Shall we see? First off, did you ever go—at any time, I mean—to Abbot's Hall?"

"Three times to be precise."

"Excellent. At whose invitation?"

"Rhoda's, of course. Not his."

"Did you ever have a meal there?"

"Of course. You don't think I'd go all that way just to look at a few bloody seagulls, do you?"

"I confess I didn't, but you could have gone for a drinks party perhaps. Then you might only get finger-eats, as opposed to a proper meal."

"Proper meal. Sit-down affair every time."

"Better and better. Did Mrs Carvell cook the meals?"

"It was her house. So who do you think...?"

Masters waited.

"Sorry. Misled you. Went there once when Molly Clippingdale cooked a slap-up affair."

"Molly Clippingdale?"

151

"Our cookery expert. Writes under the name of Bett Faring. Rhoda had some sort of clambake there—invited quite a lot of us. Molly did the food. Fork affair, really but good. Hot meal. Bourgignon with savoury rice, stuffed turkey rolls fried and all that sort of thing. Cold pudding with a bottle of good brandy in it. Never tasted better but two mouthfuls knocked you for six."

"How long ago was this party?"

"Not all that long. Earlier this year, I think. Dark night I remember."

"Just you and Molly Clippingdale from the office?"

"No. Three or four of us. I know I took two in my car."

"Females?"

"Yes."

"Any males there?"

"Not from the office. Woodruff and one or two others don't remember. Saturday night, it was."

Masters thought for a moment. "But you yourself never went into the kitchen on your visits?"

"Oh, I went in."

"But not to help with the cooking?"

"Me Cook? Listen, love, I can't boil hot water. At least I can. But I have been known to burn a boiled egg."

"I see. Then perhaps you could tell me where I could contact Molly Clippingdale. She might be able to help me."

Golly Lugano frowned. "She runs a cookery school. She's likely got lessons today."

"No matter. She might spare me a few minutes."

Golly grinned, showing lipstick-smeared false teeth. "She'd spare you a few hours. She's got an eye for the men."

"Perhaps I'll escape unscathed if Mr Green is there to protect me. Could I have the address, please?"

"Swiss Cottage way." Golly gave the address and phone number from memory.

"Thank you. Now, Mizz Lugano, could I ask just one favour?"

"What's that?"

"That you keep the fact that we have been speaking to you a close secret, and not to mention to anybody what we have just discussed?"

"Oh, come on! You've only asked me if I'd ever been in Rhoda's kitchen at Abbot's Hall."

"Even so!"

She looked at him shrewdly out of eyes narrowed against the smoke from another cigarette. "You're up to something. I can tell. You're cocky."

"Not unbearably so, I hope."

Golly got to her feet. "I'll keep quiet. I told those sergeants of yours that I liked Rhoda. And I meant it. So now I'll repeat it to you, the boss man. I want you to find whoever did it to her, and if I ever get my hands on him I'll string him up by the you-know-whats on pin-wire."

"No you wouldn't, love," said Green. "Not your style."

"Don't you be too sure."

Green shook his head. "You may act as if you were as tough as Billy Whitlam's bulldog, but you're as soft-hearted as Joe Soap underneath. Let me give you a word of advice. Until Mrs Carvell was murdered, you were against all forms of corporal punishment."

"So what?"

"Change your mind if you like, now murder has struck close to home. But don't go over the top, love. Don't let it nag you. You can take it calmly and then you'll get over it easier."

Golly stared at him for a moment.

"And what if I don't want to get over it, as you put it?"

"Meaning you feel you've got to remember?"

"Want to."

"I reckon I can guess why."

"Maybe you can." She turned to Masters. "And you, too?"

"I think so. A beautiful, clever, witty woman—the sort of person any other woman might wish she had been born like, or have as a daughter."

153

"You're on the right track, I suppose."

"Please don't forget you do an important job. You're clever, too. It's trite to say so, but we can't all be alike."

"No. But we can bloody-well dream—and regret."

"We can aid and abet Mother Nature, but we can't bilk her."

"Get out," Golly said roughly. "Go on. The two of you. And I hope I never set eyes on you again."

"Sorry, love," said Green gently.

They returned to the Yard for lunch.

"Everything's written up, Chief," said Reed. "The file's getting fatter."

"I don't like fat files," said Masters petulantly. "Any word from Robson?"

"A few minutes ago, Chief. They're searching the area with twelve men and haven't found anything yet."

Berger said: "I took a call from Professor Carvell, Chief."

Masters was interested. "To say what?"

"He said you had asked him to write out some list or other and that he'd done it."

"Go on."

"He just said it was ready for you to collect when you wanted it."

"No specific time mentioned?"

"No, Chief."

"Thank you. Right, you two. Get some lunch. Join us here in an hour from now."

After the sergeants had left them, Masters said to Green: "Shall we talk over lunch?"

"Here?"

"Why not?"

Green shrugged. "I'll have a beer and a sandwich."

"Fine. Shall we go?"

They occupied a table alone.

"What's on your mind, George?"

"Carvell. The message he sent through."

"You don't like it, do you?" Green took a large bite at

a bully-beef sandwich. "Too cheeky."

Masters nodded.

"Yet he said you could collect it whenever you wanted to."

"That alone sounded a bit too nonchalant for me. I'd have liked it better if he'd suggested a time when he would be available to receive us."

"More in keeping with his character?"

"I think so."

"He could have posted it to you or left it at the desk."

"Both courses were open to him. What I'm really saying, Bill, is that I believe he wants to see us, but tried to make it sound as though he didn't."

"Why?"

"Why what?"

"Does he want to see us?"

"There you have me. We've both known murderers who couldn't let well alone."

Green removed a strand of bully from a tooth with a forefinger. "They get big-headed. Want to see if they're beating us. Carvell would be like that. Got a good opinion of himself. Thinks the police plebs aren't up to his weight."

Masters cleared his mouth before replying. "We decided to look hard at him, Bill."

"Meaning we should take a suspicious view of everything he says and does?"

"It would be part of the hard look, wouldn't it?"

"It would." Green took up his tankard. "So we go to see him this afternoon?"

"I think not. We don't want to give him the impression we'd come running every time he opened his mouth. I think latish tonight would be better."

"Thereby giving me time to sort out the janitor at the hall of residence before we meet Carvell?"

"Can you do it?"

"I've been thinking about it quite a bit since you told me."

"Reach any conclusions?"

"Yes. It'll mean me and Berger being away this afternoon, though."

"Fair enough. I won't ask you why. But I shall take Reed with me to Molly Clippingdale's place to ask a few questions there."

"Seems a fair division of labour. What time tonight?"

"After supper. Just the two of us. I'll ring Wanda and say you and Doris will eat with us if you agree. It will save you travelling out to your place and back again, and it won't leave Doris alone."

"Sounds like a good idea. I'll tell Doris to get to Wanda's Palace by teatime, shall I? Then you and I can meet up here no later than half five."

"Excellent. Another drink?"

"Wouldn't say no."

The cookery school was the end building of a short arcade of shops with flats above. They stood well back behind the general building line so that the pavement was nearly thirty feet wide in front of the windows. A small side road ran down the side of the school, presumably to give access to the back entrances.

Obviously Molly Clippingdale had had extensive alterations done. The plate glass window had gone, to be replaced by two sashes separated by a central pillar. The shop door had been replaced by a modern house door in mahogany. The only indication that they had reached the right place was a small modern brass plate bearing the simple legend: Betta Faring.

"Doesn't advertise much, does she, Chief?" said Reed.

"Relies on the principle that good wine needs no bush, perhaps," replied Masters, pressing a bell sunk into a circular saucer of well-polished brass.

The door was opened after a few moments by a youth in shirt sleeves, wearing a white apron and chef's hat.

"Miss Molly Clippingdale?" enquired Masters.

"It's Missus actually. Who wants her?"

"We are police officers."

"In that case you'd better come in."

"You a student here?" asked Reed of the young man as they stepped into a narrow hallway obviously contrived by building an internal wall to cut off the former shop premises.

"Kitchen boy. I'm Jeff to all and sundry." He left them and went to the foot of a flight of stairs—again obviously installed afresh—which Masters presumed led to the flat above.

"Molly!" the youth called. "Molly, you've got the law after you."

There was an indistinct reply from above. "She'll be down directly," said Jeff.

"No smell of cooking," said Reed.

"Not this afternoon. They're doing cold stuff. Party pieces and what not."

"Where?"

"Through here," said Jeff, indicating a door in the new wall. "A dozen of them, all turning their noses up at caviare and getting into a mess with spun sugar. But they'll learn. They always do."

Mrs Clippingdale appeared on the stairs. As she made her way down towards them, Masters was surprised to see that she was young, plumpish and jolly-faced.

"Good afternoon. I've not put my foot in it somehow, have I?" She laughed as she spoke.

"These gents," said Jeff shrewdly, "don't look to me as if they'd be here to talk about a parking offence."

"Quite right. We're from Scotland Yard. My name is Masters..."

Jeff uttered a low whistle. "I'll be off," he said. "When the real heavy mob arrives I reckon it's time I went and opened another tin of anchovies." He departed through the door that presumably led to the kitchen.

"He's obviously heard of you, Mr Masters," said Molly Clippingdale. "Please come up. We can't talk here."

They followed her up the narrow stair into the flat.

"You've got two stories above the shop?" asked Masters,

noting that another flight ran up from the landing.

"Bedrooms," she replied. "I have to have an office with all the writing that I do. So I've got that on this floor as well as our sitting and dining rooms." She led the way into the sitting room. "Will this do for our chat about ... well, about whatever it is you've come to see me about?"

"Nice room," said Masters appreciatively as he took a deep armchair. "Cosy. And the flowers are lovely. Do you do flower arranging as well as cookery?"

She glanced around at the displays. "No, I don't do it myself. I have a woman who comes in to give instruction, but I benefit from her efforts. After she's shown the pupils, I get her demonstration pieces for use up here."

Masters nodded his understanding. Then he asked: "Has Golly Lugano been in touch with you today?"

"No." She stared at him for a moment. "This visit has to do with Rhoda Carvell, hasn't it?"

"Yes."

"I thought it must have when I heard who you were. But for the life of me I can't see why you've come to me. I don't know anything about her death."

"About her death? I'm sure you don't, Mrs Clippingdale."

She laughed with relief and then said: "For the moment you had me worried."

"About what, ma'am?" asked Reed.

She spread her hands. "I don't know. I suppose it was what you might call unreasonable fear." She laughed again. "Perhaps I thought you might be wondering whether she'd eaten one of my cakes and found it less than appetising."

"Nothing like that," said Masters. "But I want you to cast your mind back some months to earlier this year when, I believe, you went out to Abbot's Hall and catered for a party that Mrs Carvell was holding there."

"I remember. It was a very nice evening. It was just one of those spur-of-the-moment ideas. Golly had called several of her female contributors into the office to discuss a new format she was considering for the Women's Section of the *View*. We didn't often meet each other. In fact it was so rare an event that somebody said we ought to have a party to celebrate...you know how these things happen."

"It's a common enough occurrence," agreed Masters. "Somebody says it can be held at their place so long as somebody else will be responsible for the drink, somebody else for the food and so on."

"That's it. That's exactly what happened. Rhoda suggested Abbot's Hall, and all those of us who'd never been there jumped at the idea. We were all as nosey as hell to see the place, of course, so before I knew where I was I'd agreed to prepare small eats and a fork supper."

"Good."

"But I can't see why that party should interest you after all this time. It was perfectly innocuous. I don't think we even got tiddly. At any rate we all drove back perfectly safely."

"Was that the only time you visited Abbot's Hall?"

"Yes. And I must say I was a bit jealous. I reckon I could have made quite something of that house. And I liked the loneliness of it."

"In summertime, perhaps," said Reed. "It's a bit bleak at other times."

She smiled at him. "I'm sure it is. Don't they always say if you're going to buy a house you should view it on the worst possible day? If it suits you then it should suit you always."

Masters said: "If you prepared the food for the party, Mrs Clippingdale, you must have used the kitchen and the oven."

"Oh, yes! That oven!" She flapped one hand to indicate the poor opinion of the professional cook for so ordinary a piece of equipment. "Fortunately, I only needed it for heating up a few things."

"Did you use the tins in the oven—roasting tins or dripping tins or whatever you call them these days?"

She laughed aloud. "You must be joking, Mr Masters."

"I assure you I'm not."

"You're interested in my oven tins?"

"Your oven tins?"

"Yes, mine. You're not saying my tins had anything to do with Rhoda's death? They are good, high class ware."

"You said the tins were yours. You took them with you that night?"

"Yes. Rhoda told me she hadn't got a lot of pots and pans so I said it didn't matter because I'd get all the food prepared here by the pupils..."

"Ready cooked?"

"That's right. All ready cooked, in the dishes, to take in the car. I took them down there and popped them in Rhoda's oven. There was really no work to do, except to serve. But there was quite a lot of food left in the tins. I was wearing a party frock, so I didn't want to start emptying them, and washing up, so I suggested to Rhoda that she should use what she could of the left-overs during the next day or two while she was down there. She agreed and said she would let me have the tins back, but they never came. I was going to ask her for them next time I saw her, but as I said, we rarely get together at the *View* and I don't move in Rhoda's circles. And now..." She shrugged. "Am I too late?"

"I'm afraid so, Mrs Clippingdale. There are no oven tins at Abbot's Hall."

"That's odd. Perhaps Rhoda brought them back to give me after all."

Masters shook his head. "I think not. But be sure we shall look for them in the flat she has been occupying lately."

"Thank you. It will be nice to get them back. They were enamelled inside and they cost a bomb these days."

"How many were there?"

"Three. Squarish, about two inches deep. The walls were perpendicular, not sloping. Grey colour."

"I'll remember." Masters got to his feet.

"Don't go without telling me why you want to know about my pans," protested Mrs Clippingdale. "Surely a girl has a right to know when any of her rightful possessions interest Scotland Yard?"

Masters looked down at her. "I can't tell you because I mustn't. Specifically, that is. But I can tell you this. As a matter of routine, we have searched Abbot's Hall..."

"What for? Pans?"

Masters smiled. "For anything the least bit out of the ordinary. Is there anything there that we think shouldn't be there?"

"A broken cuff-link behind a chair?"

"Quite. And also, is there anything missing which we think should normally be there? Now, when we find an oven with no cooking pans, we begin to wonder how Mrs Carvell managed to do her cooking when she was there—however little she did."

"She had one tin. The one that was supplied with the oven, I think. No baking tray, but there was a grill pan."

"So five tins are missing?"

"It seems like it."

"Well, there you are, Mrs Clippingdale. It shows how right we are to wonder why there are no tins in the oven, and then to discover whether any should be there. As to what happened to them... well, their absence is just another piece of information that may or may not be relevant to our investigation. But we can't ignore them. Not yet, at least."

"So they may be completely unimportant? I'm disappointed."

"Why?"

"I don't like the idea of Rhoda being dead, but you must agree that when detectives from Scotland Yard come along and get one all agog, it is a bit of a let-down to know what they've been asking questions about is not at all important."

Masters laughed. "A lot of our work is like that, Mrs Clippingdale. We have to go around asking all sorts of

questions until one or two of the answers start to click
Then—and only then—can we start to ask the really per
tinent questions."

"You mean some cranky burglar could have pinched m
dishes?"

"Those, and a few other things that could be missing.

"Totally irrelevant, in fact."

"Possibly. But don't talk about it, please, just i
case..."

"I promise not to say a word unless..."

"Unless what?"

"Unless my dishes figure largely in the case."

"Should that happen, Mrs Clippingdale, you would b
a witness, and witnesses are forbidden to discuss thei
evidence outside the court. Your safest plan, really an
truly, is to say nothing."

She feigned tragic disappointment and agreed to follow
his advice.

Berger stopped the car close to the Shaw Theatre.

"You can't park here, lad," said Green.

"If you'll get out, I'll find a spot."

"In this traffic?"

"I know a place. If it's not taken I'll join you outside
the Hall of Residence in about five minutes."

Green got out, waited for Berger to pull away and then
looked for the best way of crossing the road. By the tim
Berger found him, he had been standing on the kerb op
posite Gladstone Hall long enough to smoke a Kensitas

"They're going in and out there like ants into a nest,
said Green, nodding as students came and went. "There'
a caff just along the road that a lot of 'em are using, too.

Berger asked: "What are we after? I know you said i
was something to do with the night porter of that iglo
opposite, but he'll not be on duty yet."

"You catch on fast, lad," grunted Green.

"I've got a reputation for it."

"I'm pleased to hear it."

162

"Come on," pleaded Berger. "What're we after?"

"First off," said Green, "I want to know his name."

"Whose?"

"The night porter's."

"Want me to go in and ask?"

Green shook his head. "I'd rather ask one of the students."

"I see. Don't want either the night man or the day man who's on now to know you're enquiring, is that it?"

"Something of the sort." Green turned to look along the pavement. "You can buy me a cup of tea, lad."

"I get it. In the café."

"Can't see where else you'd get tea round here but in the caff."

"No, I meant..."

"I know what you meant. Come on."

They bore their cups of tea to one of the little tables and sought the permission of the two occupants to join them. It caused no surprise as the little café held no more than a dozen tables and none was totally free.

Green helped himself to sugar and stirred the tea noisily. Then he took out his cigarettes and offered them around the table. The two students, surprised by such generosity, stopped their close chat to refuse the offer and immediately became entangled in Green's conversational net.

"Don't smoke, then? Very wise. Don't mind if I light up though, do you?"

"Not at all."

"Ta! Not everybody's so ready to let you these days without sniffing or making some remark."

"Well, it's not to everybody's taste."

"P'raps not." Green sighed. "Things change too much and too quickly for my liking. Still, what's the difference? Oh, by the way, you couldn't tell me the name of that janitor who's on nights at Gladstone Hall, could you? I caught a glimpse of him the other night and I thought I recognized him. Reminded me of a chap called Standish I used to know in the old days. Jim Standish? Or was it

163

Jack? Anyhow perhaps you know who he is?"

One student replied: "I honestly don't know his name. I only came into Hall a week or two ago—at the beginning of this term—and I've had no reason to speak to him."

"Nor me," said the other. "But I've heard chaps refer to him as Ticky. I don't know whether your long lost friend...?"

Green shook his head. "Can't be Standish," he said. "If he's called Ticky, his name will be Wright. Ticky Wright."

The first student said: "Now how do you know that?"

"Old army custom," replied Green. "Dusty Miller, Chalky White, Ticky Wright."

"Why Ticky?"

"Because if you get a sum right at school, you get a tick from the teacher."

The two students laughed and got to their feet. When the two Yard men were alone, Green said: "We want some students who have been in the Hall for longer than a week or two."

"Why?"

"I want somebody who knows this Wright character."

"Why?"

"I want a lever."

"You might not get one."

"Now don't start that," said Green. "There'll be something. There always is. The trouble is finding it."

Berger looked round the café. At last he said: "There's a couple over there. They're pretty thick from the look of things..."

"Thick?"

"Not stupid. Close friends. Look at them."

The male and female were conversing with heads close together.

"Go on, lad."

"They haven't got that far in the two weeks since term started. They look as if they'd known each other for a good long time."

Green grimaced. "They get that far, as you call it, in

164

couple of hours these days. But you reckon they've been around for some time, do you?"

"It's a possibility."

Green lumbered heavily to his feet. "We'll try 'em. Can't do any harm."

The two youngsters looked up after Green and Berger had been towering over them for a few seconds.

"Sorry to interrupt," said Green, "but I wonder if you could tell me when Ticky Wright, the night porter in Gladstone Hall, comes on duty?"

"Ticky you call him?" asked the male student scathingly.

"That's his name, isn't it?"

"Not to me it isn't."

Green sat down. "You sound a bit umpty-like. What's up?"

"He's a friend of yours, is he?"

"Not so's you'd notice," said Berger. "In fact we've never met him. That's why we want to know when he'll be on."

"My advice to you, then," said the boy, "is to keep your hands on your wallets."

"Kevin!" protested the girl.

"Why not tell us?" urged Green.

"You call him Ticky," said the girl. "Kevin calls him Nicky."

Green grinned. "I think I get it. love. He's a bit light-fingered, is he?"

"We have no proof that he is."

"But a moral certainty," grumbled Kevin angrily.

"Come on," urged Green again. "What's this character been up to?"

"Books," said the girl. "Or so Kevin says."

"Books?"

"Look," said Kevin, "every student in that Hall carries scads of books around. Expensive books. People are always putting them down—in the common room, in refec, in the foyer. It's one of those things. You forget them and buzz off up to your room or go out for the evening. Next

165

morning you remember them and go to where you've left them and they're gone."

"Keep going, lad."

"Rumour has it," said the girl, "that Nicky Wright collects them and then sells them to a second-hand bookshop."

"Second-hand? Ten pence a time, touch."

"No. These expensive textbooks fetch pounds untold, even second-hand, if they're in good condition and recent editions."

"I get it," said Green. "Name on the fly-leaf blacked-out and nobody knows whose it was."

"That's right. Kevin lost a brand-new book he'd just bought last week. It cost £27."

"I left it on a coffee table in the common room," said Kevin. "The number of characters in Hall who could use that book is mighty small. About six or seven of us. I asked them all if they'd got it."

"None had, and you believed them?"

"Right. So I went to the janitor's cubicle where lost property is supposed to be deposited."

"And?"

"Nicky Wright said it hadn't been handed in."

"And you accused him of scooping it up and getting a bomb for it in the bookshop."

"More or less."

"What did he say?"

"What do you think? It's well-known that books disappear mysteriously and most people reckon Wright does it. But there are several hundreds of us in residence."

"He pointed that out, did he?"

"And how."

"He also threatened to call the police," said the girl. "In view of that Kevin couldn't go on, because he'd got no hard evidence. But we all know he was right."

Green straightened up. "Don't worry, love. We are the police." He turned to Berger. "Show them your card, Sergeant."

As Berger drew out his identity wallet, the girl said, "Oh, my God. You've tricked us. He did call you in."

"No, love, he didn't. He daren't. So don't you worry. We want a word with your Mister Nicky Wright about a totally different business, but after that we'll put a flea in his ear about those books and then I don't think any more will disappear."

"I don't suppose you'll be able to get mine back," said Kevin.

"Unlikely, son, but if you'll give Sergeant Berger the title and the address of the shop, we'll have a bash. Oh, and give him your name, too, just in case we find your property."

While Kevin and Berger were conversing, Green said to the girl, "Wright doesn't come on until six o'clock. I don't want to hang around here till then. You don't happen to know where I could find him now, do you?"

"Well, I know he lives in Hall. There are staff quarters at the top, but whether he'll be there now..."

"He should be just getting up I'd have thought," said Green. "Nearly four o'clock."

"I've seen him going out to the pub for a drink sometimes at half-past five. Then he gets back for six."

"Could be a regular habit, I suppose. If so, it means he should be getting up to eat. Anyway, we'll give it a try. At the top of the building, you said?"

"Take the lift right up as far as you can go."

With these instructions to follow, it was easy enough to find the janitor's flat occupied by Wright. The name—as in every case throughout the building—was on the door. A fire bucket and an extinguisher stood on one side of the frame, and on the other a notice board carrying lists of staff duties and the like. Green glanced at it cursorily while Berger pressed the bell.

"His name," grunted Green, "is Laurence Wright. Sounds like tin-pan alley in the twenties."

The door opened.

"Mrs Wright?"

"Yes."

"Is Mr Wright in?"

"He's having his tea."

"Fine," said Green. "We can talk to him across the table."

"Who are you and what do you want?"

"We're police officers, love. Show the lady your authority, Sergeant."

"What do you want him for?"

"Don't worry, love, we don't *want* him. We have to ask a few questions about comings and goings in the foyer down below."

She let them in and led them to the small kitchen where Wright was sitting at a red melamine-topped table, eating sausage and mash and reading the sports pages of a tabloid.

"It's the police to see you. Has it to do with the one who came the other night?"

"How do I know?" Wright looked at Green. "Whatever it's about, I've got nothing to tell you."

"Can I go?" asked Mrs Wright. "I have to get to the shops." She went on to explain. "You see I do twenty bedrooms, two bathrooms and one kitchen every day. Then I come back here and by the time I've had a bite to eat and a sit down it's time to get his tea. It's all I can do to get out to buy my bits and pieces."

"You go off, love," said Green. "Your old man will still be here when you get back."

"I'll be on duty by then," grumbled Wright.

His wife merely said: "I'll get off then," and left the kitchen. Green drew up the chair opposite the janitor. "We'll talk while you go on chomping. It's about a week last Monday night and Tuesday morning early."

"What about it?"

"I want to know when Professor Carvell went out and when he came in again."

Wright speared an overcooked sausage and hacked a piece off the end. "You don't expect me to remember one

168

night from another that far back."

"I do," asserted Green. He picked up a bottle of tomato ketchup from the table and offered it to Wright. "You're out of sauce, mate. Have another dollop. Mixed with that spud of yours it'll look like murder on the Alps."

Wright took the bottle.

"I'm waiting," said Green.

"Then you'll be here a long time."

Green turned to Berger. "What was the name of that shop that sells second-hand text books?"

Wright looked up. "Now what're you on about?"

Green leaned forwards across the table to emphasize his words. "I'll give you about fifteen seconds in which to refresh your memory. After that I'll institute an enquiry into the nicking of books left lying about and how they come to end up in second-hand bookshops."

"You've got nothing on me," blustered Wright.

"Ah, but I have, chum. You see, mate, it's part of your duty to go round late at night to see all the communal rooms are safe, no fag ends burning and such."

"So what?"

"Well now, we have witnesses to prove that they were the last to leave the male common room one night—after a late night bridge session. When they went upstairs, the front doors were already locked and nobody could get in without you letting them in. But when one of them came down very early in the morning to get his books—somewhere about half-past five, he says, because he couldn't sleep—his books had gone, but the front doors were still locked. So who had taken them?"

"How should I know?"

"Who would have the opportunity to take them with you on watch?"

No reply.

"Come on chum, you're guilty either of dereliction of duty or of nicking the books. Either way you could be in the fertilizer with a good chance of losing this nice little pad." Green sat back. "However, we can soon prove it. A

169

few words at the bookshop and then dusting a few books for prints and the case will be over. You'll be out on your neck. So now, before we go any further with this particular complaint, I'll ask you again. A week last Monday night, what time did Carvell go out?"

"I don't remember."

"What time did he go out?"

"About seven," mumbled Wright.

"How can you be sure?"

"Because I allus make a note of when the tutorial staff go out."

"Why?"

"Because they get phone calls, don't they? And visitors. We don't do it for the kids. Not for them. And I looked it up after that other chap called."

"Detective Chief Superintendent Masters?"

"If he's the big bastard, yes."

"Watch it," warned Berger.

"And you make a note of when they come in, too?"

"Yes. For the same reasons."

"And what time did he get in?"

"He didn't."

"Not early the next morning?"

"Not while I was on he didn't."

"When do you finish?"

"Six."

"Twelve hour shift?"

"On nights it is. Six to ten an' two to six on days. The assistant housekeeper looks out between ten an' two ordinary days. Weekend's different."

"Right. How was the professor dressed when he went out?"

"Natty, as usual. Carrying a case."

"What sort of case?"

"Leather attaché case. He's always got it."

"How often did he stay out all night?"

"Now and then."

"How often?"

"He hasn't been living in all that long."

"How often?"

"Twice before."

"That's better. Now, you just keep your mouth shut about this, or I'll remember those missing books. As I shall if I hear any more have gone missing, or anything else round here."

"Careless little brats, they are," said Wright bitterly. "All living on the state and..."

"Existing on pittances out of which they have to buy expensive books," grated Green, "and providing you with a cushy job at the same time. Don't knock 'em, mate. They're not only your present, but your future, too." Green got to his feet. "Now, cough back those zeppelins in the clouds before they congeal any more. And remember what I've said."

Masters and Green spent the best part of an hour together at the Yard, comparing notes before setting out for Masters' cottage.

"Made any decisions about things yet, George?" asked Green as they set out to walk the few hundred yards together.

"No. I'd value your advice, Bill. You know everything. How would you proceed?"

"The keystone's missing," grumbled Green.

"There's a lot of circumstance."

"Which you don't like."

"Not normally, no."

"So what are you going to do?"

"I asked for your advice."

"Right. What options are open to you? To pull in Carvell on circumstantial evidence or to hold off until you've got one material fact to bring against him. Agreed?"

"Agreed."

"We're seeing him tonight, we hope. It could mean we get the evidence we want. In that case you'd have him."

"If not?"

"You're back where you were."

"And so?"

"Give it a day or two. You're not finished yet."

"I am, unless the search party from Chichester finds the stuff I need and, quite honestly, Bill, I can't see them being successful. Oh, I know there are things to do. We've got to search Rhoda Carvell's flat and so on, but I'm not optimistic about getting anything there."

"No. I'm not either."

They walked the rest of the way in silence.

It was as they were having a pre-dinner drink that Wanda asked: "How are you getting on with the case, darling?"

"So, so, my poppet."

Doris said in amazement: "You mean you're not getting anywhere? Bill, that can't be true, can it? Not with George?"

"He's doing well enough," replied her husband.

"That sounds as if he's not making much progress."

"He's got a long way."

"But?" queried Wanda.

"He needs a bit of luck," said Green.

"I don't think I really understand."

"Your old man knows who did it, when, where and how."

"So what is the difficulty?"

"He hasn't got one solid fact to help him plonk it on chummy's doorstep. That's the difficulty."

"But surely you'll find what you need," asserted Wanda.

"George says he's not sanguine, which in my book means it's not bloody likely."

"Bill!" Doris sounded scandalized.

"I'm right. If George says it's unlikely, you'd expect most people to say it's impossible."

"I suppose so." Doris turned to Masters. "You really are stuck, are you?"

Masters grinned. "We know what we want, and that is to find certain objects taken from Rhoda Carvell's house.

But we can't find them, and they could be anywhere between Climping and London, in a ditch, a rubbish bin, a bottle bank, a stream bed...in fact, anywhere. We have a squad of men looking for them in the area of the house, but they haven't been found. Nor, I suspect, are they likely to be. But they will constitute, in my opinion, the material evidence we need. We are swamped in circumstantial evidence, but I mistrust that when it is not supported by a single hard fact."

"And without these objects, you're up against a brick wall, darling?" asked Wanda.

"A very high brick wall, sweetie."

"But you're going out tonight. After supper. Won't you, perhaps, get something then?"

"Perhaps."

"Only that?"

"More circumstance is my guess."

"And mine," said Green. "What's on the menu, love?"

"Bill, where are your manners?" said Doris severely.

Green looked at her innocently. "I only wanted to know if I could help. Open the wine—red or white? Make the sauce—mint, horseradish or apple? Do the spuds—strain or mash? Chop the..."

"Stop it," commanded Doris. "You were only trying to hurry Wanda."

Green winked. "Not 'arf," he replied.

"You're disgusting."

Masters said innocently: "You know, Bill, I get the feeling Doris feels disgust and secret loathing as far as you are concerned."

"I've always known it, George." He slumped in his chair. "Deep weariness and unsated lust makes human life a hell."

"Now what are you on about?" demanded Doris. "Unsated lust!"

"Arnold."

"Who is Arnold?"

173

"The gent what I've just misquoted."

Wanda got to her feet. "Come on everybody, or William will be throwing the book at us."

"What book?" demanded Doris again, bewildered by the conversation.

"The *Golden Treasury*—all parts," supplied Masters. He turned to Green. "You left me—and the sergeants—in mid-air, two days ago, about some mythical character called Icicle Joe. A teetotaller, I seem to recall from the interrupted conversation at the time."

"Oh, I know that," said Doris and proceeded to recite: "Icicle Joe, the Eskimo, he lives upon the ice. And every time he wants a drink, he cuts himself a slice."

They all stared at her in silence for a few moments, so that she reddened under their gaze. Then her husband spread his hands. "That makes my point, I think. She's as bad as I am, yet she has the nerve to call me disgusting."

"I didn't. It was because..."

Green stopped the flow of protest by kissing her full on the mouth.

Wanda said: "I was wondering how ice could be cut. Now I know."

Carvell was watching a television documentary on wild life when Masters and Green called on him. He ushered them in and then crossed to switch off the set before addressing them.

"I am at home, you see, gentlemen."

"Expecting us were you?" asked Green.

"Yes." The reply was uncompromising. The sort of answer that Masters would expect from a man who wished to give the impression that he was much more often right than wrong.

Carvell waved them to seats and crossed to his desk to take up a small sheet of paper. He brought it over to Masters. "I have made sure my fingerprints are all over it, Chief Superintendent, so just take it by the corner. Shall I provide you with an envelope for it?"

174

"Yes, please," replied Masters blandly.

"So I was not mistaken when I came to the conclusion that the real reason why you asked me to write out a list of my movements was simply to obtain a set of my fingerprints?"

Masters kept a straight face. "You misjudge me, Professor, if you think that I stoop to such clumsy subterfuges."

"Do I? Why accept the envelope if not to preserve my prints?"

"Seeing you have so kindly provided them, it would be boorish of me to reject your offer. But there are a thousand ways in which I could get your prints, unbeknown to you. You handle so many books and papers that we could get samples by the simple process of elimination. And of course—and this is what I usually do—I could ask you straight out to provide them. Few people, when so requested, refuse."

Carvell sneered. "But you interpret a refusal in your own way."

"Quite. That is my job."

Masters, holding the list gingerly, glanced at it. "There appears to be nothing extraordinary here. Lecture, tutorials, committee meeting... all very useful, as there would be others present at the time." He looked up. "Why did you object so strongly to outlining your movements on the Sunday?"

"My activities are no concern of yours, particularly as Rhoda was known to be alive on the Monday."

"Ah!" Masters put the paper down. "Now for my interpretation of that particular refusal, Professor."

"Interpret it any way you like."

"I shall stick to its relevance to my case."

"I'm more than pleased to hear it."

"Mrs Carvell's murder was probably not a spur-of-the-moment killing. I say probably, because I have no factual proof of that. But it would seem that there would have to be some preparation for the actual deed."

Carvell was regarding him attentively. "My point is, Professor, that I believe our murderer would have to take certain steps before committing the crime itself. To my mind, those steps could have been taken on the Sunday."

"And my objection to telling you my movements on the Sunday is to be interpreted as an attempt to...to avoid ...what?"

"You've got the idea," said Green. "If you'd been up to some hanky-panky you wouldn't want us to know about, you'd refuse the information."

"But this is outrageous. What were these preparations that had to be made?"

Masters ignored the question. "So you refused to tell us of your movements on Sunday, and now—on the list you have provided—your have told us less than..."

"Less than what? The truth? If that is your belief, Mr Masters, you are mistaken. Every word, every time on that list is true."

"I was going to say less than the complete itinerary. I am referring, specifically, to the evening and night of the Monday and the early morning of the Tuesday. I see you say you went out at just before seven that evening, which I will accept..."

"Thank you."

"But you haven't said where you went."

"I said I went to dinner at Luciano's restaurant."

"At seven?"

"I had to call for a companion."

"I see. You didn't dine alone. Where did you park your car during dinner?"

"At my companion's house. We took a cab to the restaurant."

"So you did use your car?"

"Yes."

Masters glanced across the room to the floor beside the desk. "Is that your document case?"

"Of course it's mine. Otherwise it wouldn't be here."

"It's bigger—deeper—than the usual run of such bags."

"Because I have to carry more files and books than most people. Look here, what has my case got to do with all this?"

"You took it with you on Monday evening. Why would a man, going out to dinner with a lady companion—I take it she was a female?—carry a large document case?"

Carvell flushed angrily. "I've had enough of this. It is obvious you have been spying on me..."

"Making enquiries," said Green quietly.

"...and you come here and ask questions about matters which concern neither you nor my wife's death and to which you already appear to know the answers."

"I don't waste my time that way if I can avoid it," replied Masters. "What were you carrying in the case? Or are you expecting me to believe you were carrying a sheaf of students' essays when you went out to dinner?"

"I don't care what you believe."

"Three bottles of champagne, perhaps?"

"Keep your little jokes for those who will appreciate them more than I feel inclined to."

"And one final question—one to which I have no specific answer. What time did you return to Gladstone Hall after your outing on Monday evening."

Carvell made no reply.

"You know what Charles Lamb said," murmured Green eventually. "To be up late is to be up early. How late, or early, were you, Professor? In time for breakfast was it?"

Carvell got to his feet. "I shall not agree to see you again, either of you, except in the presence of my solicitor." He moved to the door. "I'll bid you good evening, gentlemen."

— 7 —

"We agreed last night that you've got a *prima facie* case against Carvell," said Green the next morning, when they met in Masters' office. "So what decision have you come to? Are you going to invite him in, haul him in, or let the DPP decide?"

Masters, seated behind his desk, started to fill the first pipe of the day. As he tamped Warlock Flake into the bowl he said, without looking up, "I'm not really happy about it, Bill."

"You don't have to tell me." He sat down and stretched his legs out. "I've yet to meet the Jack who didn't like to make sure. Nailing the thing down with as many solid facts as possible is the only satisfactory answer in our eyes. Even then we don't always get the verdict. When all you've got is circumstantial evidence, you're less likely to succeed. And in this case, a lot of what you've produced is not even circumstantial evidence, but theory. Good theory. We're all convinced it's sound. But a jury could find it hard to swallow without a bit of supporting material to show them in court."

"That's not really what I meant."

Masters lit the pipe. Green waited until the ritual was over before asking: "Are you trying to say you're not convinced in your own mind that Carvell is guilty?"

"I'm like the juries you spoke of, Bill. I want at least one solid, inescapable fact."

"Meaning that Carvell is too big a bug to be spiked on circumstance alone?"

"I don't give a toss how big and important he is or isn't. I just don't like charging a man with any crime so long as I am not more than a hundred per cent certain that I'm putting the guilty chap in the dock."

"And as far as Carvell is concerned, it's only about ninety-seven per cent, is that it?"

"Yes."

"You've got to make a decision."

"I've made one."

"What's that?"

"The coward's way out. Shove the responsibility on to the AC Crime and let him decide what to do."

"Anderson will love that, and I don't think."

"I know. But when you come to think about it, I have no choice. I can't tell him Carvell is not guilty, just because I can't find the little bit of material evidence I feel I need. Nor can I say that Carvell is guilty without producing the same scrap of evidence. So there has to be a fresh mind to give a ruling. It is Anderson's responsibility, so he must take it."

"It's a new departure for you, George."

"True, but it is the option that is open to me."

Green nodded. "Safety-net," he said.

"Right. So I'll ask him to see us—all four of us—this morning. I'll suggest eleven o'clock. Get what reports we can from Chichester before then, Bill, and make sure the lads have our reports written up so that I can see them before we go up."

Green got to his feet. "I'll do one on last night, and see that Reed photographs Carvell's dabs."

"Thanks."

Anderson said: "You're going to tell me the story, are you, George? Not leave it to me to ferret out for myself from the file?"

"I'd rather tell it and discuss it as we go, sir."

"Right. Everybody got coffee? Help yourselves if not, then fire away."

Masters began.

"Professor Carvell was to have divorced his wife a week ago last Tuesday morning. Rhoda Carvell had intended to be present to see and hear what went on in court so that she could later use the information in an article for the *Daily View*."

"Rag," muttered Anderson.

"However, after visiting the *View* office on the Monday morning, she went with Ralph Woodruff..."

"The feller in the case?"

"Quite, sir. They went to Abbot's Hall at Climping to spend the night, no doubt intending to motor back to London on the Tuesday morning to attend the court."

"Why! Hell of a way to go, just to come back."

"I don't know why, sir. My guess is that the two of them suddenly found themselves at a loose end after lunch on the Monday and on the spur of the moment decided to go off to Abbot's Hall."

Anderson sniffed. "Is that good enough, George?"

"Probably not, sir. But as they are both dead..."

"Quite. Can't ask them."

"But we know they did go there on the Monday, sir. We have a shopkeeper there who sold them food and drink just before closing time on the Monday."

"Fair enough. Go on."

"Abbot's Hall is an old, but strongly built house. The Carvells had renewed the windows and internal doors because, I presume, it was draughty. The new work was of a high standard. When the new windows and doors are shut the place is almost hermetically sealed.

"Rhoda Carvell was well known as a fresh-air fiend. It was her custom to sleep with her bedroom window open whenever possible. But on that Monday night a strong southerly gale blew up. The bedroom window had to be closed.

"Mrs Carvell and Woodruff drank that evening, before supper, a large amount of gin."

"Enough to make them squiffy?"

"Nearly so, I should imagine, sir. Then they had a simple, but ample supper, which could have steadied them up a bit. After supper comes the mystery."

"What was that?"

"They drank, between them, the best part of three bottles of champagne. The amount comes from the pathologist. The fact that it was champagne is my guess."

"What does the forensic examination say it was?"

"A gaseous white wine, unspecified."

"Go on."

"That amount of drink would have laid them out flat. But they were found in bed, with the room tidy and showing no signs of the disarray that one would expect to find if two drunks had gone up there."

"So what conclusion have you come to? That they drank the champagne in bed?"

Masters nodded. "It must have been that way, sir, but the odd thing was that neither the bottles nor the glasses were in the room."

"Where were they?"

Masters looked across at Green who said: "All the glasses were in the wine cupboard, sir, and the bottles had gone."

"Gone? Disappeared completely?"

"We've had a search party looking for two days, with no luck."

"Then they can't have had the champagne."

Masters shook his head. "They did, I'm afraid, sir. They had to be so drunk that their breathing would be deep and stertorous. Only in that state would they take in enough arsine gas quickly enough to kill them before they were awakened by discomfort, and vomited as one would usually expect from people poisoned by arsenic."

Anderson scratched his chin. "I see that, I think. So you're postulating the presence of a third person."

"There had to be, hadn't there?" said Green. "The murderer?"

"Of course. But am I right in believing what you're saying is that this third person brought in the champagne and cleared away later?"

"Yes, sir."

"Impossible."

"Somebody washed up all the glasses used, sir," said Masters. "And got rid of the bottles."

"To make sure we couldn't pick up his prints, you mean?"

"Yes, sir."

"But it would mean that the murderer was known to Rhoda Carvell and Woodruff. A friend, in fact. I mean it would have to be somebody pretty close if they were going to accept three bottles of champagne from this character. Three bottles! That's a quarter of a dozen. As much as I buy in a year."

"Quite," said Masters. "It is my contention that the champagne was delivered to the house with the express intention of ensuring that Mrs Carvell and Woodruff would fall into a drunken stupor."

"So that the murderer could operate without waking them?"

"Just so, sir. They were asleep, heavy with drink, in a room which—with door and window both shut—would be almost hermetically sealed. Ideal conditions for death by gassing."

Anderson shook his head. "Unbelievable," he said. "Where did the arsine come from?"

"I have here," replied Masters, "a text book on mineralogy and another on clinical toxicology." He held them up and then proceeded to open the mineralogy book at a marked page. "We will refer to this one first, sir. I don't want to bore you with all the technical detail I have ploughed through to get the continuous thread of argument and connection, so I will show you just this one section." He got to his feet and placed the open book in front of Anderson. "White iron pyrites. Occurs in chalk

182

and other sedimentary deposits. Occurs in radiating forms, externally nodular."

"What does that mean?"

"Nodules are spheres. In this case varying from the size of large golfballs up to—I imagine—tennis ball size. Radiating forms mean the spheres are filled with needle-shaped crystals, all meeting at the centre and radiating outwards."

Anderson nodded his understanding.

"I would like you to appreciate a further entry in the occurrence paragraph, sir. This bit... 'usually in concretions in sedimentary rocks such as the English Chalk or accompanying galena, blende etc. in replacement deposits in limestones."

"What are galena and blende?"

"They are of no interest to us, sir, but they are, in fact, forms of lead and zinc."

"I see."

"The important thing to note, sir, is that the shore near Abbot's Hall has a peculiar formation." Masters remained standing alongside Anderson. "It is at that point that the chalk of the inland hills behind the coast reappears. It thrusts upwards just there, and is noted for the flints and the pyrites nodules that it contains."

"You mean the things are embedded in it?"

"That's right. You can see them protruding when the tide recedes. You can pick them up, occasionally. If you cared to burrow into the chalk—which as you know, sir, is quite soft—you could come up with as many flints and nodules as you cared to collect."

"The flints they built houses with? That's where they got them from?"

"I imagine so, sir. Set in mortar they would make a strong structure."

"Sorry, George, I shouldn't digress. What's this other book? The toxicology one?"

Masters opened it. "Again, sir, I won't bother you with

183

too much technical detail. In fact, I'll read you just one sentence. It is this. 'Iron pyrites often contain quantities of arsenic sufficient to liberate fatal amounts of arsine when the ore is moistened'."

Masters closed the book and had resumed his seat before Anderson spoke.

"Let me get it straight, George. There is, for the asking—or collecting—a large supply of iron pyrites nodules within a few hundred yards of Abbot's Hall? These nodules only have to be dampened to give off fatal amounts of arsine?"

"Correct, sir, but the nodules would have to be cracked open to expose the ore before damping.

"Good God!"

Green said: "Coming up with those tit-bits wasn't too bad a job, was it, sir?"

Anderson shook his head. "I don't know how you lot do it, I really don't."

"Blame George, sir. He's the cause of all the trouble."

"Yes, yes. What next?"

"As I said, sir," continued Masters, "the nodules would have to be cracked open and laid out for watering. Quite easy to do, I believe, with any hammer that has a pointed or chisel-edged pane."

"Such as a geologist's hammer?"

"Just so, sir."

"I'm beginning to get your drift, George."

"It is almost inevitable that you should, sir. But I'll press on. What I envisaged was our murderer splitting open the nodules, a great many of them, and laying them out, close-packed on a number of trays or dishes which he could then carry to the bedroom. Because of their drunken stupor, neither Rhoda Carvell nor Woodruff would be in any fit state to interfere as he laid them about the floor and then moistened them from a can or bottle of water. He picked up the empty champagne bottles and their corks—probably because he had handled them when taking them

184

to the house—and the glasses, and then left the room, being careful to close the door behind him."

"Devilish," muttered Anderson.

"He then went downstairs and cleared away, including washing the glasses and putting them back in the wine cupboard. He was in no hurry, because he had to wait for the arsine to do its work. The vapour diffuses through the pulmonary sac and death is often delayed for up to twelve hours. But this is in a normal person subjected to a comparatively small dose. With drunken people breathing stertorously and subjected to a heavy dose in a closed and confined room, death would come much more quickly. In about half an hour the effects would be serious and then in an hour—or perhaps two at the most—they would be dead.

"But he was not to know how long his wait would be, and I suspect he dared not remove the pyrites until his victims were dead. So he had a long time to spare. But I would like to go back a bit, sir. I told you I envisaged the broken nodules being laid out on trays. My immediate picture was of baking trays and oven tins, because the picture was of little buns in their papers crowded together for cooking." Anderson nodded to show he followed Masters' reasoning.

"So I examined the oven. There were no trays or dripping tins in it nor anywhere else in the house. I found this odd, but supporting my belief that our murderer had used the trays. When we tried to ascertain whether Mrs Carvell had the customary trays in the oven, we discovered that not only had she the normal complement of her own, but also several others left there by the cookery expert of the *View* and never returned by Mrs Carvell.

"But, sir, we have been unable to find the trays and the champagne bottles. The trays were obviously lifted from the bedroom and then disposed of. Where? is the question." Masters sat back. "And that, sir, in brief is the way in which those two were murdered."

185

"You have to be right," said Anderson. "It all fits. Now you're going to tell me that Professor Carvell is the murderer, I suppose?"

"It would seem he is our man, sir. To begin with, this is a crime requiring a knowledge of geology, and he is an eminent geologist."

"Right."

"Our murderer had to have a knowledge of the house. To know, for instance, that the oven trays were available and that the rooms were virtually airtight."

"Carvell would know those things. Nobody better."

"Carvell also knew the effects that champagne had on his wife. He told me it sent her to sleep."

"He did that?"

Masters nodded. "I believe he regretted it later. But I think he delivered the champagne there in person. He went in, I suspect, on the 'no-hard-feelings' basis, that Monday evening, bearing the bottles to prove it. His wife and Woodruff were probably delighted by his attitude and happy that he should stay to take a glass with them. He probably fetched the glasses from the cupboard and poured the wine. In any case he had handled the bottles, so the glasses had to be washed and the bottles disposed of.

"He then had to leave, ostensibly. He probably suggested to the other two that they should take the champagne up to bed with them. Then he waited to give them time to drink themselves stupid."

"You can't prove this, can you?"

"Not that it was Carvell. But we have witnesses to prove that Carvell left the Hall of Residence at about seven that Monday evening. He claims he was going out to dinner with a woman companion. But he was carrying a despatch bag big enough to hold three bottles of champagne and he used his car. I find it hard to believe that a man like the Professor would take a bag with him when going out to dinner with a woman other than his wife."

"Deuced odd," agreed Anderson. "What time did he get back from this dinner engagement?"

"That's the point, sir, he didn't. Not that night."

"Didn't? Not at all?"

"Certainly not before six in the morning."

"Did he give you an explanation?"

"He refused us one."

"Damned fishy, in fact?"

"Decidedly so, sir."

"Do you attribute any motive to him?"

"There is the point that his wife died before the divorce hearing. So she was still his wife and so her estate reverts to him under the former will which would have been replaced by a new one once the divorce had been granted. There is Abbot's Hall and a large amount of valuable furniture, besides her other belongings, whatever they may be—jewellery, a bit of money, and so on."

"Quite a sum, you reckon?"

"An amount not to be sneezed at, sir."

Anderson considered this for a moment and then asked: "What's your problem, George?"

"There is a lot of circumstantial evidence, sir."

"Against Carvell? I agree."

"But no direct hard evidence."

"He has refused to help you by giving an account of himself. He can have no grouse if you assume the worst."

"True, sir."

"But you don't want to charge him?"

"I am here to ask you if I should do so, sir."

Anderson gazed at him for a moment or two. "You wouldn't come to me if you were sure in your own mind."

"I am here to ask you if I should proceed on the basis of circumstantial evidence only."

"Knowing you, I will assume you are not satisfied with your own case."

"I prefer to have some tangible evidence, sir. Something that will authenticate what we assume to be correct."

"Are you saying your investigation has been taken as far as possible?"

"There may be minor points to clear up, sir, but to all

187

intents and purposes the work has been done."

"Answer me this. Can you establish that Carvell knew his wife would be at Abbot's Hall that night?"

"No, sir. But I don't have to."

"But you do. He had to deliver champagne."

Masters shook his head. "Mrs Carvell made no secret of the fact that she intended going to Abbot's Hall on the Tuesday night. Carvell could have decided to leave the champagne there on Monday night with a note saying 'no-regrets', knowing that substantially the same opportunity for murder would be open to him after it had been drunk on the Tuesday."

"He needed the storm for his plan to succeed."

"No, sir, he didn't. At the beginning of the investigation the storm loomed large in my considerations. It helped me a great deal, in fact. But that was before I knew the two victims were completely drunk. I maintain that if the murderer could enter the room with his trays of pyrites, he could have closed the windows had they been open."

"Right enough," said Green. "I hadn't thought of that."

"Then your motive will not hold up," said Anderson, "because if the murder had been committed on the Tuesday, the divorce would have been granted."

"I don't have to prove motive, sir," said Masters.

"Neither do you, but it helps and...wait a minute, George. I'm no lawyer, but I reckon that that divorce hearing would only grant a decree nisi, wouldn't it?"

"Yes, sir."

"Would the thing be valid before the decree absolute came into effect?"

"I don't know, sir. But if what you are suggesting is right, then the motive would have been as good on the Tuesday as on the Monday."

"We should clear that point up."

"Right, sir."

"And that other point I raised. Try to find out why the woman changed her mind and went out to Abbot's Hall on the Monday instead of Tuesday."

188

Masters nodded his agreement.

"Keep on with the search for the dripping tins or whatever they are."

"That is continuing, sir."

"Good. Now, leave me with this file. I shall read all the details while you do what we've agreed. When I'm properly clued up and hear what you have to say after that, I shall make a decision. Meanwhile, leave Carvell to stew in his own juice." He got to his feet. "And let me tell you all that whether we get what we want or not, you've done a good job with this business. But, like you, George, moral certainty doesn't appeal to me. If the worst comes to the worst we may have to fall back on it, particularly if the DPP says we should, but I'm pretty sure you four can find something to make the decision easier."

"Lunch time, Chief," said Berger as they left Anderson's office. "Is there anything you want us to do immediately?"

"Have you photographed Carvell's dabs?"

"They're done. And those belonging to everybody else in the case. Mrs Carvell, Woodruff, Heddle, the lot. The first two off the corpses of course."

"Good. Have your lunch. We'll meet in my office at two."

Masters and Green made their way to the former's office. "Any ideas, George?" asked Green.

"None at all. How the hell are we to find out why Rhoda Carvell changed her mind about going to Abbot's?"

Green lit a Kensitas from a crumpled packet. "She lived in a flat. I wonder if she had a daily? Somebody she'd let know about her movements?"

"Could be. We'll put the sergeants on to it this afternoon."

"Not feeling very active yourself?"

Masters grinned. "I need a drink, Bill. Oh, and thanks for the idea about the housekeeper."

"Skip it. Where shall we go? To a pub or the mess?"

"A pub, I think, if that's all right by you."

"Pleasure."

There was a scrum in the bar and so there was no further discussing of the case. After they returned to the Yard and the sergeants had been sent about their business, Masters announced his intention of using the afternoon to clear up the paper work that had accumulated on his desk. Then he said to Green: "Take the afternoon off, Bill. I keep forgetting you're really a nine-to-five character these days. You've been working late for the past three or four nights, so we must owe you the time."

"You're sure, George? You don't have to..."

"I'm sure, Bill."

"Tomorrow's Saturday."

"So it is. I think we should all have a weekend off."

"You're nice and early, darling." Wanda kissed him. "Case finished?"

"I've thrown in my hand," he said with a grin.

"As bad as that?" She took his hand. "I'm just about to take Michael up to bath him. Come and say hello."

"Story, daddy," demanded Michael.

Masters took his son on his knee. "Story," urged Michael. "Farm."

The farm story was an on-going saga. Masters made it up as he went along and anything was permissible except the names of the characters. They had to remain the same. Michael knew them and would allow no deviation. The billy-goat was Hercules. The farm boy was Tom. Tonight Hercules found Tom's hat hanging on a gate post and ate it. The wide-eyed little chap listened avidly. When his mother came to collect him she was given an abridged version as she led him upstairs. Masters got up to pour himself a drink.

The door bell rang. Masters flicked the outside light on as he went to open the door.

Mr and Mrs Cartwright.

They all stood eyeing each other for a moment. Then Masters said: "My wife is not available at the moment."

"It's you we want to see," said Cyril.

"Yes, you, not Wanda," added Edna.

"What about?"

"A crime. A serious crime."

"Come in."

"Now what's this all about?" he demanded as he led them into the sitting room.

"We have been robbed, burgled," gabbled Mrs Cartwright.

"Somebody has broken into your home and stolen something?"

"All my jewels and the radio and the electric mixer that Cyril gave me for Christmas and..."

"Not broken in," said Cyril. "There is no sign of forced entry. Whoever did it used a key."

"Have your keys been lost?"

"They used the spare."

"I see. Tell me how they could get hold of your spare key."

"We kept it in the shed."

"Hanging on a nail?"

"No," gabbled Edna. "Under the floor."

"There is a loose piece of board," said her husband. "The key was in a tin, buried under that board. How anyone could know it was there I just cannot imagine."

"Thieves these days know all the dodges," replied Masters. "If they got into your shed—which I take it was very tidy?"

"Oh, yes, very."

"They would wonder why a man who was obviously a careful, tidy chap had not bothered to nail down a loose board. They know their business. They would realize a key would be buried there."

"I see."

"What are you going to do about it?" demanded Mrs Cartwright.

"Nothing."

"Nothing? But you're a policeman. A senior officer. No

wonder the police force can't protect our lives and property if Chief Superintendents baldly announce they are not prepared to take notice of serious crime."

"Steady, Edna," warned Cyril.

"Have you informed your local police station?" asked Masters.

"We did that straightaway."

"What happened?"

"They sent round a constable," said Mrs Cartwright scathingly.

Cyril said: "He told us there was virtually nothing they could do. He made notes of course."

"He's quite right," said Masters. "It's the climate we live in these days. You two, if I may remind you of it, have campaigned for a liberalism that leads criminals of all classes to believe they can get away with it. Non-custodial sentences, early remand, no birching, no hanging. So there is more and more crime. So much of it, in fact, that the police are swamped. There is a robbery such as the one you have just suffered every twenty seconds of every day."

"You are blaming us?" asked Edna disbelievingly.

"I am. And I would add that it is on the cards that your house will be broken into again in the not too-distant future. Possibly within the year. So my advice to you is to contact your insurance people and let them know exactly what has gone."

Neither of the Cartwrights said a word to this. After a considerable silence, Masters said: "I see. Your goods and chattels are not insured. Is that it?"

"Only the fabric of the house," replied Cyril.

"Then be thankful they did not break everything in sight, and go out first thing tomorrow and take out a policy."

"But we hope to get our things back."

"I hope you do, Mr Cartwright, but the possibility is slight."

"Won't you come round and..."

"It is not my job. First because I am already dealing

192

with a murder case and second because your local police have it in hand."

"I don't think your attitude is at all helpful, George," said Mrs Cartwright.

"If you think I have behaved in any way incorrectly, Mrs Cartwright, you can complain to my superiors. I will willingly give you the necessary details."

"I understand," said Cyril. "You must forgive my wife. She is upset. We both are."

"I am extremely sorry that this should have happened. Strictly unofficially I will ask your local police whether there is anything they can do for you."

"Good," said Edna. "I told them to expect to hear from you. I told them you wouldn't take this lying down."

Masters frowned in annoyance but said nothing. He moved towards the door to indicate the meeting was over. They followed him. He let them out and then flicked off the outside light.

"I heard most of that," said Wanda.

"Listening on the stairs, were you?" said Masters, holding her round the waist and kissing her nose.

"Not exactly. This house is very small, you know…"

"I know. Anything said downstairs can be heard upstairs."

"And I didn't want to put in an appearance."

"Quite right. Is Michael in bed? If so, I'll just pop up and see him."

When he came down again, Wanda handed him his unfinished drink and said, "I would have expected you to be blasting that woman for using your name, but you sound remarkably cheerful. Is that because you like the idea of somebody stealing their goodies, or because you think you have finally headed them off?"

"Neither, my darling. I'm extremely sorry they've been robbed, and I think you said you had already choked them off."

"I wouldn't put it quite like that, but yes, I thought I

had put an end to their visits. So why the excessive good humour?"

He kissed her again. "Because, my poppet, I believe that in their bumbling way, those two have helped me. They could prove to be the little bit of luck that Bill Green was saying we needed."

"How? They were uninsured and have probably lost hundreds of pounds worth of goods."

Masters grinned. "I believe that is the price they will have to pay for bringing to book the man who killed their beloved Rhoda Carvell. Should they ever hear about it I'm sure they will agree that it was a small sacrifice to make in so worthy a cause. Tra la la, and all such words of joy!"

"George," said his wife, "you're being frivolous and obtuse."

"And if I don't behave myself I'll get no pudding. Is that it?"

She smiled. "As it is syrup tart..."

"Marvellous woman! Now, if you'll excuse me, I must ring Bill Green and the sergeants. Their weekend off will be a weekend on, but will they mind? No, they..."

"George!"

"Yes, my sweet?"

"Don't forget to give William and Doris my love."

As Masters had foreseen, Green was in good fettle as, next morning, they sped westwards against the shopping traffic entering London.

"Incredible!" he said. "The Cartwrights! Jammy again, George. What is it about you? All these things just seem to land in your lap."

"As long as the Cartwrights don't, I'll admit that their discomfiture has afforded me a deal of pleasure..."

"Because they were turned over, Chief?"

"Not that, specifically, but because they were so fortuitously turned over. Or, rather, that they trotted round to me and told me. Few other people would presume on

194

an acquaintanceship such as the one we didn't enjoy, let alone one which was so patently nipped in the bud. Still, they came and gave me the hint, so I must not be so beastly as to rejoice in their misfortune."

"It beats me," said Green, "why you didn't see this all along, George. It's so obvious."

"Why I didn't see it? What about we?"

"Why is it so obvious?" asked Berger.

"And how can we be sure the Chief is right, even now?" asked Reed.

"He's right," grunted Green. "He has to be. It's too...too logical to be wrong."

"I'll buy that if you say so and the Chief does, too. But accepting a fact on trust is not knowing why it is a fact."

"Tell them, Bill," said Masters, who proceeded to pack the first pipe of the day.

"Our murderer," began Green.

"Carvell?" asked Reed.

"A man is not guilty until proved so," admonished Green.

"So that little chat in the AC's office yesterday morning was meaningless, was it?"

"If you remember, it was inconclusive."

"I know the Chief wasn't happy."

"Right, lad. But if it makes you happy, we'll call him Professor Ernest Carvell and risk being sued for defamation of character."

"Thanks."

"To continue," grunted Green. "Carvell had a lot of time at his disposal on the night of the murder. And when I say Monday night, I include Tuesday morning. Understood?"

"Just."

"He drove from London in his car. But he couldn't take it right up to the house."

"Why not? If he didn't know his missus and her boyfriend were there, as was suggested yesterday?"

"That may have been his belief before he set out, lad, but a light in any window of that igloo would show a mile off. So whatever he thought, he couldn't take chances. He'd stop a bit away down the track and then proceed on foot. Or would you, in his place, have driven up to the door and blown your horn?"

"I'll admit I'd have proceeded with caution in a like situation."

"Good. That's settled that. But it was a wild night. Gales, wind and rain, so he wouldn't want to make too many journeys to a car parked some distance away."

"Nobody would."

"But he had to leave those two to go to bed. So he had to get out of the house and wait for them to get stoned before he dare return. And before returning—or going indoors—he might have to do a little recce from time to time to see how things were going. If all was quiet and soon."

"Agreed."

"So where would he be? He'd need shelter as close to the house as possible."

"In one of the two tarred sheds near the gate?"

"Right, lad. And why there and not in the garage at the back of the house?"

"You tell us."

"Because from the sheds he could see the bedroom window and he'd know when the light went off or see any shadows if there was movement."

"Fair enough."

"We said he had a lot of time. He used up a bit of it breaking open the nodules and perhaps a minute or two in washing up the glasses. But what would he do with the rest of the time?"

"Keep watch."

"Of course he kept watch. But he had other things to think about."

"About getting the trays from the oven and loading them and getting the water to moisten them and how he would have to wash the glasses because he'd handled them, and the bottles and so on."

"Right. He'd go over it all in his mind, step by step, just as you said. But you didn't mention one thing, lad."

"What?"

"After the deed, son. What to do with the murder weapon. In this case, a batch of oven trays full of stinking nodules, to say nothing of three champagne bottles. All murderers are faced with the same problem if they've used a weapon. They've got to get rid of it without trace. Now, what his nibs is saying, is that one baking tray full of nodules would be quite a heavy load for one hand, so at best he could carry two. And he daren't risk falling, in case he should spill the load and not be able to find all the bits and pieces in the dark, which he'd have to do if he didn't want to give himself away. So, even if he could risk carrying two trays at a time he'd have to make three journeys to get rid of them. Could he risk stumbling down the track to the car? Would he want to in that weather?"

"The answer to that," said Reed, "is no."

"Just so, lad, particularly as, if he put them in the car he'd have to stop later to offload them, that is if he was still alive to do so. Four or five trays of pyrites giving off arsine isn't a load most people would risk driving round in a car."

"Not likely," agreed Reed.

"So he's standing in an old tarred shed, keeping his eyes open and thinking things over. Out of the wind and the rain and wondering what to do with all the stuff he's got to get rid of. But he begins to get a bit cold in there, with no heating on a wild night. He stamps his feet to keep them warm. And guess what? He's stamping on soil. Hard packed, probably, but still capable of being dug up with the gardening implements in either the shed he's in or the one next door. So, time being no object, he clears some of the rubbish out of the way and he digs a hole. A good big one. Not hard to do once the top two inches of hard stuff have been picked away. When the time comes, he puts all the stuff he wants to get rid of in there and replaces as much soil as he can. He stamps it down and

197

pulls the garden roller and other stuff on top of it and carries outside the bucketful he's got over and chucks it on a flower bed where it'll never be noticed."

"Just like that?"

"Two or three trips from the house to the shed instead of long walks to the car. No danger of the arsine affecting him as he carried it in the open air with a gale to blow the gas away. And the whole operation carried out in the comparative comfort of a shed where he could safely use a torch to see what he was doing."

"Simple when you think about it," said Reed.

"And obvious, as the Chief said," added Berger.

"And yet it took the Cartwrights and the story of where they had hidden their spare back door key to make me see it," said Masters. "Now what we have to hope for is that we're not on a wild-goose chase."

"We're not," said Green firmly. "It gels."

"Stop for coffee, Chief?" asked Reed as they approached Haslemere.

"Good idea. There's a nice little place close to the car park I seem to remember."

"Chief?" said Berger when they were sitting at the table drinking coffee and eating home-made scones, "if the shed is the hiding place and it is as obvious a place as you say it is, why haven't the locals who are searching the area found it?"

"Probably because it is so obvious."

"The answer's easy," said Green with his mouth full. "We've asked them to look for a heap of things. Enough to fill a big cardboard box, in fact. Some of the locals will have been into those sheds and looked round. What are they hoping to find? If we'd asked them to locate a thimble, they'd have been through everything there with a louse comb. As it is they've just made sure that the big items we want aren't tucked in among the other stuff. A glance would tell them that. The idea of digging up the floor wouldn't occur to them, particularly if miladdo made sure his excavation was covered over so that they couldn't see the earth had been disturbed."

Berger nodded his acceptance of this explanation and then asked: "Have you warned Mr Robson we're going to Abbot's Hall, Chief?"

Masters nodded. "He'll be there with Middleton."

"Probe gently," said Masters to Reed and Berger and the two local constables who were to help them. "At the first sign of disturbed earth, you will evacuate the hut where it is found, and don the masks. Remember that there could be poison gas seeping up either through the earth or ready to escape once the pyrites are uncovered."

Reed and Berger took a hut each with a helper apiece. Immediately, all manner of items were being carried out. Garden tools, boxes of junk, a broken clothes horse, heaps of plant pots, paint tins and seed boxes.

Reed appeared with a door. "Five or six of these inside," he puffed. "The old ones from the house, I suppose."

Robson said: "My men looked in those huts."

"I'm sure they did. But they weren't looking for buried treasure."

"We're not complaining, chum," said Green. "We only thought of it last night and even so we could be on a hiding to nothing."

"What makes you think the things could be here?"

"Logic," replied Green airily, and proceeded to give Robson and Middleton, who had joined them, a shortened version of the reasons he had given to Reed and Berger in the car. When he had finished, Middleton said: "I reckon you're right. There's a spot a bit of a way down the lane where a car has been pulled off recently."

"The traces are still there?"

"Just. An oil drip from the back end drew our attention to it. We reckoned we could just make out where it had stood with the oil mark to help."

Reed and his assistant carried out the last of the doors.

199

"I think we've got something, Chief. Behind this lot. I'll just go in and probe." He took up the thin metal rod. "Back in a moment."

"Something here, Chief."

From the doorway, Masters asked, "How deep?"

"About eight inches."

"Right, you and Berger. You'll only need trowels. Do it very, very carefully. In masks."

"There could still be dabs we could pick up, Chief. On some of the stuff at any rate. On the underside away from the overlying soil."

"That's what I'm hoping. Right. Plastic sheet. Work one at a time. The one not working watch the other like a hawk for any sign of distress. In you go."

Green offered a new packet of Kensitas round. "I'm feeling nervous," he confessed. "But why the hell I should, I don't know." He turned to Masters. "It's all your fault, George."

"Why his?" demanded Robson. "Dammit, he's been playing guessing games ever since he first arrived here, and as far as I can see he's..."

"Bottles, Chief," called Berger. "Moet et Chandon. One so far."

"I thought old Carvell would at least have risen to Krug," said Green.

"Three," called Berger. He poked his head out. "All dry on the outside, Chief, so we'll be able to dust them."

They hadn't much longer to wait before Berger called for the camera. "We'd better have a shot of the trays as they are, Chief."

"Yes, please."

After a number of flashes, Berger announced the hole to be clear. Five baking dishes, three champagne bottles and a heap of segments of nodules which Green estimated would make up to fifty or sixty of the spheres.

"They still pong, Chief, even in the open air," said Reed. "Garlic."

"Oblige me by keeping your nose away from them. Wrap

200

each of the other things very carefully in a plastic sheet, and then put the pyrites in a bag and seal it. Then put that bag in a second one and seal that. And continue to wear your masks while you're doing it."

"Is that it?" asked Robson, as the parcels were laid gently in the boot of the Rover.

"I think so, Mr Robson. Or should I say I hope so. We shall no doubt be meeting later over this business, but I should like to thank you, and Sergeant Middleton here, and indeed all your people, for the willing and helpful co-operation you have afforded us."

Robson scratched one ear. "I still don't know how you've done it, sir. I mean to say, I didn't believe half of it as you went along."

"Jam jars, chum," said Green. "Full ones. He uses them like weather forecasters use seaweed."

Robson looked bewildered.

"Come on," ordered Masters. "With a bit of luck we can get half way home before we stop for a ploughman's."

"Farm manager's for me," said Green as they entered the car.

"That's a new one on me."

"It's the socially divisive lunch," explained Green. "Much bigger and more variety than a ploughman's—as one would expect. One lunch for the boss and another for the workers."

"I'll bet it costs more," said Reed.

"True, lad, but as you'll be buying my beer, I can afford an extra 40p for the grub."

"You wouldn't like me to buy that for you, too, would you?"

"All offers gratefully accepted," replied Green, putting his hands together in an attitude of prayer and closing his eyes.

"Now what?"

"I'm giving thanks for my food. Saying grace if you like."

"Grace? You? This I must hear."

"So you shall, lad."

Green waited a moment and then intoned. "Rub a dub dub, Thanks for the grub." He then opened his eyes and lowered his hands. "Come on, lad, lead me to it. Chop, chop."

Reed snorted with disgust and eased the handbrake.

Masters and Green were in the former's office. They were sitting back, smoking and talking. It was half-past three in the afternoon, and they were waiting for Reed and Berger to report on fingerprints found on the morning's haul.

"But you always go to the Isle of Wight for your holidays," said Masters. "Doris likes it. Why the West Country next year?"

"Doris liked it when she was down there with you and Wanda."

"In that case, would you like me to talk to Frank about letting you his cottage?"

"P'raps. Would he mind?"

"The enquiry? Not at all."

"In that case..."

The internal phone rang.

"Chief?"

"Yes, Berger?"

"Not a sign of Carvell's prints anywhere."

"I thought there might not be. Are you hoping to surprise me."

"I reckon so, Chief. You'd never guess."

"Let me try. Those of Mr Derek Heddle."

"I should know better than to take you on, Chief. Are you coming down?"

"Straightaway."

"Heddle?" asked Green in disbelief. "How the hell did you know that, George?"

"I didn't. But you know I've been plagued with the possibility of Carvell not being our man. So I spent last night trying to fit in a parallel character, if I can call him

202

that. And you'd be surprised, Bill, at how much of what we have ascribed to Carvell can be equally well ascribed to Heddle—if we accept that he told us the odd lie at the outset."

"So we start again."

"Not quite. But there are a few things to sort out." He got to his feet. "We'd better see Reed's evidence."

"Nothing of any use on the bottles and pans, Chief, but beauties on these nodules. Look, I'll show you." He took one up in a pair of forceps. "They're all coated in chalk. I expect he couldn't crack them while wearing gloves, or else he marked them when he collected them. Probably the latter, because they were damp when he handled them, and I reckon he'd be careful not to moisten them the night he used them. So, if you look, you can see the prints in the thin coating of chalk. Done when wet. Once they dried out they'd be set in a sort of concrete. As easy as anything to bring up and photograph and enough of them to compare with all his prints several times over." He put the nodule down, picked up a number of photographs and started to point out the more obvious comparison points on the various sets.

"No doubt about it, then?"

"We'll get over the minimum number of points on virtually every finger, Chief. I've never had one so easy."

"Thank you. You and Berger pack up and go home. I'll have your written report on Monday."

Masters and Green returned to the office. "Carvell, I think," said Masters picking up the phone. "Let's hope he's at home."

When they reached Carvell's set in Gladstone Hall, Carvell had three cups and a plate of biscuits waiting on the coffee table.

He was dressed in slacks and sweater and looked as though he was about to go for a workout in a gym. But his manner was relaxed.

"I gathered from what little you said on the phone that

you are not here to arrest me? That being so, I suggest we have a celebratory cup of tea. The kettle is boiling. If you will park yourselves, I'll make the brew."

He rejoined them a moment later. "The joy of a set is that one has a mini-kitchen of one's own. I don't have to join the throng in the public kitchens."

As he poured, Masters said: "Your action in providing us with so complete a set of your finger prints, Professor, has enabled us to eliminate you from our investigations."

"Totally?"

"Totally. Although I must say that your refusal to tell us your movements made the elimination somewhat more difficult."

Carvell handed him a cup of tea. "I'm sorry about that, of course, but I knew you would check whatever I told you, and there are some secrets any man would wish to preserve."

"I have been told that you are most discreet in your affairs."

Carvell shrugged. "That way lies safety. But I was intrigued as to why you should imagine I was carrying champagne that evening."

"When you were, in fact, carrying toilet articles and other necessities for sleeping the night other than in your own bed?"

The professor grinned. "I couldn't have told you, could I, except as a last resort? But why champagne?"

"Because we knew that somebody had, that evening, taken three bottles of champagne to Abbot's Hall and handed them to Mrs Carvell and Mr Woodruff."

"You're joking."

"No, sir. That is what happened, and whoever did so not only knew of Mrs Carvell's liking for champagne, but also the soporific effect it had on her."

"Good Lord!" exclaimed Carvell. "I can remember telling you it made Rhoda sleep like a babe."

"Do you wonder we had you in mind?" asked Green, carefully choosing from the selection of biscuits.

"I wouldn't have told you if... but I am forgetting that all murderers make mistakes, am I not?"

"Something of the sort. Good biscuits these. Fresh and crisp."

"Help yourself to more." Carvell turned to Masters. "I can't think that the sole object of your visit is to tell me that you are satisfied I did not kill my wife. First, because you are under no obligation to do so and, second, the phone call achieved that object."

"Here to grill you," said Green through a mouth full of biscuit. "And now you're off the hook we want proper answers. No evasions."

"No promises," said Carvell. "But try me."

"Cast your mind back," said Masters, "to one Sunday last June when you went collecting rock samples or fossils down in the area of Abbot's Hall, and found your wife in residence there, entertaining a young male visitor called..."

"Heddle? Is that the one? Cub reporter type?"

Masters nodded. "I'd like to know about that day."

Carvell leaned back. "To give you the full report Mr Green demands, I must go back a number of years. As you may or may not realize, certain areas in this country, as in all others, offer more in the way of geological specimens than others. Dorsetshire, for instance. The marble beds there yield a great harvest of fossils every year. You'll have heard of Blue John in Derbyshire. And so on. The nearest such spot to London—at any rate to the west—is part of the coastline of West Sussex. So, when Rhoda and I, who owned no house in London, thought to buy a property of our own as a second home, I was keen to go to the district which had so much to offer me professionally. As the area where we fetched up was of no great importance to Rhoda, we kept our eyes open until a suitable property in the chosen spot became available. That is how and why we came to buy Abbot's Hall.

"It was a fruitful area for me. I could potter about, virtually on my own doorstep, mixing business with pleasure. Unfortunately things began to go wrong for Rhoda

205

and me. A couple that has two homes never really knows how the other is being used."

"Unless you literally stay in each other's company, you mean?"

"Precisely. But there is no need to go further into that. Later, Rhoda and I both used Abbot's for our own purposes. Or rather, she used the house and I used the fossil-hunting ground close by.

"And that is how it was on the Sunday you mentioned. I didn't realize Rhoda had gone there for the weekend. I went down for the day and collected a number of bits and pieces. I proposed to return quite early as I had an engagement in the evening, so I came up off the beach opposite Abbot's because there is a beaten path there and I could follow that to the track that serves the house, and then down the track to where I had parked the car.

"As I neared the house, I saw a strange car there. As I was still co-owner, I was naturally interested. It could have been an intruder."

"Quite."

"So I went there and found Rhoda sunbathing on the lawn with a youth who, quite frankly, didn't strike me as being exactly her type. Out of courtesy I stopped to pass the time of day."

"Is that all?" asked Green. "Heddle said you looked fearsome, with a hammer in one hand and a cloth bag of rocks in the other."

Carvell laughed. "Thus armed, and probably displaying a deal of hostility for any man spending time alone with Rhoda, I could well have appeared less than friendly. To begin with, that is. When I learned who the lad was and why he was there, I feel sure the meeting became more amicable."

Masters said gravely. "Tell me about the meeting. What you talked about and so on."

"Nothing very earth-shattering. Rhoda asked if I had had a good day's hunting. Heddle seized on that and asked 'hunting for what?' So I tipped the samples out of the bag.

For some reason he seemed impressed, or at least interested, so I told him what they were. I remember I had two or three nodules of iron pyrites, which one can chip out of the chalk there. He asked what they were and I said fool's gold. Then I split one for him, using the hammer and showed him the construction of the thing. The crystals are needleshaped, and radiate from the centre. Quite remarkable to anybody who hadn't seen one before. And, of course, they are brassy coloured—hence the name, fool's gold. And I think that's about all. I left soon after."

"You told him where you found the nodules?"

"Yes, I suppose so. I certainly told him everything I had in the bag had been found within a drive and a chip of Abbot's."

"Why had you collected the nodules, Professor?"

"For lab use. I gather them regularly, so that students can break them open and see the formation." He stared straight at Masters. "That's how she was killed, isn't it? When dampened, they can give off toxic amounts of arsine."

"You knew that?"

"Of course I knew it. That's why I collect fresh supplies. I don't like too many old ones left in the lab—except perhaps a few in a fume chamber."

"Did you mention arsine or arsenic to Heddle?"

"I am positive I did not. It is not the sort of thing I would tell a layman."

"You guessed from the outset that iron pyrites nodules were the source of the arsine that killed Mrs Carvell?"

"I confess I did."

"Yet you didn't tell me."

"I was wrong not to give you the hint. But look at it from my point of view. It was the crime of a man with a knowledge of geology, and I am a geologist. I was her husband. I knew the house. And so on. I fully expected to be arrested for murder the moment you knew the likely source of the arsine."

"So you decided to what? Hold me off in the hope that

I would never discover the source?"

"Not quite that. I didn't murder Rhoda. But I suspected —probably mistakenly—that once you had arrested me, you would probe no further. I held back because, being innocent, I had everything to gain from a prolonged and thorough enquiry."

"Our enquiry hasn't been all that prolonged," protested Green. "Far less than a week."

"But if I'd been arrested after twenty-four hours?"

Green grinned. "You'd have had to spill the beans about your...er...dinner companion."

Carvell laughed. "But I didn't have to, did I?"

"An' a damn nuisance you were to us, too."

"To get back to Heddle..." began Masters.

"One moment, Chief Superintendent. Am I to take it that Heddle killed Rhoda?"

"Such is our belief. But he's innocent until proved guilty."

"Of course. Please ask your question."

"At the time you spoke to him, Heddle appeared to know nothing of rocks and fossils in general and iron pyrites in particular?"

"Nothing. Nothing at all, I'd have said."

"He must have gained some knowledge in the intervening months."

"Nothing easier, I'd have thought. He's a budding journalist. They're taught to be investigative. Any public library—the reference section—would yield the knowledge he used. The trick is knowing of the existence of iron pyrites nodules and where to collect them. I suspect that after he saw my samples he was moved by a certain enthusiasm to go and read about them and, thereafter, to make a journey or two to Climping to collect them."

Masters nodded. "It is more or less what I did myself, to learn about the nodules. But I started from the other end. A toxicology text book told me that arsine could be obtained from iron pyrites. It was then I went to a book on mineralogy."

208

"I see."

"But I believe the motive for collecting the nodules, in Jeddle's case, was that it provided an excuse for his presence in the area of Abbot's Hall, should he be seen there."

"You mean he went there for some other reason?"

"I believe he went there in the hope of seeing Mrs Carvell, should she happen to be there alone."

"To kill her?"

"No, no."

"You mean...you mean he was in love with her?"

"So I believe."

"Incredible."

"Why incredible?" demanded Green. "She was a good looking woman by all accounts, witty and charming. And he used to talk to him where she didn't talk to the other men on the *Daily View*. Used to call him her Little Stinging Nettle..."

"Her what?"

"Stinging Nettle. A joke to her perhaps, but a sign of friendship—perhaps even of intimacy—to a young impressionable lad."

"I had no idea," said Carvell, "that this lad was in any way involved with her...no, dammit, I'm putting this badly. I could tell he was besotted with her that Sunday, but I took it to be a youthful crush, nothing more, though God knows I was myself only too aware of how she could attract a man. I married her, so I should know what I'm talking about. But knowing Rhoda as I did, I would be more than surprised if she had led that young man on or caused him to believe in any way that his passion for her was returned."

"I'm sure you're right," agreed Masters. "No blame could be placed at your wife's door. The boy is deranged in some way."

"Deranged? That's putting it a little mildly, isn't it?"

"You said he loved her, yet he killed her."

Green murmured that somebody had made just that point about us all.

209

"Why did he kill her, Chief Superintendent?"

"It is not any part of my duty to provide an answer to that question, but I imagine that it was the shock of learning that Mrs Carvell, on being divorced from you, intended to cohabit with Mr Woodruff, as opposed to with him, Heddle. I can only assume that so long as she was married to you, he accepted it, because you had got there first. But he was not prepared to let a third man intervene."

"Funny thing, love," said Green.

"It must be," agreed Carvell, "if, as Mr Masters postulates, it has turned an apparently harmless and normal young man into a homicidal maniac." Carvell gritted his teeth. "But he isn't a lunatic. From what I have heard from you two gentlemen, I should say he had executed his little bit of mayhem with a great deal of thoroughness and good planning, and particularly so if he did it more or less on the spur of the moment."

"He did," said Masters assertively. "I don't believe the idea had entered his head until he overheard Mrs Carvell talking to Golly Lugano that Monday morning."

"He worked fast, then."

"He had all the means to hand. His store of pyrites gathered over the weeks of visiting the area. His basic knowledge of how to produce arsine. His knowledge of the house after spending a day there—every detail etched in his mind because that was the setting where Mrs Carvell had entertained him. He probably went into the kitchen and saw the baking trays there. As for the champagne—well, I suggest Mrs Carvell had told him of her great liking for it while they sat and ate strawberries together."

"Nothing surer," said Carvell. "Strawberries would go with champagne in Rhoda's mind. She would certainly chatter about it in a picnic situation like that. You know the sort of thing: 'If only we had a bottle of iced bubbly to wash these down...'" A youth like Heddle would automatically ask her if she liked the stuff. He might even

210

have made a mental note to take a bottle for her should he ever again have cause to go to Abbot's."

"Good point," said Green. "He'd probably splurged on a quarter dozen for her just in case the call came. He could have had it in his possession for weeks or months."

Masters nodded. "There'll be a lot of points to clear up. His buying the champagne and so on." He got to his feet ready to leave.

"Wait a moment," said Carvell. "He must have lied about when Rhoda said she would be there. He said she mentioned she was going there after the divorce."

"Immaterial," said Masters. "He could have gone down there on Monday to prepare his project. When he discovered Mrs Carvell in residence he could have decided to make use of the opportunity. After all, who would be more welcome than an unexpected caller bearing loads of champagne? He would be let in and made much of. No, I don't believe the day matters in the slightest. But we shall speak to Golly Lugano again, to try to check whether Mrs Carvell did actually mention Monday or Tuesday."

On the Monday morning the AC Crime listened attentively as Masters and Green told their story, bolstered by the minor points they had cleared up on the Sunday.

"You've arrested him?"

"He was taken into custody and charged yesterday morning."

"Has he made a statement yet?"

"No, sir, and I haven't insisted."

"So we have no motive to ascribe to him, other than his frustrated love of Rhoda Carvell? If he couldn't have her, nobody else was going to? Is that it?"

"A psychologist spent several hours with him yesterday, sir. I have a preliminary report from him with me, sir. It will be entered as supplying an explanation for Heddle's actions."

"The shrink says he's crackers, does he?"

211

"More or less, sir. Shall I read it to you?"

"Yes, please. The relevant bits. Not all the jargon."

Masters took the paper from a file cover. "I'll pick out bits as I go along, sir."

"Thanks."

"'Heddle is suffering from emotional incongruity. The outcome of his belief that Mrs Carvell cared for him, as evidenced by the attention she paid him and the nickname she gave him, could mean that, when she announced her divorce and intention to set up home with another man, Heddle became obsessed with suspiciousness or persecutory delusions. In turn, the outcome of such delusions may have become impulsive, murderous attacks.'"

Masters went to another paragraph lower down the page. "'In a person with Heddle's state of mind, love and hate, trust and suspicion, joy and sorrow, terror and confidence co-exist and alternate so rapidly that the patient is bewildered. The chaos of mental and emotional feelings have led to impulsive action which, to the normal mind, can only appear as eminently bizarre and incomprehensible behaviour.'"

Masters turned the page.

"The psychologist then goes on to talk of Heddle's paranoia. He has distinguished three kinds. The first, paranoid jealousy. 'Paranoid jealousy is no different from ordinary jealousy, except that, in Heddle, I have discovered it to be much more profound and relentless. It is pathological in that the reason for it is inadequate to everybody but himself. It is, in fact, merely a projection of his own wishes and desires.

"'Paranoid eroticism is easily perceived in Heddle, who has projected his own desires on to another person, namely Mrs Carvell, whom he has regarded, however incorrectly, as the object of his passion.

"'Paranoid grandiosity, in the face of frustration such as Heddle felt when Mrs Carvell chose Mr Woodruff instead of himself, placed him in an imagined position of omnipotence where desires can neither be diminished nor denied without punishment to those responsible.'"

Masters looked up. "Finally, sir, there is a short note about a point that had been troubling me. Heddle seemed a fairly normal youth. So I had wondered about signs of mental disorder not appearing on the occasions of earlier interviews. The psychologist says, 'Heddle is, in my opinion, suffering from paraphrenia or paranoid schizophrenia. Such people have strong delusions—such as the mistaken one that Mrs Carvell loved him—which might be accepted as reasonable, if true. Such delusions may exist in the mind and be strongly held for long periods of time without any noticeable deterioration or disintegration of the personality.'" Masters looked up. "He goes on to say that he does, however, expect progressive mental disorder to become apparent from now on, as a result of the crisis caused by the murder and the arrest."

"Heddle will become overtly schizophrenic?"

"That is the psychologist's belief, sir."

Anderson nodded and turned to Green. "Well, Bill, that seems to be that."

"It worries me," replied Green. "She was merely being nice to him and he got hold of the wrong end of the stick. If she'd slapped him down, she'd still be alive. We none of us know when we're signing our own death warrants these days."

"Innocence and decency bring their own dangers," agreed Anderson sagaciously, and got to his feet to indicate the meeting was over.

213

THE PERENNIAL LIBRARY MYSTERY SERIES

Ted Allbeury

THE OTHER SIDE OF SILENCE   P 669, $2.84
"In the best le Carré tradition . . . an ingenious and readable book."
                                        —*New York Times Book Review*

PALOMINO BLONDE   P 670, $2.84
"Fast-moving, splendidly technocratic intercontinental espionage tale
. . . you'll love it."   —*The Times* (London)

SNOWBALL   P 671, $2.84
"A novel of byzantine intrigue. . . ."—*New York Times Book Review*

Delano Ames

CORPSE DIPLOMATIQUE   P 637, $2.84
"Sprightly and intelligent."
                                —*New York Herald Tribune Book Review*

FOR OLD CRIME'S SAKE   P 629, $2.84

MURDER, MAESTRO, PLEASE   P 630, $2.84
"If there is a more engaging couple in modern fiction than Jane and
Dagobert Brown, we have not met them."   —*Scotsman*

SHE SHALL HAVE MURDER   P 638, $2.84
"Combines the merit of both the English and American schools in the
new mystery. It's as breezy as the best of the American ones, and has
the sophistication and wit of any top-notch Britisher."
                                —*New York Herald Tribune Book Review*

E. C. Bentley

TRENT'S LAST CASE   P 440, $2.50
"One of the three best detective stories ever written."
                                                —Agatha Christie

TRENT'S OWN CASE   P 516, $2.25
"I won't waste time saying that the plot is sound and the detection
satisfying. Trent has not altered a scrap and reappears with all his old
humor and charm."   —Dorothy L. Sayers

Andrew Bergman

THE BIG KISS-OFF OF 1944   P 673, $2.84
"It is without doubt the nearest thing to genuine Chandler I've ever come across. . . . Tough, witty—very witty—and a beautiful eye for period detail. . . ."
—Jack Higgins

HOLLYWOOD AND LEVINE   P 674, $2.84
"Fast-paced private-eye fiction."
—San Francisco Chronicle

Gavin Black

A DRAGON FOR CHRISTMAS   P 473, $1.95
"Potent excitement!"
—New York Herald Tribune

THE EYES AROUND ME   P 485, $1.95
"I stayed up until all hours last night reading *The Eyes Around Me,* which is something I do not do very often, but I was so intrigued by the ingeniousness of Mr. Black's plotting and the witty way in which he spins his mystery. I can only say that I enjoyed the book enormously."
—F. van Wyck Mason

YOU WANT TO DIE, JOHNNY?   P 472, $1.95
"Gavin Black doesn't just develop a pressure plot in suspense, he adds uninfected wit, character, charm, and sharp knowledge of the Far East to make rereading as keen as the first race-through." —Book Week

Nicholas Blake

THE CORPSE IN THE SNOWMAN   P 427, $1.95
"If there is a distinction between the novel and the detective story (which we do not admit), then this book deserves a high place in both categories."
—New York Times

END OF CHAPTER   P 397, $1.95
". . . admirably solid . . . an adroit formal detective puzzle backed up by firm characterization and a knowing picture of London publishing."
—New York Times

HEAD OF A TRAVELER   P 398, $2.25
"Another grade A detective story of the right old jigsaw persuasion."
—New York Herald Tribune Book Review

MINUTE FOR MURDER   P 419, $1.95
"An outstanding mystery novel. Mr. Blake's writing is a delight in itself."
—New York Times

THE MORNING AFTER DEATH   P 520, $1.95
"One of Blake's best."
—Rex Warner

A PENKNIFE IN MY HEART P 521, $2.25

"Style brilliant . . . and suspenseful." —*San Francisco Chronicle*

THE PRIVATE WOUND P 531, $2.25

"[Blake's] best novel in a dozen years . . . . An intensely penetrating study of sexual passion. . . . A powerful story of murder and its aftermath."
—Anthony Boucher, *New York Times*

A QUESTION OF PROOF P 494, $1.95

"The characters in this story are unusually well drawn, and the suspense is well sustained." —*New York Times*

THE SAD VARIETY P 495, $2.25

"It is a stunner. I read it instead of eating, instead of sleeping."
—Dorothy Salisbury Davis

THERE'S TROUBLE BREWING P 569, $3.37

"Nigel Strangeways is a puzzling mixture of simplicity and penetration, but all the more real for that."
—*The Times* (London) *Literary Supplement*

THOU SHELL OF DEATH P 428, $1.95

"It has all the virtues of culture, intelligence and sensibility that the most exacting connoisseur could ask of detective fiction."
—*The Times* (London) *Literary Supplement*

THE WIDOW'S CRUISE P 399, $2.25

"A stirring suspense. . . . The thrilling tale leaves nothing to be desired."
—*Springfield Republican*

Oliver Bleeck

THE BRASS GO-BETWEEN P 645, $2.84

"Fiction with a flair, well above the norm for thrillers."
—*Associated Press*

THE PROCANE CHRONICLE P 647, $2.84

"Without peer in American suspense." —*Los Angeles Times*

PROTOCOL FOR A KIDNAPPING P 646, $2.84

"The zigzags of plot are electric; the characters sharp; but it is the wit and irony and touches of plain fun which make the whole a standout."
—*Los Angeles Times*

John & Emery Bonett

A BANNER FOR PEGASUS   P 554, $2.40
"A gem! Beautifully plotted and set. . . . Not only is the murder adroit
and deserved, and the detection competent, but the love story is charming."   —Jacques Barzun and Wendell Hertig Taylor

DEAD LION   P 563, $2.40
"A clever plot, authentic background and interesting characters highly
recommended this one."   —*New Republic*

THE SOUND OF MURDER   P 642, $2.84
The suspects are many, the clues few, but the gentle Inspector ferrets out
the truth and pursues the case to its bitter and shocking end.

Christianna Brand

GREEN FOR DANGER   P 551, $2.50
"You have to reach for the greatest of Great Names (Christie, Carr,
Queen . . .) to find Brand's rivals in the devious subtleties of the trade."
                                                  —Anthony Boucher

TOUR DE FORCE   P 572, $2.40
"Complete with traps for the over-ingenious, a double-reverse surprise
ending and a key clue planted so fairly and obviously that you completely
overlook it. If that's your idea of perfect entertainment, then seize at once
upon *Tour de Force.*"   —Anthony Boucher, *New York Times*

James Byrom

OR BE HE DEAD   P 585, $2.84
"A very original tale . . . Well written and steadily entertaining."
—Jacques Barzun and Wendell Hertig Taylor, *A Catalogue of Crime*

Henry Calvin

IT'S DIFFERENT ABROAD   P 640, $2.84
"What is remarkable and delightful, Mr. Calvin imparts a flavor of satire
to what he renovates and compels us to take straight."
                                                  —Jacques Barzun

Marjorie Carleton

VANISHED   P 559, $2.40
"Exceptional . . . a minor triumph."
—Jacques Barzun and Wendell Hertig Taylor, *A Catalogue of Crime*

George Harmon Coxe

MURDER WITH PICTURES   P 527, $2.25
"[Coxe] has hit the bull's-eye with his first shot."

—New York Times

Edmund Crispin

BURIED FOR PLEASURE   P 506, $2.50
"Absolute and unalloyed delight."

—Anthony Boucher, *New York Times*

Lionel Davidson

THE MENORAH MEN   P 592, $2.84
"Of his fellow thriller writers, only John Le Carré shows the same
instinct for the viscera."   *—Chicago Tribune*

NIGHT OF WENCESLAS   P 595, $2.84
"A most ingenious thriller, so enriched with style, wit, and a sense of
serious comedy that it all but transcends its kind."

—The New Yorker

THE ROSE OF TIBET   P 593, $2.84
"I hadn't realized how much I missed the genuine Adventure story
. . . until I read *The Rose of Tibet*."   —Graham Greene

D. M. Devine

MY BROTHER'S KILLER   P 558, $2.40
"A most enjoyable crime story which I enjoyed reading down to the last
moment."   —Agatha Christie

Kenneth Fearing

THE BIG CLOCK   P 500, $1.95
"It will be some time before chill-hungry clients meet again so rare a
compound of irony, satire, and icy-fingered narrative. *The Big Clock* is
. . . a psychothriller you won't put down."   *—Weekly Book Review*

Andrew Garve

THE ASHES OF LODA   P 430, $1.50
"Garve . . . embellishes a fine fast adventure story with a more credible
picture of the U.S.S.R. than is offered in most thrillers."

—New York Times Book Review

THE CUCKOO LINE AFFAIR   P 451, $1.95
". . . an agreeable and ingenious piece of work."   *—The New Yorker*

Andrew Garve (cont'd)

A HERO FOR LEANDA P 429, $1.50
"One can trust Mr. Garve to put a fresh twist to any situation, and the ending is really a lovely surprise." —*Manchester Guardian*

MURDER THROUGH THE LOOKING GLASS P 449, $1.95
". . . refreshingly out-of-the-way and enjoyable . . . highly recommended to all comers." —*Saturday Review*

NO TEARS FOR HILDA P 441, $1.95
"It starts fine and finishes finer. I got behind on breathing watching Max get not only his man but his woman, too." —*Rex Stout*

THE RIDDLE OF SAMSON P 450, $1.95
"The story is an excellent one, the people are quite likable, and the writing is superior." —*Springfield Republican*

Michael Gilbert

BLOOD AND JUDGMENT P 446, $1.95
"Gilbert readers need scarcely be told that the characters all come alive at first sight, and that his surpassing talent for narration enhances any plot. . . . Don't miss." —*San Francisco Chronicle*

THE BODY OF A GIRL P 459, $1.95
"Does what a good mystery should do: open up into all kinds of ramifications, with untold menace behind the action. At the end, there is a bang-up climax, and it is a pleasure to see how skilfully Gilbert wraps everything up." —*New York Times Book Review*

FEAR TO TREAD P 458, $1.95
"Merits serious consideration as a work of art." —*New York Times*

Joe Gores

HAMMETT P 631, $2.84
"Joe Gores at his very best. Terse, powerful writing—with the master, Dashiell Hammett, as the protagonist in a novel I think he would have been proud to call his own." —*Robert Ludlum*

C. W. Grafton

BEYOND A REASONABLE DOUBT P 519, $1.95
"A very ingenious tale of murder . . . a brilliant and gripping narrative." —*Jacques Barzun and Wendell Hertig Taylor*

S. B. Hough

DEAR DAUGHTER DEAD   P 661, $2.84
"A highly intelligent and sophisticated story of police detection . . . not
to be missed on any account."   —Francis Iles, *The Guardian*

SWEET SISTER SEDUCED   P 662, $2.84
In the course of a nightlong conversation between the Inspector and the
suspect, the complex emotions of a very strange marriage are revealed.

P. M. Hubbard

HIGH TIDE   P 571, $2.40
"A smooth elaboration of mounting horror and danger."
                                                        —*Library Journal*

Elspeth Huxley

THE AFRICAN POISON MURDERS   P 540, $2.25
"Obscure venom, manical mutilations, deadly bush fire, thrilling climax
compose major opus.... Top-flight."
                                        —*Saturday Review of Literature*

MURDER ON SAFARI   P 587, $2.84
"Right now we'd call Mrs. Huxley a dangerous rival to Agatha Christie." .   —*Books*

Francis Iles

BEFORE THE FACT   P 517, $2.50
"Not many 'serious' novelists have produced character studies to compare with Iles's internally terrifying portrait of the murderer in *Before
the Fact,* his masterpiece and a work truly deserving the appellation of
unique and beyond price."   —Howard Haycraft

MALICE AFORETHOUGHT   P 532, $1.95
"It is a long time since I have read anything so good as *Malice Aforethought,* with its cynical humour, acute criminology, plausible detail and
rapid movement. It makes you hug yourself with pleasure."
                                        —H. C. Harwood, *Saturday Review*

Michael Innes

APPLEBY ON ARARAT   P 648, $2.84
"Superbly plotted and humorously written."   —*The New Yorker*

APPLEBY'S END   P 649, $2.84
"Most amusing."   —*Boston Globe*

THE CASE OF THE JOURNEYING BOY   P 632, $3.12
"I could see no faults in it. There is no one to compare with him."
—*Illustrated London News*

DEATH ON A QUIET DAY   P 677, $2.84
"Delightfully witty."   —*Chicago Sunday Tribune*

DEATH BY WATER   P 574, $2.40
"The amount of ironic social criticism and deft characterization of scenes and people would serve another author for six books."
—Jacques Barzun and Wendell Hertig Taylor

HARE SITTING UP   P 590, $2.84
"There is hardly anyone (in mysteries or mainstream) more exquisitely literate, allusive and Jamesian—and hardly anyone with a firmer sense of melodramatic plot or a more vigorous gift of storytelling."
—Anthony Boucher, *New York Times*

THE LONG FAREWELL   P 575, $2.40
"A model of the deft, classic detective story, told in the most wittily diverting prose."   —*New York Times*

THE MAN FROM THE SEA   P 591, $2.84
"The pace is brisk, the adventures exciting and excitingly told, and above all he keeps to the very end the interesting ambiguity of the man from the sea."   —*New Statesman*

ONE MAN SHOW   P 672, $2.84
"Exciting, amusingly written . . . very good enjoyment it is."
—*The Spectator*

THE SECRET VANGUARD   P 584, $2.84
"Innes . . . has mastered the art of swift, exciting and well-organized narrative."   —*New York Times*

THE WEIGHT OF THE EVIDENCE   P 633, $2.84
"First-class puzzle, deftly solved. University background interesting and amusing."   —*Saturday Review of Literature*

Mary Kelly

THE SPOILT KILL   P 565, $2.40
"Mary Kelly is a new Dorothy Sayers. . . . [An] exciting new novel."
—*Evening News*

Lange Lewis

THE BIRTHDAY MURDER   P 518, $1.95
"Almost perfect in its playlike purity and delightful prose."
                                   —Jacques Barzun and Wendell Hertig Taylor

Allan MacKinnon

HOUSE OF DARKNESS   P 582, $2.84
"His best . . . a perfect compendium."
  —Jacques Barzun and Wendell Hertig Taylor, *A Catalogue of Crime*

Frank Parrish

FIRE IN THE BARLEY   P 651, $2.84
"A remarkable and brilliant first novel. . . . entrancing."
                                   —*The Spectator*

SNARE IN THE DARK   P 650, $2.84
The wily English poacher Dan Mallett is framed for murder and has to confront unknown enemies to clear himself.

STING OF THE HONEYBEE   P 652, $2.84
"Terrorism and murder visit a sleepy English village in this witty, offbeat thriller."   —*Chicago Sun-Times*

Austin Ripley

MINUTE MYSTERIES   P 387, $2.50
More than one hundred of the world's shortest detective stories. Only one possible solution to each case!

Thomas Sterling

THE EVIL OF THE DAY   P 529, $2.50
"Prose as witty and subtle as it is sharp and clear. . .characters unconventionally conceived and richly bodied forth . . . . In short, a novel to be treasured."   —Anthony Boucher, *New York Times*

Julian Symons

THE BELTING INHERITANCE   P 468, $1.95
"A superb whodunit in the best tradition of the detective story."
                                   —August Derleth, *Madison Capital Times*

BOGUE'S FORTUNE   P 481, $1.95
"There's a touch of the old sardonic humour, and more than a touch of style."   —*The Spectator*

Julian Symons (cont'd)

THE COLOR OF MURDER P 461, $1.95
"A singularly unostentatious and memorably brilliant detective story."
— *New York Herald Tribune Book Review*

Dorothy Stockbridge Tillet
(John Stephen Strange)

THE MAN WHO KILLED FORTESCUE P 536, $2.25
"Better than average." — *Saturday Review of Literature*

Simon Troy

THE ROAD TO RHUINE P 583, $2.84
"Unusual and agreeably told." — *San Francisco Chronicle*

SWIFT TO ITS CLOSE P 546, $2.40
"A nicely literate British mystery . . . the atmosphere and the plot are exceptionally well wrought, the dialogue excellent." — *Best Sellers*

Henry Wade

THE DUKE OF YORK'S STEPS P 588, $2.84
"A classic of the golden age."
— Jacques Barzun and Wendell Hertig Taylor, *A Catalogue of Crime*

A DYING FALL P 543, $2.50
"One of those expert British suspense jobs . . . it crackles with undercurrents of blackmail, violent passion and murder. Topnotch in its class."
— *Time*

THE HANGING CAPTAIN P 548, $2.50
"This is a detective story for connoisseurs, for those who value clear thinking and good writing above mere ingenuity and easy thrills."
— *The Times* (London) *Literary Supplement*

Hillary Waugh

LAST SEEN WEARING . . . P 552, $2.40
"A brilliant tour de force." — Julian Symons

THE MISSING MAN P 553, $2.40
"The quiet detailed police work of Chief Fred C. Fellows, Stockford, Conn., is at its best in *The Missing Man* . . . one of the Chief's toughest cases and one of the best handled."

— Anthony Boucher, *New York Times Book Review*

Henry Kitchell Webster

WHO IS THE NEXT? P 539, $2.25

"A double murder, private-plane piloting, a neat impersonation, and a delicate courtship are adroitly combined by a writer who knows how to use the language." —Jacques Barzun and Wendell Hertig Taylor

John Welcome

GO FOR BROKE P 663, $2.84

A rich financier chases Richard Graham half 'round Europe in a desperate attempt to prevent the truth getting out.

RUN FOR COVER P 664, $2.84

"I can think of few writers in the international intrigue game with such a gift for fast and vivid storytelling."

—*New York Times Book Review*

STOP AT NOTHING P 665, $2.84

"Mr. Welcome is lively, vivid and highly readable."

—*New York Times Book Review*

Anna Mary Wells

MURDERER'S CHOICE P 534, $2.50

"Good writing, ample action, and excellent character work."

—*Saturday Review of Literature*

A TALENT FOR MURDER P 535, $2.25

"The discovery of the villain is a decided shock." —*Books*

Charles Williams

DEAD CALM P 655, $2.84

"A brilliant tour de force of inventive plotting, fine manipulation of a small cast and breathtaking sequences of spectacular navigation."

—*New York Times Book Review*

THE SAILCLOTH SHROUD P 654, $2.84

"A fine novel of excitement, spirited, fresh and satisfying."

—*New York Times*

THE WRONG VENUS P 656, $2.84

Swindler Lawrence Colby and the lovely Martine create a story of romance, larceny, and very blunt homicide.

If you enjoyed this book you'll want to know about THE PERENNIAL LIBRARY MYSTERY SERIES

Buy them at your local bookstore or use this coupon for ordering:

Qty	P number	Price
_____	_____	_____
_____	_____	_____
_____	_____	_____
_____	_____	_____
_____	_____	_____
_____	_____	_____
_____	_____	_____
_____	_____	_____
_____	_____	_____
_____	_____	_____
_____	_____	_____
_____	_____	_____
_____	_____	_____
_____	_____	_____
	postage and handling charge	$1.00
	_____ book(s) @ $0.25	_____
	TOTAL	

Prices contained in this coupon are Harper & Row invoice prices only. They are subject to change without notice, and in no way reflect the prices at which these books may be sold by other suppliers.

HARPER & ROW, Mail Order Dept. #PMS, 10 East 53rd St., New York, N.Y. 10022.

Please send me the books I have checked above. I am enclosing $_____ which includes a postage and handling charge of $1.00 for the first book and 25¢ for each additional book. Send check or money order. No cash or C.O.D.s please

Name_____

Address_____

City_____State_____Zip_____

Please allow 4 weeks for delivery. USA only. This offer expires 1/31/86 Please add applicable sales tax.